MW00480288

SNAP
ZAP
MURDER

D.B. ELROGG

A MILO RATHKEY MYSTERY

Snap Zap Murder
A Milo Rathkey Mystery

Copyright © 2021 Alyce Goldberg, Harvey Goldberg
All Rights Reserved

ISBN 978-0-9998200-7-0 (paperback)
ISBN 978-0-9998200-8-7 (eBook)

No part of this publication may be used, reproduced in any manner, or published in any form or by any means, electronic, mechanical, photocopying, recording or otherwise, without the prior written permission of the publisher, except brief quotations to be used in the production of critical articles and reviews.

If you wish to contact the authors, you may email them at:
authors@dbelrogg.com

This is a work of fiction. All characters and incidents are totally from the minds of the authors and any resemblance to actual persons, living or dead, or incidents past and present are purely coincidental.

Cover Art by Jason Orr

Dedicated to Elena

SPECIAL THANKS TO

STAN JOHNSON
JODY EVANS
DR. ELENA CABB
DOUG OSELL
NICK GOLDBERG
PIPER GOLDBERG

1

Milo Rathkey stepped away from the body of Charles Dawson. The noxious smell and Dawson's charred hands reinforced the medical examiner's preliminary verdict of death by electrocution. Police Sergeant Robin White handed the victim's phone to Lieutenant Ernie Gramm, while the forensics people maneuvered around each other in the all too crowded room. The circumstances of his demise were no longer of concern to Charlie Dawson, but the possibility that Charlie had been murdered was just what Milo needed.

§

Several days earlier on his sprawling estate along the Lake Superior shores, Milo, alone and bored, was digesting his dinner in the Lakesong library. The calendar on his phone was blank. Lakesong's co-owner, Sutherland McKnight and his girlfriend, Agnes Larson, Milo's personal assistant, had taken off for three weeks in Hawaii. To make matters worse, Milo was eager to investigate a human finger bone found in his neighbor's attic, but the neighbor, Mille Greysolon, had flown to her Florida house for a month. Her departure was frustrating for Milo. He was looking forward to beginning his first interesting case since resuming his PI business for interesting situations only.

Even blue-eyed beauty Mary Alice Bonner had jetted off somewhere for sun and fun. In Milo's former world, no one jetted off anywhere in January. Besides, he hated hot weather and loved Lakesong, especially in the winter.

"The front gate is opening," Lakesong's intercom announced, startling Milo. Checking the app on his phone, he watched a limo cruise through the gate and stop at the front door. He hurried out of his cozy library, past the double staircase, into the foyer, and pulled open one of the heavy mahogany front doors just in time to see Sutherland and Agnes emerging from the limo's backseat.

Artic cold had descended on Duluth two days earlier, dropping temperatures to fifteen below zero with a wind chill of thirty below. Sutherland's frosty breath was clearly visible.

"Thank you, Milo. You're just in time to help get our suitcases in from the car."

"Hi, Milo," Agnes said, popping out of the limo with too over-the-top glee considering the late hour and bone-chilling temperature.

"Brr, it's freezing," Sutherland said to Agnes as he pulled his knit hat down over his ears. "Go! Run inside. Milo and I can handle the luggage."

"You're right. I'm so delicate I could freeze," Agnes joked, grabbing a large suitcase from the open trunk, and bumping it up the stairs.

"I'm delicate too," Milo complained, stopping his feet, and rubbing his arms, trying to stay warm.

"Go, grab three or four suitcases. It'll warm you right up, and we can get it all done in one trip," Sutherland suggested, handing Milo two roller suitcases and a duffle bag. Without waiting for more, Milo threw the duffle bag over his shoulder, and bumped the suitcases up the steps into the warmth of the house. Sutherland stumbled in behind him, dropping the remaining suitcases. Both Agnes and Milo shouted at him to close the door.

Sutherland stared at the suitcases and then shifted his gaze up to Milo and Agnes. "Sure, I'll get right on that," Sutherland snarked, tripping over the suitcases on the way back to shut and lock the twin mahogany doors.

"So, I guess your vacation was enjoyable," Milo said, joining Agnes standing at the foot of the stairs.

"How can you tell?" Sutherland challenged.

"You're both tan and smiling. It's my job to notice these things."

"Well, you're right." Sutherland proclaimed, standing tall and proud. "And Agnes is here to stay."

"You mean remarkable, enjoyable, attractive Agnes is here to stay?"

Sutherland did a double take, realizing Milo was parroting the exact words he used to describe Agnes after their first date a year ago. "How do you remember that?"

"It's a gift."

Here to stay? What is that—male speak? Agnes waited for a reaction to Sutherland's muddy description of their status. Hearing none, she added, "I hope the 'Agnes here to stay' part is not a problem."

Milo shrugged. "Problem? Why would it be a problem? It's an easier commute since you work here."

"Glad you're on-board, Milo," Agnes said, rolling her suitcases to the stairs before pausing, closing her eyes, and scrunching up her face. "It may not have been clear that Sutherland's 'here to stay' is code for 'we're married.'"

"Milo, you shouldn't stand there with your mouth open. It's not a good look," Sutherland kidded, rolling several more suitcases, joining Agnes to begin their trudge up the stairs.

"Wait!" Milo yelled.

Agnes froze on the second step. Sutherland turned to look at Milo.

"Wait you two. I have a question," Milo said with what sounded like—to Agnes and Sutherland— a tinge of anger in his voice.

Agnes glanced at Sutherland. The anger was unlike Milo. "What question?" Sutherland asked, stepping in front of Agnes as if to protect her.

"Why do you refuse to use the elevator? You never use it. What has that elevator ever done to you?" Milo exhibited a rare Milo grin while rolling the two suitcases in the direction of the elevator.

Sutherland muttered, "I keep forgetting about that damn elevator."

Arriving at the elevator door, Milo turned and opened his arms. "Welcome to Lakesong, Agnes!" Agnes abandoned the suitcases to give him a hug.

"Don't I get a hug?" Sutherland asked.

"Let me think. No."

Both of Lakesong's cats, Annie and Jet, shot through the gallery and the foyer on their way to the kitchen. "The cats are celebrating too it seems," Agnes said.

Milo, Sutherland, and Agnes jammed all the baggage into the elevator, leaving little room for humans. Annie the cat slinked in unnoticed, hiding between a suitcase and the wall. Agnes crawled over the top of the suitcases, perching herself on the largest roller bag. That left enough room for Sutherland to squeeze in between the gate and Milo's smiling face.

Milo waved bon voyage to the newlyweds as the elevator doors closed. He returned to his beloved library, stoked the fire, and relaxed into his favorite leather chair. Talking to his benefactor, Sutherland's late father John, Milo said to the empty room, "Well, John, in your will, you said my job was to get Sutherland out of his uneventful, predictable life. He ran off and got married. How'm I doin'?"

After an hour of reading, Milo began to crave a taste of the raspberry revel ice cream Mary Alice had given him a month ago. He rose and headed to the kitchen only to stop, not wanting to intrude on the laughing voices making pizza and plans.

Jet saddled up to him and squeaked. Milo looked down at the shiny, black cat. "The times they are a-changin', Mister Jet."

2

Milo spent a restless night. He loved Lakesong and was grateful to be reconnected with the place, but now wondered if he would be in the way. Sutherland and Agnes made a good match, but Milo had expected more tradition from Sutherland, an engagement, a few parties, and then a blowout wedding—time for Milo to get used to the idea, and possibly find another place to live.

After his swim, he walked into the morning room with his parade of cats. He was disappointed to find an empty table, no Sutherland pouring over his newspaper. He greeted Martha, Lakesong's resident chef, and asked why she was in the kitchen on her day off.

"I want to hear about Hawaii," Martha said.

"They came back last night, but they're not up yet," Milo said, grabbing a cup of coffee from the urn Martha always set up for Sunday morning.

"I'm awake. I can give you the whole story, and I come with pictures," Agnes proclaimed as she walked into the morning room.

"All the better," Martha said. "Berry smoothie?"

"No! It's Sunday—Ilene's pastry day, your day off. Come join us." Agnes said. "Milo where's your creampuff?"

"It's Sutherland's job to bring them in from the front porch. I'm just waiting patiently."

Martha sat down with her coffee cup. "Truthfully, I'm escaping. Darian has a science project and has requested Jamal's help in constructing something or other on the kitchen table," she said, referring to her two brothers who lived with her in the cottage on the estate. "I didn't want to watch."

As Agnes joined the group with her coffee, Sutherland arrived with the box of Ilene's goodies. "You know, Milo, you could have brought them in. They were delivered a half hour ago. Now they may need to be thawed."

"Not my job."

"And what is your job, Milo?"

"Sparkling conversation."

"Did you sparkle Martha with our news?" Agnes asked Milo.

"You have news?" Milo played stupid—he thought quite well.

Martha lifted her coffee cup but froze in mid-sip. She set the cup back down. Agnes followed Martha's gaze to her left hand and nodded. Martha smiled, picked up her coffee, and sipped in silence.

Seconds went by. Sutherland filled his coffee cup, chatting about the pros and cons between a frozen jelly-filled Bismarck or an almond paste Danish. Hearing no one chime in, he looked up and asked, "Why is everyone so quiet?"

"I don't know about them, but I was enjoying watching the icy branches bounce off the frozen snow," Milo said. "Last I heard, Agnes was sparkling Martha with some news, then everything went quiet. I think they are communicating by silent mind waves now."

"Oh, yes," Sutherland said, "our news!"

"I know!" Martha exclaimed. "Congratulations to both of you!"

"See, I told you—mind waves," Milo insisted.

Martha did a double take. "Wait, I see two rings."

"An engagement ring and a wedding ring," said Agnes, waving her hand. "But that's not all, I have a third ring."

Martha stared at Agnes' trying to figure it all out.

Agnes reached into her fleece pocket and withdrew a shiny metallic washer. "This is my original wedding band."

"We got married on a sailboat," Sutherland took up the story. "It was a spur-of-the-moment. We hadn't purchased rings, so the captain made do with washers. We have matching ones." Sutherland showed his washer.

"Lovely," Martha laughed.

"When we came ashore, Sutherland insisted we get proper rings." Agnes did an eye roll. "I made him propose to me in the jewelry store."

"Did you say yes?" Milo asked.

"I took my time—walked around the store for a while."

"I will make you both a special dinner tomorrow night," Martha said, getting up from the table. "What would you enjoy? Mrs. McKnight?"

Agnes laughed, thinking Martha was kidding being so formal. Then she realized Martha was not kidding. Agnes felt a pang of loss. This needed to be fixed.

Someone is at the front gate, the intercom interrupted.

Sutherland looked at his phone and jerked his head back. "Good grief. No one besides Ilene delivers on Sunday morning!" Sutherland said, looking at the squared-jaw, long-haired man in an oversized white van displayed on his phone. "Who is this guy?"

"You could ask him," Milo urged.

Sutherland pushed the talk button. "Yes?"

"I'm Ethan Marsden. I'm here from Gibbs Industries to set up a prototype bike."

"Oh yeah," Milo said. "Some guy in a truck delivered a bunch of boxes while you were in Hawaii. I had him put them in your exercise room."

"With all the excitement, I forgot all about that. A cycling partner, Gabe Gibbs, is developing a special stationary bike, and I'm one of the testers." Sutherland told the group. He opened the gate using the app and went to meet the bike man at the front door.

Agnes joined Martha in the kitchen. "The 'Mrs. McKnight' thing is weird."

Martha smiled. "You're my employer. Like it or not, I call my employer by his or her surname. Now, would you like me to call you Ms. or Mrs. Larson or McKnight?"

"Agnes. Call me Agnes like you've done since we met. Seriously, we're friends."

"And we still are and will continue to be."

"Okay, I guess I get it, but please call me Agnes in private. If someone else is here, someone from outside, you can be more formal if that makes you more comfortable."

"Formal as in Mrs. McKnight?"

Agnes shook her head. "I don't know. To be announced. This is so confusing. I need to talk to my friend—you."

Left alone in the morning room, Milo was also taken aback by hearing the name, "Mrs. McKnight." To Milo, Mrs. McKnight was Sutherland's mother, Laura, the lady of Lakesong, where Milo grew up, the son of Lakesong's widowed cook.

§

On their way up to the exercise room, Ethan Marsden informed Sutherland the unit came in six boxes, and he was sent to assemble it. "I'm a little bit electrical engineer, quality control, and customer service," Marsden joked.

Sutherland showed him to the exercise room where six boxes were set against the far wall. Marsden carried a tool kit which he set on Sutherland's weight bench. "Do you mind?" he asked.

"Not at all. That bench hasn't gotten much use. I mainly ride bikes for exercise."

Marsden removed his parka, folding and placing it neatly alongside the tool kit. He was dressed to work, wearing a sweatshirt and jeans with his shoulder length dark blond hair pulled back in a ponytail.

"Could you help me move this treadmill and the stair stepper?" Marsden asked, looking around the room. "The prototype will take up double the space of an ordinary bike."

Sutherland helped Marsden, and then sat back to watch the man work. Marsden arranged the boxes with the largest one in the center and the others surrounding it. Beginning with the large box, he cut it open and pulled out a larger-than-usual, bright-red stationary bike which came assembled. Each of the five remaining boxes held a monitor, stand, and cords.

"What is all that equipment for?" Sutherland asked.

"The experience of a lifetime," Marsden grinned. Sutherland didn't know if he was being facetious.

Sutherland was impressed as he watched Marsden work. There was no wasted motion. He was exacting and smooth, as if he had done this a million times before. Tools were taken up, used, and returned to their place in his toolbox making the cleanup effortless.

To make conversation, Sutherland asked, "How long have you worked for Gabe?"

He shrugged. "He's my step-brother."

Sutherland thought it was Marsden's second odd answer to a conversational question.

"Sorry for not being chatty. I have two more of these bikes to set up today. Gabe wants the first test tonight at six."

"On a Sunday?"

Marsden smiled. "That's Gabe. He wants this first test group finished as soon as possible—first twenty-five miles tonight. One hundred miles total by Wednesday."

Sutherland eased past the right-side monitor and looked over the bike as Marsden finished the assembly and pressed the on button. The center console lit up, displaying the usual information: miles, time, pulse rate, plus several other features.

"Cameras are encased in the monitors," Marsden explained. "As we ride, we will be able to see the others riding with us, ahead of us, and behind us. They can see us the same way."

"Impressive!" Sutherland exclaimed. "Just like real life. So, you will be joining us?"

"Absolutely—experience of a lifetime," he repeated again, grinning. "Only ride the bike during the tests. No offline riding." Marsden reached over and turned off the bike. "That's important. Here is an instruction sheet Gibbs prepared."

"Great!"

Marsden shook Sutherland's hand, "Good to meet you."

§

After breakfast, Sutherland and Agnes made a quick trip to the wine cellar for packing boxes to take to Agnes' Lakeside bungalow. Sutherland thought packing would take an hour or two. Agnes knew differently.

Once back on her home ground, Agnes took command. "Your job is to put these wine boxes back together. There's packing tape with the rolls of giftwrap in my closet."

"Found it," Sutherland announced. "I also found an entire role of Milo's matching luggage—black garbage bags. When he joined me at Lakesong last year that's how he transported his limited wardrobe." Sutherland looked back in Agnes' bedroom closet and murmured. "Did we bring enough boxes? We may need to use some of Milo's *luggage*."

"I prefer no garbage bags." This was not the day to have the foster kid, black garbage bag discussion with Sutherland.

Sutherland put his arms around his new bride, and tucked Agnes' hair behind her ear. "Have I told you in the last thirty seconds how much I love you."

"No! I think you're overdue!"

"Yes ma'am. I love you."

"I like that. Set your alarm for another thirty seconds," Agnes urged. Sutherland was not the traditional romance hero she enjoyed reading about when she needed an escape. He was far from perfect, but he was perfect for her. "We've got all day to finish packing. We could take a break." She smiled suggestively.

Several hours later Sutherland resumed putting the boxes together while Agnes made them cocoa. "Big or little?" she yelled to him.

"Big or little what?"

"Marshmallows of course."

"Big cup, little marshmallows."

"I'd like to take my painting to Lakesong."

"Which one?"

"The real one, the Zuckerman Hartung. The one I got last summer from your good friend Morrie Wolf," Agnes said, giggling, and handing him his steaming big cup of cocoa with little marshmallows bobbing on top.

"My friend, the gangster. How did that happen? Oh wait, I know. Milo happened."

Agnes looked up from her packing. "I know Mr. Wolf has a reputation, but when I met him at his granddaughter's wedding, he seemed nice. And he did give me that wonderful painting."

He and three cherry pies from Milo kept my legs from being broken. Sutherland thought. "I agree. He seemed...nice."

"I just thought, he never gave anything to you."

Sutherland waved off the thought. "No problem. We're good."

Agnes cocked her head. "Something you want to share, oh husband of mine. How are you and Morrie Wolf 'good'?"

"We were experiencing a bit of nastiness from a competitor on the Kiner Project. Let's just say Mr. Wolf intervened on our behalf."

"Should I know more about this?"

"Naw, ancient history." Quickly changing the subject, Sutherland asked, "Do you want to take any of your furniture? Maybe we should hire a moving company to do this properly."

Agnes sat down on the bed. "I love my furniture, but where would we put it?" Thinking about the cozy little bungalow that had been her home and her safe place, she said, almost to herself, "I don't want to sell this house."

"Don't," Sutherland said. "Keep it."

"I..." Agnes felt a pang of fear. She was no longer self-sufficient, independent Agnes Larson; she was...well, Agnes didn't know who she was right now. Agnes Larson, wife. Who is that? Agnes' eyes began to water.

"What's wrong?"

Sutherland would never understand. She didn't understand. "I guess I'm sad. I'm going to miss my little house."

Sutherland sat next to her. "Does it help that you're getting a much bigger house."

She looked at him like he had grown a third eye. "No."

"Bigger isn't better?"

Agnes sighed. "This was my first home. It was created by me for me. I'm moving to a home you were born into. I have had nothing to do with it."

"True. If it matters, I didn't have much to do with it either, so we're alike that way. I did remodel part of the second floor to fit me, but we can remodel it again to fit us. It will become our house, your second house. Besides, Lakesong loves you as do I. Am I late on the thirty seconds?"

Agnes brightened. "You're good," she said, kissing his cheek, "making me feel that *we're* an *us*. And you're right about Lakesong—she likes me best." Agnes leaned against him, put her finger on his lips, stopping him from objecting. "So, this is really happening?"

"Oh yes! It's already happened! I'm excited!" Sutherland said.

"I am too. It's just a lot to deal with. Every now and then, I need to stop and breathe."

"We'll take it at your pace. If you need to come back and sleep in the bungalow for the night, we'll come together."

Agnes squeezed his hand.

"Him," Sutherland whispered.

"Him?"

"Lakesong. He's a him."

Agnes gave Sutherland a loving poke. "No, dear. Lakesong is a she. I know; she shows me her secrets."

3

Milo spent the better part of the morning looking for a secret Jet door. When the young, black cat first came to Lakesong, Milo awoke to find him curled at the end of the bed despite the fact the bedroom door was always closed. Now, Jet turns up most nights stretched out where Milo wants to put his feet.

"How did you get in?" Milo asked Jet repeatedly.

Jet squeaked in response but otherwise would not give away any secrets. Milo used to put him out of the bedroom and go back to sleep, only to find Jet back on the bed in the morning. Now he didn't bother moving the sleeping furball, but felt it was a personal mystery to be solved.

Sutherland was no help. He didn't know if any of the Annie cats throughout the years were allowed in his parents' bedroom at night. If the current Annie knew the secret, she wasn't using it.

Agnes laughed at Milo when he suggested that someone had built a secret door for cats, much like the secret door in the library. "Who would do that?" she asked.

Milo had to admit it was a strange idea, but how else could the cat get in? Defeated, Milo sat in the park-like gallery and glared at the current Annie who was perched in her Guiana Tree. "I bet you showed Jet how to sneak into the bedroom, didn't you? I feed you bacon, and you betray me?"

Annie blinked, yawned, and stretched out on her tree limb. Jet chewed and pulled on Milo's shoelaces. Milo's phone buzzed with a text from Mille Greysolon stating she would be returning home tomorrow and would like to meet with Milo concerning the finger bone in her attic.

At last!

"Oh, there you are," Sutherland said upon entering the gallery. He sat down across from Milo.

"Shouldn't you be upstairs helping Agnes unpack?" Milo asked.

"I've been unpacked from my rooms."

"Already? What did you do?"

"I thought I was helping. Agnes pointed out that newly married couples often live in small, cramped apartments making it hard to get away from each other, but we have Lakesong, and Lakesong has many rooms."

"She suggested you find one of those many rooms primarily away from her." Milo guessed.

"Exactly." Sutherland sighed.

"One of the keys to a successful marriage is knowing when to be helpful and when to find another room."

Sutherland look at him. "How long does it take to learn that?"

"I don't have a clue. I'm divorced, remember. Speaking of helpful, would it be helpful if I moved out?" Milo offered, not that he wanted to move out, but he felt it was the right thing to do.

"No! Why would you do that?"

"A year ago, after John's will reading, we had lunch at that overpriced cafeteria."

"I remember. I had hummus and you ate two hamburgers with a bloody hand."

Milo ignored the bloody hand comment. "You said John gave me half of Lakesong to double the chances it would remain a home and not become a museum. It looks to me like you and Agnes are making Lakesong a home."

"I don't want the whole house. It's huge, far too large for just Agnes and me."

"Don't you think the lord and lady of the manor should have the master bedroom? It's built with massive his and hers closets."

"That was my parents' bedroom and now it's yours along with that stuffy library. Besides, my father made you and me a team."

"Should we have team t-shirts?"

Sutherland rolled his eyes. "Like it or not we're a team, just like Agnes and I are now a team, except different. Wait. That's a bad analogy." Feeling like he was going down a rabbit hole of his own making, Sutherland changed tacks. "On a different note, I will need to expand my...our...the rooms upstairs and repurpose some of the guestrooms—three or four."

"What!" Milo exclaimed. "That would cut us down to only five unused bedrooms on the south side of the house. What will we do when the circus comes to town?"

Sutherland assumed that was Milo-speak to do whatever it was he needed to do, just don't touch his library.

§

"Back so soon?" Agnes chirped, watching Sutherland go into the bedroom closet.

"I'm not really here. I'll be gone in two seconds. I just need my bike gear. Have to do that first ride on that new bike tonight before dinner."

Several minutes went by. Agnes was putting her toiletries into the bathroom. "We are going to have to expand and update this bathroom," she yelled. "One sink, no bathtub, and a tiny shower. That's a problem."

"I have a problem too. Where's my bike gear?" Sutherland yelled back. "I can't find it."

Agnes stepped out of the bathroom to see where he was looking.

"I keep it on this shelf," he said, pointing to a shelf that now held multicolored yoga pants.

She took Sutherland's hand and led him down the hall to his exercise room. "I made an organizational decision. As of today, exercise clothes belong here in this closet. See, they are nicely folded and placed on this unused shelf."

Sutherland was new to this. "Aren't your yoga pants exercise clothes?"

"Yoga pants are a fashion statement,"

Sutherland laughed. "And my bike shorts are not?"

Agnes put her arms around him and batted her eyes. "Do you like how I look in my yoga pants?"

"Yes!" Sutherland responded with too much eagerness.

Agnes smiled her Cheshire Cat grin.

Sutherland thought about asking if she liked him in his spandex shorts but thought he may not like the answer. "Okay then. I'll now get dressed for exercise in the exercise room—makes so much more sense."

Agnes laughed as she returned to the bathroom.

"Can I request a tour of the rest of my rooms tonight?"

Agnes stuck her head out the bathroom door, "You mean *our* rooms, dear? Sure."

Sutherland grimaced at his faux pas as he changed into his spandex shorts, a dry fit shirt, and his bike shoes, He turned on the five monitors, one by one per the instruction sheet. Mounting the bike, he turned on the main console and waited for Gabriel Gibbs to appear in the front monitor—a strange moment, reminiscent of waiting at the start line for a major race.

At six o'clock sharp, the smiling, familiar Gibbs, welcomed everyone. "Good evening and thank you all for agreeing to participate in beta test number one—twenty-five miles tonight, data to record, adjustments to be made."

Gibbs had joined the Zenith City Riders several years ago, and his riding buddies knew his fiercely competitive side. His boyish good looks and smile often ran opposite to his character. In Sutherland's front monitor, Gibbs was on his bike, facing the group like the start of every other exercise class. Sutherland was not impressed—certainly not the "experience of a lifetime" promised by Ethan Marsden. This was supposed to be new and innovative.

As if reading his mind, Gibbs announced, "I'm going to now begin the program." Gibbs suddenly was facing the other way. "You should all see my back and if you look left and right, you should see the other riders."

Glancing at his left monitor, Sutherland saw Charlie Dawson checking all the toys on the handlebars. Leah Davis was next to him. She waved. "This is cool! Hey Nora, hurry up get on your bike!" Sutherland could hear the excitement in Leah's voice.

"Where's Nora?" Sutherland asked.

"She *should* appear on your right," Gibbs said.

"Who decides that?" Sutherland asked.

"The program sets it up. Marsden, do you have anything to add?"

"Not a thing Gabe. Just excited to begin the experience of a lifetime. It was a pleasure meeting you all this weekend." His voice came from behind Sutherland who turned around and saw the man on a bike in one of the rear monitors. Marsden gave him a salute. Sutherland nodded back.

"I can hear everybody," Nora said, "but..."

"You're too short. We can't see you Nora, get on the bike." Leah urged. "We're all in the monitors."

Nora seated herself and looked. "Oh, there you all are! Hello Sutherland. Everybody."

"Hello Nora," Sutherland responded.

"Hello Gibbs," Nora said.

"Are we ready, ready for the experience of a lifetime?" Gibbs asked.

Sutherland smiled. That "experience of a lifetime" was clearly the ad tag line.

"I live in a small room," Nora explained. "Getting these cables and monitors to fit was my experience of a lifetime."

"As virtual bikers, we've never been able to see or talk to each other— have a total social experience—until now," Gibbs said. "That's why I invented this biking system."

"Is this the way the bike is going to be sold?" Nora asked. "It's cumbersome. Like I said, I rent a room—a small room. I had to move my dresser out in the hall just to get this in."

Gibbs' jaw tightened at the criticism, "Nora, the bike size will of course be reduced. The monitors will be replaced by holograms. Anybody else with a problem? Leah, do your legs hit the electronics box?"

"My knees are fine, Gabe."

"Great. I didn't want to spend the money on the micro-electronics that will reduce the box size until we have all the bugs worked out."

"How much is this bike going to cost?" Charlie asked, eager to make a pitch to get this ad account and possibly invest.

"In the neighborhood of 10K."

Nora Swenson whistled. "Out of my price range."

"Payment for helping is a free bike. Groups that ride together in the summer want to stay together when they ride virtually in the winter. We've done the research. There is a market for this kind of bike, again, a total social experience.

If no one else has any questions or complaints let's begin beta ride number one, our first twenty-five miles."

Sutherland saw his front screen change announcing the course was the Loire Valley of France. Gibbs was leading the pack. "Let's go!" he yelled, waving them forward.

Sutherland began to pedal. Not only could he hear the sounds of bicycle wheels on pavement, but a hidden fan in the control console blew an increasing wind in his face.

"What, no frogs or crickets?" Charlie Dawson asked.

"Can we get crickets?" Nora echoed.

"Only if you run over them," Gibbs shot back.

Charlie passed Sutherland on the left and appeared in the front monitor behind Gibbs. Sutherland saw Leah and Nora were pedaling on either side of him. "I like this!" he exclaimed.

"It will be even better once we get the hologram projectors. You will see the scene and the other riders around you—360 degrees. The monitors are only there to approximate what the final bike will do." Gibbs hollered.

"Oh, look at the sunflowers!" Leah laughed. "I want to get off and see if they're taller than me."

Gibbs sighed. "If you get off, Leah, the flowers will disappear."

"Vineyards to the left!" Nora exclaimed.

Beyond the vineyards, Sutherland could see a hill in the distance and prepared to shift into a lower gear. Charlie, caught up in a discussion with Nora, did not see it. Sutherland passed him and was inching up on Gibbs.

"Charlie, push the map button on your panel. You will see our trip. You can anticipate the hills and curves. It was on the instruction sheet," Gibbs said harshly. "Don't you read?"

"How do you know I missed my gear change? You're ahead of me!" Charlie complained.

"Look at those monitors behind you, one on the right, and one on the left. I can see everybody and everything."

They all checked their rear monitors. Sutherland saw Charlie sprinting, catching up on the left. Once Charlie passed him, he looked behind to see Sutherland and grinned.

"Charlie, before the next ride, read the damn instructions!" Gibbs shouted.

"You got a winner here, Gibbs, an experience of a lifetime," Charlie parroted, bolting ahead on his agenda of grabbing this advertising account.

"Everybody—especially Charlie—check your maps! Hairpin turn to the right. Tell me if the lean feels good. Is it real?"

Leah caught up to Sutherland and they leaned into the curve together. "Mine is smooth, Gibbs. Nice."

Nora came up alongside Leah and Sutherland and they were all riding side by side through the small village of Montsoreau. "This is like the Tour de France," Nora yelled. "We don't have to ride single file anymore."

The group rode for about an hour when Marsden stopped pedaling. "Ouch! Dammit! I've got a leg cramp."

Sutherland looked behind him and saw Marsden's empty bike.

"Marsden! Where the hell are you?" Gibbs demanded.

"Leg cramp, Gibbs. I'm walking it off."

"Let's keep going, people," Gibbs shouted. "Marsden, catch up when you can." Gibbs went another mile before calling a cool down mile and stopping. Gibbs was now facing them again. "So, any glitches?" he asked. "Besides newbie Marsden's leg cramp."

Sutherland said Nora and Leah's video stuttered a bit when they were on his left.

"When I was trying to pass you, Gibbs, you froze," Charlie said. "Did you put something in there that keeps us from passing you?"

"You weren't passing me, Charlie. You caught up to my frozen video. Your short legs could only pass me if I were standing still."

"My nature sounds cut out. Birds, wind, it all went silent when going through the wheat fields," Nora said.

"Are you guys getting all this?" Gibbs called to his staff.

A disembodied voice said, "Making a list Gibbs."

"Marsden?" Gibbs asked.

"Looked good from the rear," Marsden said, "until the cramp."

"Before the next ride, Marsden, make sure you're hydrated. Tomorrow we will do twenty-five more miles. Remember do not ride the bike on your own, only in our group session."

"What difference would it make?" Charlie asked with defiance.

"It's above your pay grade. Don't do it because I told you not to do it."

"Not good enough."

"Anyone want to fill Charlie in?" Gibbs asked.

One of the disembodied technicians began to explain how the test worked. It was a lecture on variables, servers, moving bits of information, and mechanical compliance.

Halfway through, Charlie surrendered. "Okay, okay. By the way, Gibbs, who's handling your advertising?"

"Come on, Charlie, this is an international product. You're small potatoes."

Sutherland thought that was nastier than it needed to be.

4

Sutherland opened his closet door with trepidation, fearing his suits might have disappeared, and he would have to wear bike shorts to the office. He was pleased to see his suits hanging in their usual place.

Agnes remained curled up in bed. "Do you have to go to work today?" she murmured through a yawn. "We only had a week of honeymoon time."

"We had three whole weeks in paradise."

"We weren't married for the first two. They don't count."

Sutherland sat down next to her. "This may come as a shock. As much as I love you, I am afraid you are in competition with Ilene for my Monday morning affections."

Agnes groaned. Ilene of Ilene's bakery was formidable competition indeed. "What has stolen your heart? An éclair, a Bismarck, or a bear claw?"

"I would not leave you for a mere éclair," Sutherland said. "It's a goat cheese-filled, honey-fig muffin."

"Ick! That sounds terrible!"

"I love it, and when it arrives in Ilene's Monday morning pastry box of goodies no one else touches it."

Agnes leaned up and kissed him. "Well, dear one, your goat-figgy muffin will also be safe here at home also."

Sutherland resumed dressing. Seeing only a few of Agnes' things hanging in the closet, he asked her where she put the rest of her clothes.

"I made use of one of the spare bedrooms. I thought I could bring in the clothes I plan to wear for a couple of days and then switch them out. Did you miss that part of the tour last night, my dear?"

"I was too mesmerized by your beauty to pay attention to the *tour*."

"Nice save."

Sutherland bowed.

Agnes giggled.

"Let the renovations begin. We'll need an architect and contractor and probably a..."

"Slow down. Remember *our* pace. I'd be happy with a nearby closet and a bigger bathroom. Besides, I can only handle one surprise a day and your figgy goat muffin was too much for me. Have you mentioned renovating to Milo?"

"He had some concern about circus clowns."

Agnes laughed. "Of course. As do we all."

§

Milo's breakfast constants for the past year had been his half lumberjack breakfast, Sutherland reading his Wall Street Journal, and the cats. With the addition of Agnes, he figured that might change, but how he didn't know. As he walked toward the morning room, he was joined by Annie and then Jet. Check. He said hello to Martha. Check.

"Hello, Mr. Rathkey," Martha said from the kitchen. Jet ran up to her and squeaked. "And hello to you, Jet."

Sutherland was in his place, reading his Wall Street Journal. Check. Milo poured himself a cup of coffee and sat down.

Martha arrived with his breakfast. Milo handed out bits of bacon to the cats and decided to ignore Sutherland. He took out his phone and texted Mary Alice Bonner. *I know something you don't. Na na na.*

Milo had finished re-buttering his already buttered toast when Agnes arrived looking like she always did, crisp and professional—just tanner. She grabbed her cup of coffee as Sutherland put down his paper.

Milo's phone played 'Uptown Girl,' the ringtone for Mary Alice. She began immediately without salutation, "If you're talking about Agnes and Sutherland getting married in Hawaii, you're late by fifteen minutes. Sutherland updated his country club membership at eight this morning. Let me talk to Agnes."

Milo glared at Sutherland.

"What?" Sutherland wondered aloud.

Milo returned to his phone. "Well, in my defense, I didn't know Jack Rabbit Slim over here was going to notify the world before I could talk to you."

"Excuses, always excuses. Put Agnes on."

Milo handed his phone to Agnes and turned to Sutherland. "Your marriage was probably the only piece of Duluth gossip that I could have beat Mary Alice to but you..."

"What did I do? How did she find out?"

"Let me roll back my phone conversation," Milo said as he pressed an imaginary rewind button. "Oh, here it is, *Sutherland notified the Country Club...*"

"Oh."

"Yeah, oh."

Agnes hung up with Mary Alice and handed back Milo's phone. "She's putting a notice in the paper."

"A notice about what?" Sutherland asked.

"I've run away. She's putting my picture on a milk carton," Milo suggested.

Sutherland shook his head. "I'm confused."

"Our wedding, Sutherland. Mary Alice is putting a notice in the paper announcing our wedding."

Sutherland brightened up. "Oh, that's nice—I guess."

§

Having spent the past month in Florida, Mille Greysolon was settling into the realities at Wardline, her estate on Lake Superior, south of Lakesong. Wardline and Lakesong were often referred to as the twins, having been built in almost identical Jacobean style before the turn of the last century.

Snuggled in a heavy, red sweater that set off her short-cropped, wavy white hair, Mille sat in her great room drinking hot coffee, vowing to extend her Florida stay until

March next year. Milo Rathkey, whom she met once last fall, was due any minute. Mille was looking forward to Milo's investigation, something to keep life exciting until spring when she could enjoy being outside again.

§

Mia Dawson did not share her husband's love of long-distance cycling. She thrived on short-burst, heart-pounding, intense work outs. Sweat was dripping down her face and back as Cliff Cardeo, her favorite trainer, shouted from her bike monitor. Bits and pieces of his patter permeated her brain.

"Yas, come on! You're beautiful! You're beautiful!"

Mia's breathing was hard and deep.

"Lean on it! Push it! Push it! Push it!"

Mia tasted the salt on her upper lip.

"You're gonna be ready for the runway. Twerk it! Twerk it up! Twerk it up!"

This was her cue to go for the final burst, and she poured it on until she heard Cliff's mantra for cool-down time: "Finished, fine, done and dusted." Mia grabbed her towel from the handlebars to wipe her face and neck until the music faded—the class was over.

She was heading downstairs for more water when she heard her husband's biking music coming from his study. Ten years ago, when they were first married, Charlie was a cross-training exercise fanatic—not so much in the last couple of years. She crossed the living room and opened the door to the study. Charlie was biking on the new bike, the one provided by Gibbs, but the monitors were off.

"I thought you're not supposed to ride that thing without the group," Mia complained.

"How do you know?" Charlie challenged between breaths.

"I'm not deaf. Last night, I heard Gibbs tell everyone to ride it only as a group at night. Riding it alone will throw off everything he's measuring."

"Yada yada yada. What about what I need?"

Mia rolled her eyes and released her long brown hair from its twisty.

"You don't think so, but I got a lot of stress—working on a big deal," Charlie complained.

"But why ride his bike? Because he told you not to?" Mia knew her husband. Charlie didn't listen.

"This bike is smooth. I like it. I think Gibbs has a winner here. I'm not only going to get the ad account for this puppy, I'm going to buy in. This will get us in the money, honey."

Mia shut the door on the promise she had heard all her married life; a promise she no longer believed. She also failed to believe Charlie's excuse for riding the bike. Mia didn't know what he was up to, but she knew he was up to something.

§

Arriving at work, Sutherland hung up his coat and walked down the row of empty, glass-enclosed offices to the conference room. All the chairs around the large, rectangular table were filled except for Sutherland's. Lorraine, Sutherland's administrative assistant, handed him his goat cheese-filled, honey-fig muffin complete with a lit birthday candle as everyone broke into one verse of belated "Happy Birthday."

After blowing out the candle, Sutherland took a bite of his birthday muffin. "I'm glad to see everyone. I was worried when I saw empty offices," Sutherland said as a way of a joke. "I've been gone a long time."

There were several 'welcome back' and belated 'happy birthday' murmurings.

Sutherland removed his agenda from his coat pocket, as Lorraine passed out copies. "So, let's begin…"

Marion Caldwell, the head of residential real estate, cleared her throat.

"Marion?"

"Well, as long as you called on me…"

Sutherland did an invisible eye roll in his mind thinking *as if I had a choice.*

"Cybil, my old friend, over at Nelson Realty, told me that her old friend Janet, at Bonner Development told her that you're not single anymore. Are Cybil and Janet in error?"

"Marion, I am so glad you mentioned that. If you look at the agenda for this meeting, item number one is new developments. This is my new development. I married Ms. Agnes Larson last week in Hawaii. I am not single, and Cybil and Janet are correct. Now, moving on, Piper—our head of development—gave birth to a son, Jack, about the time I was being married. Mother, son, and dad are doing well."

"Whoa! Hang on there, boss," Marion said. "We know about Piper. She's old news. Jack's a week old. Your marriage is breaking news. Congratulations!"

Others echoed the same. Helen Munger, the head of HR, reached into her purse, and pulled out a five-dollar bill.

Sutherland watched the bill move up the table to Loraine who smiled. "I win."

"You win what?" Sutherland asked.

"Five dollars. I bet Helen five dollars that you were going to Hawaii to get married," Lorraine said.

"What? I didn't even know I was going to Hawaii to get married."

"You should have asked me. I could have told you."

"Okay," Sutherland laughed. "Enough of the personnel developments. Let's talk brick and mortar. Bill, how are we doing on the Kiner Development?"

§

Mary Alice Bonner called Milo back and invited him to dinner.

"This is a pleasant surprise," Milo said.

"Of course, I love your company all the time, but I'm trying to get you out of the way so Sutherland and Agnes can have a nice dinner alone. Martha and I have talked."

"Good idea."

"I know it is. Now, where is Agnes this morning?"

"In her office. Why?"

"I'm coming over. She and I need to talk."

"I won't be here. I'm going over to Mille Greysolon's. You remember, the finger bone in the attic."

"You say the cutest things. Your presence, always charming and delightful, is not required."

Agnes was glad to be busy. She had invoices to pay, appointments to make, and repairs to check on. Even though she was officially Milo's personal assistant, in reality she was also Lakesong's house manager. Agnes was about to grab a needed second cup of coffee from the kitchen when she heard the intercom announce the gates were opening. Agnes' brow wrinkled in concern. No one was scheduled that would know the code.

Agnes watched from her ground floor office as a flashy red, top-up convertible drove by the private entrance and stopped. Mary Alice, elegant in a hooded black, faux fur belted long coat, and black boots, strode into the office. She flipped down her hood, unbelted her coat, and sat down in front of Agnes, removing her gloves without a word.

Agnes, used to Mary Alice time, waited.

"I'm here because we need to talk," Mary Alice announced. "You should have told me you were going to marry Sutherland. We have repair work to do."

The wrinkled brow returned. "What?"

It was Mary Alice's turn to be nonplussed. She stared at Agnes.

"I don't understand what you mean by repair work, but I was going for coffee. Can I offer you a cup?" Agnes said.

Mary Alice followed Agnes into the gallery. "Chose an area; I'll get the coffee." Agnes continued into the kitchen making two cups of coffee using the French press. Martha had taught her how to use it and now it was her midmorning go-to pick-me-up. She found some cookies and rolled the cart out to the table area. Mary Alice had paper and pen in front of her.

"Okay, let's begin with the fun stuff. Tell me about the wedding," Mary Alice said.

Agnes began to gush. "It was wonderful. We decided to elope on a whim. The big wedding I planned last summer for Mr. Wolf's granddaughter was fun, but so much work and stress. Sutherland had rented a boat for a day of sailing. We had kidded and teased about getting married the night before, and we mentioned it to the captain. He said we could get married onboard, so we did. The captain married us. The first mate and the chef were our witnesses."

"Spectacular!" Mary Alice smiled.

"It was impulsive, so out of character, but it felt so right."

"I'm glad for you both. I really am. Also, I'm sorry. I realized when I offered to place an announcement yesterday that you may have people to do that. I didn't mean to intrude."

"People?"

"Family."

"No. I'm my people, and Sutherland is his people."

"Then you also have me," Mary Alice declared, "and we need to write up an announcement. I'll get it into tomorrow's paper."

"I appreciate your help, but why?"

"Not to announce would be impolite."

"Impolite? To whom?"

Mary Alice smiled. "It's news, Agnes, and people need to know."

Agnes scrunched up her nose. "Do they really? Isn't love a private thing? To tell you the truth, I'm still trying to get used to all of this."

Mary Alice cocked her head to the side. She didn't disagree with Agnes. Sipping her coffee, she thought about how to approach the situation. "I agree, love is private, but you and

Sutherland have made your love official and legal—brought it into the public spaces. Normally, couples get engaged. There are parties. Then couples get married. You and Sutherland fast tracked it on a tramp steamer somewhere in the Pacific Ocean, so we have to improvise."

Agnes laughed. "Tramp steamer? More like luxury yacht. Mary Alice, if you think it's important, go ahead, put the notice in the Duluth Paper."

"And Minneapolis and St. Paul," Mary Alice added.

"Really? Why?"

Mary Alice considered the question as she drank her coffee, broke off a piece of cookie, and tapped it into crumbs. "Sutherland went to the University of Minnesota. I'm sure he has friends there who would want to know."

"I guess it makes sense."

"Good. I need middle names and details."

"Mine is Rose. Can you believe it? Agnes Rose. I should have been born in the eighteen hundreds. I have no idea about Sutherland. With a first name that long, maybe he doesn't have a middle name."

5

Milo waited for Wardline's gates to open before following the tree lined drive to Mille Greysolon's front door. He couldn't help but notice the similarities between Wardline and Lakesong. On the outside they were almost identical: same red brick, same multiple windows, same roof line except for Lakesong's singular glass-domed gallery.

A distinguished looking man with dark hair but silver-grey temples met him at the double door. "I'm Robert, sir," the man said. "Mrs. Greysolon is expecting you."

Following Robert through the house, Milo noticed Wardline's interior was much different from Lakesong— dark entrance, closed doors to cutoff rooms whose purposes were not clear. Craning his neck, Milo could not identify a library or a billiard room, and certainly no glass domed, tree filled, park-like gallery. He realized just how much renovation Lakesong had undergone.

If Sutherland thinks Lakesong's first floor is dusty, musty, and old, he needs to take a stroll in here, Milo thought.

Robert led Milo into a large, dark paneled great room. The room's gloom was lifted somewhat by a roaring fire, and the weak winter sun filtering through the three banks of windows that gave a panoramic view of the lake.

Mille Greysolon's plumpness filled out a large wingback chair alongside the fire. She nodded at Milo and held out her hand, offering him a matching chair facing her.

Robert stopped by Mille's chair and asked, "Can I bring you and your guest some refreshment, Madam?"

Mille looked at Milo, "Tea? Coffee? Soft Drink? Or something harder?"

"I'm good." Milo said.

"Coffee, Robert, and get it right this time, two sugars and a one pour of cream."

Robert smiled. "No, Madam."

"What?"

"The doctor said no sugar, Madam."

Mille turned to Milo. "I should have sacked him in '94." Mille gave a full-throated laugh that woke up a small, black-and-white spotted horse that had been sleeping behind the long couch facing the fireplace. The animal bumped his hip cornering the couch, lopping over to Mille's chair. He laid his head in her blanket-covered lap, her cue to pet him. "This is Chester, my clumsy Great Dane. He can't help it. He doesn't realize how big his body has gotten. He's the one you need to interrogate about the finger bone. He found it."

Chester lifted his head to stare sadly at Milo. Finding the barrel-chested detective uninteresting, the dog laid his head back down on Mille. Robert returned with Mille's coffee and snapped his finger at Chester who slid down and laid at Mille's feet. Then to Milo's surprise, Robert brought up a nearby chair and sat down.

Mille, who rarely missed anything, saw Milo's reaction to Robert. "Robert is my butler. His job is to simply buttle, but he butts in these days where he's not needed."

"I buttle to all people in this house. If there is a dead person in the attic, I need to know."

Not caring to understand the dynamics of the exchange, Milo asked to see the finger.

Robert stood up, went to a nearby end table, open the drawer, and removed a red felt cloth and handed it to Milo. Milo unfolded the cloth with care to reveal a single white bone.

"It's the metacarpal bone of the middle finger," Mille stated.

"How do you know that?" Milo asked.

"In my youth, I was trained as an archaeologist, an acceptable course of study for wealthy ladies of my era who wanted to appear worldly. Also, my late husband was an orthopedist. When I tell you it's a metacarpal bone of the middle finger, that's what it is."

"Is there anything else I should know?"

Mille paused. "What I have is family folklore and gossip, not facts. I want facts Mr. Rathkey. That's why I hired you. Impress me." Mille was as crusty today as she was last fall when Milo met her at the Chester Park Fall Festival.

Undaunted, Milo continued. "How was the bone found?"

"I was up in the attic, rummaging. My granddaughter was graduating from medical school this past December. I thought my husband's first stethoscope would be a nice gift. I was channeling my sentimental side. The stethoscope's no longer useful of course, although it would connect the two generations of doctors. She could hang it on the wall, but it will probably end up on the back of a door somewhere. Don't care. I've done my job. Apparently, Chester followed me up there, got to wandering, and fell asleep. I locked him in the attic not knowing he was up there."

Robert picked up the narrative. "I heard him barking, trotting, and scratching later in the day and let him out. He dashed to Mrs. Greysolon who showed me the bone."

"Chester is an old dog. When he was younger, he would have swallowed that bone," Mille said. "As a puppy, he ate everything. We would go to the vet every other week. He's pickier these days."

"I went up to see if there were more bones," Robert said, "but the attic is large, and I may have missed some areas."

"We were hoping you could not only find the skeleton, if there is one, but tell us whose skeleton took refuge in my attic."

"I would like to see the attic," Milo urged.

Robert led the way up to the second floor and down a long hallway to another set of stairs behind a locked door. Milo could feel a wave of frigid air telling him the attic was not heated. He rebuttoned his coat. At the top of the stairs, Milo, Robert, and Mille proceeded down another hallway with four rooms off to either side. No skeletons greeted him there. The hallway opened into a larger room with plaster walls and cut-glass globes covering several ceiling lights illuminating unneeded furniture, chests, and boxes.

"This is one full attic," Milo said.

"You know, it's not really an attic," Mille explained. "It's a third floor, but we never used it as such. I think it was originally meant to be a playroom or sectioned off to be servants' quarters. I call it the attic. I retrieved my father's medical bag from that chest by the rocking chair."

Milo walked over to the chest, opened it, and closed it again. He stood up and looked around the room. "From all this storage, I would guess there has been traffic up here in the last hundred years, yet no one has found this body?"

"Thus, the mystery," Robert said.

Milo turned to Mille, "Lakesong has secret rooms triggered by kicking the baseboards. Maybe there was a fire sale on secret rooms."

Mille laughed. "Start kicking."

Milo went up and down the baseboards kicking as hard as he could. Nothing moved. "Okay, good theory, but incorrect. I need to go through those other rooms, but that can wait. Could I take the bone, and have it analyzed?"

"Certainly," Mille said. "Meanwhile we will interrogate Chester again."

§

"Doesn't Milo Rathkey live with you?" Bill Bingham, the head of commercial real estate, asked Sutherland.

Sutherland looked up from his desk. "He does. My dad willed him half the estate. Why do you ask?"

"Have you read the Sunday New York Times?"

Wondering where this was going, Sutherland asserted, "No. I've been a little busy."

Bingham dropped the book review section on Sutherland's desk. "Someone wrote a book about him."

"About Milo?" Sutherland picked up the paper and read aloud, "*The Life and Death and Death Again of Harper Gain by Ron Bello.* It's Ron's book on Harper Gain, not Milo."

Bingham pointed to a paragraph in the review. "It says 'much of the book concerns itself with the investigation by Duluth Police Consultant, Milo Rathkey, who solved the mystery surrounding the poisoning death of a woman and, in so doing, dropped the Harper Gain bombshell. Being a suspect, author Ron Bello was on the inside when it all came down.'"

"Interesting. Does it mention me? I was at the reveal. I served the sherry," Sutherland boasted.

Bingham laughed. "I have no idea what that means, but if I were you, I'd keep the day job."

"Sherry pourers are treated so shabbily these days," Sutherland lamented. "And it was good sherry too. All of the suspects asked for seconds, except, of course, for the murderer."

§

Police Lieutenant Ernie Gramm was enjoying the beginning of his second month without a suspicious death when Deputy Chief Sanders called. "Ernie, is our consultant around?"

How had Milo graduated from my consultant to our consultant? "If you mean Milo, he hasn't been in for a couple of weeks. Healing from our last case, I guess."

"He's healed enough! Get him in here. I need to talk to him." The phone went dead.

Gramm yelled for Sgt. Robin White whose desk was in the general bullpen but within shouting distance to Gramm's office. It was a quiet day, so Gramm's bark was unexpected. White grabbed her coffee and stood in the doorway. "You yelled?" she asked as her heartbeat returned to normal.

"Sanders wants to talk to Milo. Why?" Gramm asked.

"No idea."

"Give him a call and get him in here ASAP?"

"Will do." As White turned to leave, Gramm caught sight of the stocky bodied, curly haired, police consultant strolling into the bullpen.

"Never mind, he's here,"

White turned back and claimed a chair in Gramm's office, interested in the reason for Milo's trip to the deputy chief—anything to break up the monotony of the paperwork Gramm had passed to her.

Milo walked into Gramm's office. "I have a finger bone I need someone to look at."

Gramm looked at White. "Did Milo just ask us to look at his finger?"

"I heard it too," White agreed.

"Not my finger," He took out the red cloth as he sat down, placed it on Gramm's desk, and uncovered his prize. "It belongs to a dead guy."

Lifting his bushy eyebrows, Gramm said, "I figured that out myself, Milo. Before we get into your dead guy finger mystery, you need to go up to Deputy Chief Sander's office."

Gramm managed an uncharacteristic grin. "He's demanding to see you."

Milo was uncomfortable with Gramm's glee. "What about?"

"Maybe he has another finger," White said. "A couple more, you two could have a whole hand."

Gramm laughed and pointed at White, approving of her humor. "Milo, go deal with Sanders. Your finger bone can wait here for you."

White picked up the cloth holding the bone and held it out, saying, "No, it can't. This isn't the morgue, take this with you. It's creepy."

Milo put the cloth in his pocket. He had never talked with Deputy Chief Sanders before. What did Sanders have to say that couldn't come through Gramm? Maybe he was getting fired. No, that was something he would have Gramm do.

Sanders wasn't at all what Milo pictured in his mind. The man was short, slight, a little paunchy with a bald head, and a nervous broad smile. He pumped Milo's hand for a long time—too long for Milo's liking. When the handshake was finally over, Sanders pointed to a comfortable padded chair across from his desk.

"Let me get to the point. I assume you have had a number of requests for interviews already."

Milo thought it best to keep smiling. "About what?"

"That book of course," Sanders said.

The smile was waning. "Book? What book?"

Sanders moved some papers around on his desk revealing a portion of a newspaper. "*The Life, Death, and Death Again of Harper Gain, by a Ron Bello.*"

"Oh, Ron's book. It's been published?"

Sanders smiled, "Oh, it's been published. According to this article, a good portion of the book details—I'm quoting here—'brilliant revelations by Duluth, Minnesota Police Consultant, Milo Rathkey.'"

"Oh crap. I'll get Ron to change that."

"Change it? No!"

"He seems to give me credit and…"

Sanders held up his hand signaling Milo to stop talking. "You are missing the point. The key words here are *Duluth Police Consultant*. This is good publicity for us. Even better, good national publicity. On this frigid, gray day in February, Chief Moore is smiling. When Chief Moore smiles, I smile; we all smile. He wants to milk this as much as possible, and to that end, I am going to have our PIO work with you on interviews, as many as possible."

Milo was about to object when Sanders rubbed his shiny, bald head, gave Milo a no-humor stare that said it was non-negotiable. Milo returned to Gramm's office.

White leapt up from the paperwork and followed Milo, glad for a second interruption.

"Did you get fired?" Gramm asked, not worried, but curious.

"Worse. I have to shoot someone."

"Anyone I know?"

"Ron Bello. Of course, Martha will object; they're old friends. Maybe I'll just wound him."

"Your life gives me a headache. Let's talk finger bone."

"You don't want to know why I have to shoot Ron Bello?"

"I know. The PIO just called. It seems you are the dog and pony show for the force. Congratulations!"

White began a slow clap.

"Thank you for your support," Milo said, fishing around in his pocket. "Here's that creepy bone again. It was found in Mille Greysolon's attic by her dog who looks like a pony."

"He's both the dog and pony for your show," White laughed. She was either on a roll or hysterical from paperwork overload.

"Who is Mille Greysolon? Where is her attic? And does the size of the dog matter?" Gramm asked.

"The size of the dog is key to this entire investigation. Mille lives next door to me."

"Where the couple was murdered with arrows?" White asked. "I thought the woman who owned that house died before those murders."

"Wrong neighbor. This estate is on the other side of Lakesong, Wardline."

"You live in a bad neighborhood," Gramm said.

"Tell me about it. Her dog found this bone, but her butler's brief search of the third floor didn't turn up any more bones. I think there's a skeleton hiding up there somewhere— another search is needed, but for now I want to know male or female, age, and anything else I can learn."

"Are you thinking homicide? Do we have to investigate? Is this Mille person capable of murder?"

"At the moment suspicion falls on Chester."

"Is Chester the husband?"

"No, Chester is the dog. He looks guilty."

Gramm took the cloth-wrapped bone. "I'll have Doc Smith take a look, meanwhile get out of my office and let me resume my calm day."

Milo stood up. "Who's the department PIO?"

"Kevin Richards. He's one of us. Don't abuse him."

"Who me?"

"Have fun."

§

When Sutherland arrived home, he checked on the special Martha-made dinner with Agnes. Martha shooed him out of the kitchen. He grabbed two slices of celery and an olive on the way out. He had his second ride scheduled on Gibbs' bike before dinner.

Turning on the monitors and the main bike console, Sutherland heard Gibbs talking. He realized he was late. "It's about time, McKnight! What if I showed up late for a real estate closing?" Gibbs said in an annoyed voice. "I was reminding others not to ride by themselves."

Sutherland thought Gibbs' tone was a bit testy. After all, they were doing him a favor. *What happened to that smooth charmer who schmoozed me at the club and on Saturday bike rides?*

After the shot at Sutherland, Gibbs moved on to abusing his staff. "Do we know if anyone is riding by themselves?"

An unknown man popped up in a small box on the screens. "No. If the bike isn't connected to the server, we have no idea."

"Why not?"

"Because it's not being recorded. The server only records the sanctioned rides. We all agreed to set it up that way. The riders are your..."

"Don't explain your job to me."

Sutherland, who never abused his employees, checked the monitors to see if anyone else was shocked at the Gibbs' outburst. Leah just shrugged. Marsden smiled and shrugged. Nora was with Sutherland, looking shocked. Charlie was playing with the ride route buttons on the screen oblivious to Gibbs.

"We're losing time, and I have other things to do. Let's ride!" Gibbs yelled. His bike spun around, and the ride began.

Sutherland turned to Leah Davis riding on his right. "What's going on with Gibbs?"

"You're seeing the real Gabriel Gibbs. Don't be fooled by that baby face—uber alpha in the worst way."

Sutherland heard Leah's comment, but her lips didn't quite match her words. "You're lip sync is off."

"So's yours," Leah said.

Charlie came up on Sutherland's left.

"Say something to me," Sutherland requested.

Charlie laughed. "Your lips are weird. What's going on?"

"I think there's a problem," Sutherland said, "but only when we talk."

"Keep up people!" Gibbs yelled. "Twenty-five miles shouldn't take two hours." He was almost out of sight.

The ride began where the previous day's ride had stopped in the Village of Montsoreau. Some villagers stopped along the street to watch the riders. A young boy waved.

"If we go through this village again, would the little boy still be there waving?" Leah asked.

"For these beta tests, yes," Gibbs said. "We sent bike riders out with small cameras strapped everywhere. Eventually, we will have computer generated effects mixed in, so the scene changes as well as the seasons and the weather."

The beginning of the day two ride took them through colorful streets narrow enough to be alleys. Flowers bloomed on either side with café patrons sipping their wine and coffees on outdoor terraces. The row of buildings on the riders' left gave way to a gothic style castle—built in white tufa stone—clinging to the riverbank.

Leah said she was sad as the ride left the village behind and progressed into the countryside. Wheat fields hugged both sides of the ever-tapering road until the riders came to a wooden bridge that passed over a fast-flowing stream.

"The bridge is a nice touch, Gibbs," Charlie Dawson said, "but the water has stopped moving. Oh, wait, it's now flowing backwards!"

Gibbs did not comment.

When the ride ended, and Gibbs was facing them once again, he asked if there were any problems besides their lagging behind.

"Could you hear what we were saying about our lips not matching the words at the beginning?" Sutherland asked.

"No. I was too far ahead. You laggers were out of range. The program is set so you can only hear another rider if they are close to you."

"It looks fine now," Leah offered.

Gibbs rolled his eyes and yelled. "Okay code mavens, why was the lip sync off? I want to know, and I want to know now!"

The riding group heard a voice but there was no picture. "It's the latency problem we've discussed, Gabe. When you're riding, looking straight ahead, it's not noticeable, but when you're looking at the face beside you, the moving lips will be a split second off. There is no getting around it, but you only see it when you're riding side by side."

"So, what do you suggest?" Gibbs yelled.

"Don't talk. Ride."

Gibbs smiled. "There you go people. In the future, don't talk even though that's the whole purpose of the bike! What is wrong with the lot of you. My office—now!"

"Hey Gibbs, don't forget your stream was flowing backwards!" Charlie Dawson yelled.

If Gibbs heard, he didn't react.

§

Continuing her busy day of catching up on bills, and scheduling kept Agnes' mind off the chat she had with Mary Alice this morning. It was bothersome, and Agnes didn't want 'bothersome' ruining Martha's special dinner for her and Sutherland. She was looking forward to their first official dinner together at Lakesong. The giggle-fest pizza fiasco last night was fun, but hardly up to Martha's standards. A small kitchen in their rooms might be nice so they wouldn't mess up Martha's official Lakesong kitchen.

Agnes took a long soaking bath in the en suite of the bedroom where she stored her clothes. The small kitchen was a maybe, but a soaking tub was a must on Agnes' remodel list.

Sutherland finished his ride a few minutes before seven, showered, dressed in his usual dark-gray slacks and navy sweater, and went down to make sure all was right for their special dinner. The appetizers were on the coffee table, the entrees were in the warming drawer, and the wine was chilling. Martha waved as she left for her cottage.

Agnes had texted him earlier to tell him where she would be, so he was not alarmed at her absence. She dressed for dinner in her single-life splurge, a soft white, Lilly Pulitzer sweater with pearls everywhere complimented by a pair of gray slacks, and metallic pewter ballet flats. The sweater made her feel fancy.

When she entered the family room, Agnes gazed at the tall, handsome, sandy-haired, young man behind the bar making her dirty martini. She sighed and thought tonight was special enough to have two.

Sutherland looked up, came out from behind the bar with her drink, and grinned. "The perfect drink for my perfect bride." He clicked a remote control and the beginning strains of Ed Sheeran's "Perfect" floated into the room.

Agnes smiled at the cheesiness of the moment, but hugged and kissed him anyway, knowing he was trying his best. Sutherland did well to kiss Agnes and not spill her drink. He spun her around, set the drink on the bar, and did a proper job of continuing the kiss.

The spin put the family room coffee table in Agnes' direct line of sight. "Is that what I think it is?" she asked Sutherland after they disengaged.

"It is. Beluga and Golden Ostera caviar and, of course, oysters."

"My favorites. How did Martha know?"

"I may have suggested a few things for this evening," Sutherland said with a sly smile, happy Agnes was pleased as he led her to the sectional. "I wanted our first official meal at Lakesong to be filled with our favorites."

She picked up her dirty martini and they toasted to all the good things life would bring. Agnes sank back into the sectional. Sutherland mirrored her. Their shoulders snuggled together.

When the drinks were drained and the hors d'oeuvres consumed, Sutherland disappeared into the kitchen, and reemerged rolling a cart with two plates of lake trout in garlic butter sauce, small red potatoes, and green beans along with a lovely bottle of chilled pinot blanc.

"The Pickwick," Agnes whispered, remembering the first dinner she and Sutherland shared together.

Sutherland grinned again. He looked about fifteen years old. "That was the night I discovered how special you are—so special," Sutherland murmured, a little embarrassed, not sure his words were enough as he poured the wine. They were. They toasted again to this night and many more to come in their lives.

Maybe it was the martini and wine, or the crackling fire, but Agnes felt another warm embrace as if Lakesong itself was welcoming her.

6

"That Gibbs idea will be money in the bank!" Charlie Dawson announced to Mia, as he entered the kitchen wearing his bike riding shorts and dry fit shirt. "Save your lecture. I'm taking another solo trip again this morning."

Mia flicked her long black hair out of her face and took a drink of her coffee.

"Did you hear what I said?" Charlie demanded. "I love that bike!"

Mia looked at him as if he was a stranger.

There was a time when Charlie thought his wife was the most beautiful woman he had ever seen—a tall, tan, fearless panther, powerful and determined. In the past few years, however, her distain for him had put him off. "Well, I know you think I'm just a loser...a clown. I'm telling you;

you should be interested because I'm investing in something even better—and cheaper—than Gabe's bike."

"You're not using my money, and you don't have any of your own."

"I'll find some somewhere. This is a sure thing. When it takes off, if you're smart enough to invest, you'll have enough money to divorce me and marry your lover boy, Ivan."

Mia sighed. "You're tiresome."

"I hear the late-night phone calls. If not with my boss, you're having an affair with someone," Charlie spat.

Mia laughed and shook her head.

"I'm going to my study to ride the money bike—research for my investment."

Mia yelled after him, "Do you really think Gibbs doesn't know you're breaking the rules? He's going to get rid of you."

Charlie ignored her.

§

Mia watched for Charlie's car to leave the garage before picking up her phone and calling a familiar number.

"Mia," the male voice crooned.

She smiled. "One o'clock?"

"Works for me."

§

After a delightful afternoon, Mia drove back to her house in Duluth's fashionable Hunter Park. She plugged her Tesla into its outlet, closed the garage door behind her, and shuddered as she walked into the house. She never liked this house. When they bought it twelve years ago, Charlie called it a starter home. Mia was anxious to make it their "ender" home. She was tired of being the mortgage payer, and wife of a clown who fell for get-rich-quick schemes such as eco-friendly fireplaces gone bust, and heat-absorbing wall-paper that peeled off the wall. Every time she walked into the living room, their presence was a testament to her poor choice in men.

Needing an energy boost before catching up on a client presentation for tomorrow, Mia stopped in the kitchen, grabbed a frosted sugar cookie, and warmed the morning's unfinished coffee in the microwave. The microwave buzz was drowned out by a loud thump. Mia froze, listened. Another thump. Someone was in the house! Not Charlie, his car wasn't in the garage. She briefly debated whether to call the police or deal with the intruder herself. She did both. Rushing into the garage, she called the police from her cell phone, and grabbed a nine iron from her golf bag. The thuds seemed to come from the family room. There was another bang like something falling.

Armed with the club, she inched her way toward the noise. The family room was empty. A loud crash, followed by swearing, told Mia the intruder was in Charlie's study. Worried the intruder was about to come through the open study door, Mia sprinted though the family room, paused by the study, flattened herself against the wall, and raised the golf club over her head. Another loud thud frightened her. She jerked. The golf club bumped the wall behind her. Everything went silent.

Fearing she had given herself away, Mia went on the offensive, charging into the study screaming. She swung at the intruder. He lurched to the side, the golf club missing his head but connecting with his shoulder. Yelping in pain, he lashed out, pushing Mia down. Her head struck the handle of the bike. Dazed, Mia saw her attacker rush through the broken French doors, disappearing toward the rear of the house.

She hurt. Her hand touched the warm liquid streaming down her face. It was red. She blinked and tried to stand. Wobbly, she grabbed the bike and paused on her knees to get her bearings. Rising, she stepped over two fallen monitors, and stumbled to the kitchen where she sat down at the kitchen table. Wobbly gave way to dizzy. Police sirens were approaching the house. Still sitting, she reached into the freezer grabbing a cold pack and placed it on her forehead. Several minutes later a policeman was at her door.

Leaning against the walls for balance, she managed to open the door and point toward the study.

He called for EMTs, walked her over to the couch in the family room, and asked if anything was taken.

"I don't know. It's my husband's office. It's over there. I think the guy was messing with the bike. Two monitors are on the floor."

"I'll check it now. The EMTs are here to check you over."

Mia settled back as her vitals were taken and her head was cleaned up—no stitches, just a bandage.

The officer walked into the study, spent five minutes looking over the scene, and returned, saying, "I've never seen a bike like that."

"It's a prototype. Look, can we hurry this up? I don't feel well. I know the name of the punk who broke in." Mia wanted everybody gone.

The officer pulled out his note pad. "That should make this easier."

"His name is Xavier something."

"Last name?"

"Don't know. Contact my husband, Charlie Dawson at the Babin Ad Agency."

"I see you have a camera outside the door. Can I get that video?"

"Yeah. Sure. I need to lie down."

"One other thing. Your husband is going to want to get that door fixed as soon as possible."

Yeah, right, the husband who can't do anything useful, Mia thought as she said goodbye to the officer and the EMTs. She grabbed a bottle of water, two ibuprofens, and started the ecofriendly fireplace which, to her surprise, stayed lit. Taking out her phone, she called Mr. Mitchell, her handyman asking him to fix the door, ASAP. He said he could do a temporary plywood fix today. Wrapping herself in her winter coat and the couch throw, Mia laid her head down, forgetting about the client presentation, and slept.

§

"How are we all feeling?" Gibbs asked the assembled group.

"Energized," Nora said.

"Ride three. The next twenty-five miles. Let's go Gibbs," Leah added.

"Sutherland?" Gibbs asked.

"Oh sorry, I was adjusting my seat—finding the sweet spot."

The others laughed. Sutherland rolled his comment back in his mind to find the funny part. "Grow up people," he chided.

"We have," Nora said. "That's why it's so funny."

"Charlie? Are you with us?" Gibbs asked.

"Let's get this ride started. I'm cold." Charlie said. "Some idiot broke into my house this afternoon and I only have plywood covering the door. Drafty. By the way, those are some sturdy monitors you have. The idiot knocked two of them down. I picked them up, and they're working fine."

"A break-in? Is anything missing?" Gibbs demanded.

"Nothing missing from my study."

"The bike!" Gibbs shouted. "Is anything missing from the bike? I don't care about your study!"

"Thank you for your concern," Charlie shot back.

"You should have told us about it. Marsden could have made sure all the connections were tight."

"If there are glitches with Charlie's bike, I'll be glad to go and check it out, Gibbs," Marsden agreed.

Sutherland was going to ask more about the break-in when Gibbs cut him off. "We all have problems. You're sitting on mine. Let's move people!" Gibbs said. The program turned him around and they all began to pedal. "We are going to go over the same stretch again. It should be smoother this time."

"Oh look! It's the waving kid!" Leah exclaimed. "Hi, kid." She waved back.

Toward the end of the ride, they crossed the bridge and the water flowed in only one direction this time. Charlie didn't comment.

Sutherland wanted to see if the program would allow Gibbs to be bested so he poured it on. Charlie was thinking the same thing and crept up on Sutherland's left, not to chat, but to beat them both.

"The boys are having their alpha moment," Leah said to Nora as they rode side by side.

Nora looked at Marsden in one of the rear monitors. "Are you going to join them?"

He smiled and said, "It's my job to pull up the rear."

Sutherland was almost up to Gibbs when he heard a sizzle and snap followed immediately by a muted yell. "What's that?" He turned around to see Nora, Leah, and Marsden shaking their heads in the rear monitors behind him but no Charlie. He slowed his pace. "Where's Charlie?" he asked.

Leah and Nora turned to look. "I can't see him."

"He's not behind me, or in front of me." Marsden reported, checking all the monitors. "I don't understand. He's disappeared and his bike has disappeared."

"Charlie?" Sutherland yelled.

Gibbs was being told by his technicians the other riders had slowed down. "What's wrong with you people? We only have a few more miles to go!"

"Gibbs! Charlie's disappeared. I heard a shout!" Sutherland said, miffed at Gibbs' attitude.

A disembodied voice said to the group, "His bike is not responding. It's offline. Charlie, we need you to continue the ride, or our data will be skewed. We're not putting enough pressure on the servers."

"What the hell does that mean?" Gibbs demanded.

"We've set up the ride for six bikes. We need six bikes. Stop the ride."

Gibbs stopped. "He said his room was cold. Don't tell me cold affects the electronics."

"We tested these bikes for extreme heat and cold. No problems."

"Maybe he turned the bike off," Sutherland offered.

The voice said, "We pinged the bike; even a turned off bike should answer the signal. There's nothing."

"Wait," Gibbs said, "what does that mean?"

"The bike is offline. He unplugged the bike."

"Screw him. I'll deal with Charlie later. Let's ride!"

"Gibbs! We need six riders!"

"Deal with it! I was going to bounce Charlie anyway."

"I don't mind resuming the ride," Leah said, "but I heard a scream. Someone needs to see if Charlie's okay."

"It's just like Charlie to screw with me," Gibbs spat.

The group, minus Charlie, continued to ride. Sutherland poured it on, passing Gibbs in the final quarter mile.

"I see your butt found it's sweet spot,"

Sutherland laughed but recognized that Gibbs was miffed at being passed. Maybe volunteering to help Gibbs on this project had not been the best idea.

§

After his turbulent ride, Sutherland called Charlie, leaving a message on his voice mail. Looking forward to a pleasant evening, he showered, dressed for dinner, and came downstairs.

Agnes was in the kitchen talking with Martha. Sutherland made himself a martini then called to Agnes to find out if she would like a cocktail.

"That would be lovely," Agnes responded from the kitchen as Martha gave her the back hand wave of get out. Agnes backed out, bowing to her friend.

She looked around the family room, seeing Sutherland behind the bar, the table set for two, and the fireplace warm and crackling. "Did we chase Milo away again?"

"He had a second night invitation he couldn't refuse."

Agnes laughed. "Is Mary Alice going to keep him away forever?"

"I think this is our last reprieve. If we want a romantic dinner, it has to happen upstairs. We can't foist Milo on Mary Alice forever."

"I don't want Martha carrying food upstairs?"

"There's an elevator, and wheeled carts" Martha yelled from the kitchen. "I excel in popup romantic dinners to go."

§

Milo awoke to the da-dunk sound on his phone, the ringtone for Ernie Gramm. The room was dark except for the light of the phone. Milo took a moment to get his bearings before answering. "Ernie?"

"We need our famous police consultant to do actual work today,"

"It isn't today. It's tonight. Dark."

Gramm gave him an address. "We got a partial crispy critter over here. From what I've been told we could also use Sutherland. Get moving!"

"Sutherland isn't here."

"We'll worry about him later." The phone went dead.

7

Milo left a text for Mary Alice and nodded to Luna glad that the other, noisier dogs were crated in Mary Alice's late husband's office—now the in-house kennel. He made his way through the perpetual construction zone, to the garage, slipped into his '87 Mercedes 560SL and drove up the hill to the Hunters Park neighborhood.

Milo's teenage dream car, which he gifted himself last year, was never meant to be a go-to-a-murder car. Trying to wake up, he stopped at a twenty-four-hour gas station for coffee but passed on any food. Decaying bodies no longer bothered him, but burnt flesh always made him queasy.

The sun was rising as his map app identified his destination: a traditional, yellow stucco, two story house in the middle of the woods. He parked behind the line of three official vehicles, leaving room for the medical examiner's body car to exit.

Milo flashed his ID at the patrol officer manning the front door. Officer Butler recognized the stocky detective and pointed in the general direction of the crime scene, thrusting a box of gloves in Milo's face.

Gramm was waiting with Sgt. White in the doorway, while Doc Smith, the medical examiner, knelt by the body of Charlie Dawson. As the first wave of burnt flesh brushed past him, Milo closed his eyes, held his nose, and turned his back to the crowded room.

"Forget your nose salve, newbie?" White said, handing him her tube. "Here. They're $8.99 on Amazon."

Milo applied the salve under his nose and breathed in the fresher scent. "I left my tube in my other car," he explained as he gloved up, knowing that was an excuse that had never passed his lips before.

Gramm, who went old school with Vicks under the nose, looked around and back toward the front door. "Where's Sutherland? I want to talk to him."

"In bed, I suppose. That's where most people are at this hour."

"Yeah...well...it looks as though Mr. Dawson here was shocked."

"Electrocuted," Doc Smith corrected. "One survives a shock. Could you all move back, your dainty smells are contaminating my crime scene." Doc Smith disliked the use of odor blockers, especially Vicks, preferring to take in the noxious odors au naturel in case they provided a clue.

Milo maneuvered around Gramm to peek into the room. He saw a fried bike surrounded by TVs. "What the hell is this? A stationary bike fatality?"

"Seems so," Gramm grunted.

Milo noticed the charred hands and arms on the body that was lying behind the bike. "Who's the crispy critter?"

Doc Smith looked up. "A guy named Charlie Dawson."

White added, "His wife found him. She's in the kitchen with Officer Preston."

"Was there an explosion?" Milo pointed to the plywood over the door.

Gramm shook his head. "No. Why do you ask?"

"Plywood is out this year."

"That, I am told by the wife, was from a break-in earlier yesterday."

"Robbed and fried on the same day?"

"Could be," Gramm said.

"Why did you need Sutherland? You want his bike expertise?" Milo asked.

White tapped him on the shoulder and held a phone in front of his face. "The victim's last call."

Milo backed up against the door jamb to focus and read *Sutherland McKnight* on the caller ID. "Small world." The phone burst into life. Sutherland was calling again. Milo took the phone from White asking Sutherland if he was sipping his smoothie.

Sutherland paused. "Milo? Did I call the wrong number?"

"Not if you were calling a Charlie Dawson."

"Why are you answering…" Sutherland began. "Oh hell! What's happened to Charlie?"

Gramm grabbed the phone out of Milo's hand and put in on speaker. "Gramm here. Why are you calling Charlie Dawson?"

"I wanted to see if he was okay."

Agnes propped herself up and tapped him on the arm. Sutherland turned. The look on his face told her something was wrong. Sutherland put his phone on speaker.

Gramm continued, "Why were you concerned?"

"He left the ride last night."

"Is your phone on speaker?" Gramm demanded.

"Yes."

"Who's listening?"

"Agnes."

"Agnes Larson?"

"Well, um, yes."

White rolled her eyes and mouthed, "Again?"

"What ride?" Gramm asked.

"What?"

"You said Charlie Dawson left a ride. What ride?"

"Oh, we were testing a new bike for a friend of ours, still are—Gabriel Gibbs. There was crackle and Charlie disappeared. He didn't come back."

"Well, he's here now," Gramm said. "When you say he disappeared, what do you mean?"

"We were all riding and chatting. Then we heard a sound, and we were all questioning what it was, but Charlie wasn't one of the questioners. He just disappeared. One of Gibbs' technicians said he unplugged his bike. I began to wonder about a heart attack or something like that, but Charlie is healthy, fit."

Gramm looked at the body. "Tell me about this test. How many people are involved?"

"Four, five counting Gibbs, six counting Gibbs' guy Marsden." Sutherland could have stopped there, but given his penchant to over explain, he went on. "Most of us ride together in person in the summer, and ride virtually in the winter. We're part of the Zenith City Riders. Well, not Marsden, but maybe this summer. We got a big write up in the..."

"Getting back to the test," Gramm interrupted, "you rode yesterday evening?"

"Yes. About halfway through, Charlie disappeared. I've been calling to find out why."

"Give Sergeant White the names, numbers, and addresses of the other riders including this guy Gibbs."

After Sutherland gave her what information he had, White hung up and re-bagged the phone. Doc Smith was still leaning over the body.

"Anything yet, Doc?" Gramm asked.

Smith looked up. "Yeah, he's still dead."

The odor block was wearing off, plus Milo was not pleased being roused in the early morning for nothing. "Why am I here?" Milo asked Gramm. "Looks like an electrical accident. I only solve murders."

"Hang on Sherlock. The paramedic thought it looked suspicious and told our people. They called me and Doc Smith."

"The paramedic?" Milo questioned.

"I didn't get it all, but he said these bikes shouldn't have enough volts to kill someone. He said the bike was missing a...ah..."

"Transformer," White filled in from her notes.

"Anyway, the EMT said it looked suspicious or at least dangerous," Gramm added. "That's why we're here, and I wanted to share the fun." Gramm moved from the doorway toward the kitchen. "Forensics is going to be a while. Let's go talk to the widow,"

Mia Dawson, still in her winter coat, was sitting with Officer Preston. The widow had her hands around a coffee cup, staring into the cold, black liquid, trembling as if she were cold.

Gramm made the introductions.

Mia looked up. "Why are you here?"

White, not sure if the Mia Dawson was in shock, exchanged glances with Preston who had been with the widow for much of the morning. Preston shrugged, took out her pad, and prepared to take notes.

"Your husband is dead," White answered. "We have some questions. How did you happen to find your husband in the middle of the night?"

"I fell asleep on the couch. I woke up to a strange smell." Mia shivered. "I was cold and thought Charlie left the door open to his study. Those French doors were broken. I found him there on the floor and called for help. I'm still cold. That doggie draft-stopper, could somebody put it against the door to the garage?"

White was puzzled. "Doggie draft-stopper?"

Mia was annoyed. "Yes, that thing," she snapped, pointing to a black-and-white fuzzy cloth worm.

White stood up and saw the round cloth tube with the face of a dog. She shoved it up against the bottom of the door while looking through the window into the garage. "Oh, you have one of those electric cars."

Mia nodded, still trembling.

Gramm moved the conversation. "Did your husband have any health issues—any heart trouble?"

"No. None."

"Did your husband have any enemies?"

"Why would you ask me that?"

"It's procedure," Gramm said.

"Look!" Mia pushed her fingers through her hair in exasperation and fatigue taking care to avoid her bandages "I'm not having a very good day. You people need to talk to each other. I told them how that kid broke in here and attacked me. Look at me," she said, pointing to her forehead. "That kid didn't even hate me, but I've got bandages and bruises. Charlie was the one he hated."

"Why would that person want to harm your husband?" White asked.

"Charlie was a louse and a thief. I'm not feeling well. Just leave, please."

"We have a person to help you. She's on her way. She'll explain what happens next," White said.

The interview ended. Gramm told Mia to stay out of the study as it was for now considered a crime scene.

"Fine. Just leave and close the door. I'm so cold."

§

Annie didn't get her bacon this morning and stomped off with a meow.

Sutherland expelled a deep breath. "Poor Mia,"

"I assume that's Charlie's wife," Agnes said. "Do you know her well?"

"Not well, I've met her a few times at the club. She's not a Zenith City Rider—indoor bike person only."

"What happened?"

Sutherland stared at Agnes blankly. "Now that you ask, I don't know. Gramm didn't say, but he was interested in the bike, that new one we're testing for Gibbs."

"The same one you're riding? Is it safe?"

"Good question. I don't know. I don't know anything. I do know Charlie disappeared from our ride last night—maybe his heart, but then why would Gramm or Milo be involved?" Sutherland asked, taking a sip of his smoothie.

Martha walked into the morning room with Agnes' fruit smoothie. "If you want something other than blender food in the morning, let me know."

Agnes laughed. "One of these days I'm going to try Milo's lumberjack breakfast. I won't have to eat for a week." She opened her pad and began to read the local paper.

Sutherland went back to his Wall Street Journal.

"Oh my! Here it is!" Agnes exclaimed.

Sutherland looked up. "What's where?"

"Our wedding announcement. It's in the paper." Agnes handed her pad to Sutherland who began to read: *"Mary Alice Bonner is pleased to announce the marriage of her friend, Agnes Rose Larson, to Sutherland Moray McKnight. The couple wed in Hawaii…"*

"Moray?" Agnes laughed. "Your middle name is Moray? Are you named after an eel?"

Sutherland straightened up in wounded pride. "Moray is a Scottish name and is one of the three stars on our family crest: Moray, Freskin, and Sutherland or so my mother told me."

"Impressive. You have a family crest. Somebody in my family loved antique names and flowers—Agnes Rose."

Sutherland handed back her pad. "Well, Ms. Agnes Rose, don't forget to ask your boss for tomorrow off. We have an appointment with Creedence Durant our financial advisor."

"I don't know. My boss is such a stickler for the rules."

"Right. He's a real rules guy. Tell me again, why did Mary Alice put that announcement in the paper?"

"She said people would have considered no notice to be impolite." Agnes sipped her smoothie and waited for a response.

"Mary Alice—the arbitrator of society's rules," Sutherland said.

"But at the same time, she's with Milo." Agnes said.

"Complicated lady."

§

Milo was following Gramm to Gibbs Industries when "Uptown Girl" began to play on his phone. "Hi Blue."

"I woke up and you were gone."

"I left you for a murder."

"You say the nicest things."

"I'm a charmer."

"You're not welcome tonight, I've got a meeting," Mary Alice stated.

"Are you saying I have to return to that cramped house down the road?"

"Sad but true. If you get claustrophobic, take a walk outside."

"You say the nicest things."

"I'm a charmer too."

§

Gibbs Industries was located in an avant-garde, two story building on Arrowhead Road near the university. Gramm and White arrived first, driving under the second floor which stretched over the access road. Gramm parked the Police Interceptor in the circular driveway. Milo was pulling up behind when his phone began to ring.

"Rathkey," he said to the unidentified caller.

"Kevin Richards here. I'm the police PIO, public information officer."

"I know what PIO stands for," Milo said, not disguising the annoyance in his voice. "Kinda busy right now."

"Right—don't care. The first interview will be tomorrow with NPR at ten-thirty in the AM."

"I'm on a murder case right now, and…"

"The deputy chief made it clear—interviews before murder."

Milo huffed. "Where do I go?"

"Minnesota Public Radio on Superior Street. I'll text you the exact address. That's the first of several. The Duluth News Tribune wants you. Good Morning America is thinking about it. You may have to go to New York for that one."

"I don't like New York, too many restaurants, I can't choose, forget to eat, and then I just faint."

"They're only thinking about it."

"If I murder Ron Bello, would these interviews stop?"

"Well, you'd be locked up and not available for interviews."

Milo didn't respond.

"Mr. Rathkey?"

"I'm thinking about it."

"Tomorrow is interview number one. Be at the radio studio at 10:15."

Gramm and White saw Milo on his phone and decided not to wait out in the cold, They entered the office and informed the woman at the information desk they were there to see Gabriel Gibbs. The woman, who never looked up, matter-of-factly told the two that Mr. Gibbs was a busy man and was not available to anyone except by appointment. Gramm tossed his badge down on the computer keyboard. It got her attention. He never tired of the badge trumping the wall of no appointment.

Milo burst through the double doors and waved off the same objecting information desk person. He rushed to join Gramm and White just as a young male intern was leading them past a security door and into a long hallway. "Mr. Gibbs hasn't come into the office yet. He's working in his residence," the intern said, looking over his shoulder.

"His residence?" Gramm echoed. "How far away is that?"

"It's just upstairs." Glancing up from his phone, the intern smiled. "He just needs only to get on the elevator. Mr. Gibbs is wondering what this is all about."

"I bet he is," Gramm said, offering no information.

77

They were led into a white conference room with a long irregular driftwood table, surrounded by orange padded armchairs. Unlike the many other white conference rooms, this one sported a number of electronic games and pinball machines along one wall. "Feel free to play," the young man said, looking at his phone. "Mr. Gibbs says he'll join you shortly."

Milo took him up on the offer, sending the first pinball through six rapid fire bumpers on a machine called Houdini. White began exercising her flipper button fingers while she checked out Octoberfest, plotting the best attack strategy. Gramm took a seat at the table, crossed his arms, and watched them spin numbers and ring bells.

After about fifteen minutes of arcade sounds, a tall, boyish looking man, with slicked-back, product-filled, blond hair, and a trendy stubble walked into the room. He stared at the group, waited for the pinball music to stop, and asked why they were there.

Gramm didn't see this guy as Gabriel Gibbs. He looked more like an older intern who brought bad news and bad coffee. "Are you Gabriel Gibbs?"

The man whose hair did not move, nodded.

"Do you know a Charlie Dawson?" Gramm asked as White and Milo joined Gramm at the table.

"Sure. Why do you ask?" Gibbs said, leaning on the back of one of the orange chairs.

"He's dead."

"Good. I was going to kick him out. Solves my problem."

"Cold." White thought. "The man died. Do you want to know how?"

"I assumed you were going to tell me. Just make it quick."

Gramm sat back. "Your bike killed him," Gramm said, looking for a reaction. He got it.

Gibbs stepped back, fists clenched at his side. "What the hell are you saying?"

"He was electrocuted while riding your bike. What would you call it?" Gramm persisted. "When did you last see Dawson?"

"Last night on the ride. Well, I wasn't with him. He was just a person in my monitor, and my bike didn't kill anyone." Gibbs shook his finger at Gramm. "I don't need this."

"Neither did Mr. Dawson. I am told that most bikes use a…" He looked at White.

"Transformer," White added.

"Your bike seems to be missing that device," Gramm said.

Gibbs smiled, relieved. "My bike's not missing anything. That step down is inside the electronics box under the handlebars. I've seen it. It provides twelve volts like every other exercise bike ever made. We were all riding identical bikes. This is all on Charlie. According to my people, Charlie pulled the damn plug."

"How would you know he pulled the plug?" White asked.

"I don't know! My people know. It's why I pay them." Gibbs shouted as though White were his employee, not a police sergeant.

"I suggest you change your tone, Mr. Gibbs, unless you want to be hauled out of here in handcuffs," White admonished. "This is an initial visit to inform you of Mr. Dawson's demise. Answer my question. How did your people know Dawson pulled the plug on the bike?"

Gibbs curled his lip as though she were lowly vermin, switched his gaze to Gramm, and continued. "My techs do something called pinging the bike. The bike should answer. It didn't. They told me he pulled the damn plug. Is that clear enough to all of you?"

"Oh, it's clear, but from the evidence it was more like Charlie's plug was pulled," Gramm said, not liking Gibbs' tone.

Gibbs just shook his head. "Just not possible."

Milo knew that Gramm was probing just to be irritating. Doc Smith didn't even have the corpse back to the autopsy room yet.

Gramm continued. "We are still at the beginning of the investigation, but we would like one of your bikes for our forensics people to check out."

"I won't do that. These bikes contain proprietary information."

Gramm leaned forward, folding his hands on the table and stretching out his shoulders. "We're not in the bike business, Mr. Gibbs. We're in the homicide business. I don't care about proprietary information. If you refuse now, I'll get a warrant. But having to get a warrant makes me cranky."

Crankier, White thought.

Gibbs took out his phone and ordered the person on the other end to come to the conference room.

"While we wait, tell us about this test," Milo asked.

"Six of us ride for about an hour a day, twenty-five miles. After each ride, my crew analyzes the data and fixes the bugs in the code. That's why Charlie's stupid pulling of the plug was a serious complication. He took the bike offline during the ride. His ride data was lost."

Gramm started smoothing the bushy hair on his left eyebrow, a Gramm exasperation tell. "Maybe I wasn't clear on this. Charlie Dawson was electrocuted while riding your bike. When we found the body, the bike was still plugged in. He didn't pull any plug," Gramm said.

Milo added, "You seem upset by Charlie. Did Charlie upset you a lot?"

Gibbs rubbed his blond, nearly invisible chin hairs, debating how to answer, when Ethan Marsden entered the room. "What do you need?"

Gibbs turned to him. "These people are police. Charlie's dead."

"Charlie? Charlie Dawson? I…I…I am so sorry."

Gramm nodded.

"That explains the glitch last night. Please extend our sympathies to his family." Marsden shook his head in disbelief. "Was it a heart attack?"

"They say electrocution," Gibbs said.

Gramm interrupted. "Who are you?" he asked Marsden.

"Ethan Marsden. How? While riding the bike? That can't be. I assure you the bike had nothing to do with Charlie's death unless it was a heart attack."

Not wanting to go down the corporate party line once again, Gramm said, "We will need one of these bikes for our investigation."

Marsden looked at a scowling Gibbs who reluctantly nodded. "I will personally deliver one to you and set it up." Marsden advised. "They have to be set up properly."

Gramm gave him the address of the forensic warehouse.

After the police left, Marsden reminded Gibbs that all participants signed a health waiver and offered to contact the corporate lawyers.

"Not your call, errand boy!" Gibbs snapped.

8

Glad to be done with Gibbs, the trio stood huddling outside in the parking lot. White complained about the penetrating cold. Gramm didn't want to discuss the weather. "I've been up half the night, I'm freezing, and have had nothing to eat. I need food...now!"

White stared at him. "I've been with you the whole time. Do you think I've been snacking?"

"You're younger. You have energy. Where do we go around here?"

"This isn't my neighborhood."

"I know a place," Milo said.

"Of course, you do," White sighed.

"Everybody's House. It's only a mile from here."

"If they serve food, let's go, now!" Urged Gramm. "We'll follow you."

Milo led them to a house-like restaurant with a large sign advertising Everybody's House. "I hope you like hamburgers," Milo said. "There are thirty-six varieties."

"And you, of course, have eaten them all." White said.

"I stopped at the mushroom Swiss burger. It's my favorite."

"I don't care if it's a cardboard and coffee grounds burger, as long as it's big and hot, I'll eat it," Gramm said.

Milo was accosted at the front door by a spritely, short woman. She was wearing a bright and cheery, yellow mock turtleneck. "Milo!"

"Maude!"

"You've lost weight. Not healthy! Have you been eating sour cream with your scallions?"

White looked at Gramm who shrugged.

"I haven't been eating scallions, Maude, or sour cream."

"They're good for your heart."

White mouthed the word 'scallions?'

Gramm almost laughed.

"Maude, these are my associates, Police Lieutenant Ernie Gramm, and Sergeant Robin White," Milo said.

Maude shook their hands. "I'm Maude. Welcome to Everybody's House which is really my house." They followed her to a table near a side window.

After peeling off the winter layers, White perused the menu. "Milo wasn't kidding. They have thirty-six hamburgers."

Gramm leaned toward White. "I don't see scallions on the menu."

"No, the scallions are only on Maude's menu for me," Milo said. "Maude has boundary issues."

"Says the man who insults every server in every restaurant he goes to," White muttered while responding to a text alert. "Burglary says they've arrested a suspect in the Dawson break-in. I told them to hold him for now, we're going to want to talk to him."

Gramm grunted. "Not until eat something."

Maude came back to take their orders. White opted for a veggie burger and a bowl of minestrone. Gramm thought the double Duluth Blizzard Burger and fries would fill his empty places. Milo didn't quibble as he did in other restaurants. He asked for his mushroom Swiss burger, fries, and a diet coke.

As Maude left, White said they should come here more often because Milo didn't take five minutes to order.

"Maude scares me," Milo said.

Gramm asked White to read off the names of other beta riders in Charlie Dawson's group. "Nora Swenson, Leah Davis, Sutherland McKnight, Ethan Marsden, and the delightful Mr. Gibbs," White said.

"This McKnight guy sounds like a criminal," Milo quipped.

"He has come up on our radar several times," Gramm added. "He always claims he didn't do it, but I'm suspicious."

White asked Gramm why he pressed Gibbs so aggressively. Gramm said he didn't care for Gibbs' insulting attitude. While the two discussed egocentric personalities, an unordered appetizer of scallions and sour cream appeared in front of Milo.

Maude arrived with their burgers. "Eat the scallions!" Maude ordered. White looked around the restaurant. No other patron had a plate of scallions.

"Anybody got a breath mint?" White asked. "Milo's going to need one."

"I want more background on that blond bike maker. Also, the other people on that ride," Gramm said, biting into his double Blizzard Burger. "Mmm. This is good!" he managed between chews.

White picked up her phone. "I'll get Preston on that."

Gramm caught Maude's attention and ordered a black coffee to go, unusual for him at lunch. "It's gonna be a long day, and I'm already tired," he said, by way of an excuse. "I also want to know more about our victim. What's the name of Dawson's boss? We should probably question him too."

"Ivan Babin," White said. "I'll get an address."

Gramm sipped his coffee. "I could use a nap before I continue with my favorite part of an investigation."

"Watching Milo not eat onions?" White joked.

"That too and learning about the victim and the suspects. Why can't murderers just come forward and confess?"

"You are tired," Milo laughed.

"Okay, we talk to the victim's boss next," Gramm said.

"I looked him up," White said. "The Babin Group has offices in the new building at Lake and Superior."

Maude eyed Milo and the still not touched side plate. To keep her from coming over, he held up two scallions and with a great flourish, dipped them in sour cream, and wedged them into his mushroom Swiss burger, making sure Maude saw him.

"How is that good for your heart?" Gramm asked.

"Don't question it!" Milo said. "If I don't eat these, she'll bring more."

"Aww, she's worried about you." White mocked.

"I think she hates me. It's hard to tell, but the burgers are outstanding even with onions and sour cream."

§

Gibbs stepped into the pinball conference room where all the bike technicians had been assembled. He informed them that Dawson had not unplugged the bike but died while riding. "How could that have happened?"

There was murmuring and shock, but no answers.

Gibbs moved on. "Recalibrate the test parameters for five riders instead of six."

Marsden, standing in doorway, shook his head. "Shouldn't you be more concerned about your friend than recalibrating the bike's parameters? He hasn't even been buried yet."

Gibbs clenched his teeth and turned to Marsden. "Do you see all these people, Marsden?" His hand swept the room. "They all receive *needed* paychecks, needed paychecks that come because of this bike." Moving closer to Marsden, Gibbs stood nose to nose, and whispered, "Unlike you, you crazy SOB, who are only here because your mommy felt sorry for you."

Marsden stood his ground, smiling. "I was only thinking about you, Gabe, and the company."

Gibbs walked to the door, turned, and shouted, "Okay, we'll delay it a day or two, but I want the tests to resume by the first of next week! Get on it, now!" Gibbs stormed out of the room.

§

Xavier Cullen sat in the police interview room nervously running his clammy palms over the top of his blue-jeaned thighs. He was anxious, waiting for a new attorney to arrive. Originally, an overworked public defender had been assigned to his case, but he was dismissed in favor of Saul Feinberg. Xavier didn't know Feinberg, but Marlene Budack, the owner of the Tip Top Tavern, said he was top notch and would probably not charge him.

Xavier was a favorite of Marlene's because she loved his neon signs. She was one of Xavier's biggest clients.

Feinberg sporting new tortoise shell glasses, shook his new client's hand, introduced himself, and opened his leather folder. Looking at Xavier, Feinberg thought the young, nervous, suspect was a juvenile. The prosecutor had sent him the file only minutes before. He had enough time to print it, but not look at it. Taking the booking sheet out of his folder, Feinberg checked the kid's age. He was nineteen, an adult in Minnesota.

"Let's start at the beginning," Saul began. "It says here you are charged with breaking and entering, and assault at a house on Featherstone Lane. Why?"

"That wasn't me. I wasn't there." Xavier said, avoiding eye contact.

"You weren't where?"

"At Dawson's house."

Feinberg shook his head. "Okay, that's a problem because how do you know who lives there?"

"I don't. You're supposed to be my lawyer."

"I am your lawyer. I'm not the cops. You need to tell me the truth. What you tell me goes no further. It's like a secret I can't tell."

"I'm not a child," Xavier whined.

"No, you're not. You're old enough to go to an adult jail. If you don't start telling me the truth, that's where you'll go."

"Okay, okay, I know Charlie Dawson, but I wasn't at his house on Tuesday."

Feinberg rolled his eyes. He expected a nineteen-year-old kid to be a better liar. Most of his clients were savvy; this kid had convicted himself at least twice in the last five minutes. "Okay, according to you, you weren't at the Dawson house, but you know *who* lives there, and you know *when* the burglary took place. You're two for two, and not in a good way."

"I wasn't stealing. I was trying to get my stuff back. He's the one who stole my stuff."

Feinberg wrote several notes. "Now we're getting somewhere. Tell me about your 'stuff.'"

"It's my drawings and ideas. I tried to get a job at that ad agency Dawson works at. He was interviewing me to be like his assistant. I showed him some of my ideas, so he could see how good I am. He took them and said he would get back to me. That was two months ago. Then I see one of my ideas in an ad on TV."

"Did you confront him?"

"Yeah," Xavier blurted.

"Want to elaborate?"

"Sure. I went to his agency two or three times. He was always out or with a client. Finally, I see him, but he just sits there smiling. He says I learned a valuable lesson: don't trust anyone. I tell him I want my other drawings back. He laughs at me and throws me out of his office."

"Then what?"

"I left, but I was freaked. Look, he stole from me, so I figured I had a right to take my stuff back. I waited in my car for him to leave. I watched him. He had my portfolio under his arm like it was his. Made me mad."

"What did you do next?"

"I followed him to his house. It was dark. I parked down the road, snuck back to his house, and looked in the windows." Cullen stopped talking—again.

Feinberg rolled his eyes. "And?"

"My portfolio was on a chair in a back room that sorta looked like an office, but it had this weird bike with all sorts of TVs around it. I tried the door, but it was locked. I made a plan to get it the next day when the house was empty."

"But it wasn't empty."

"I got delayed...that other guy. I messed up. I thought no one would be home all afternoon, but the delay screwed me up. That woman came screaming in, swinging a golf club. I defended myself. She popped me in the shoulder. It hurt!" Xavier said, rubbing the place where the nine-iron had made contact with his body. "Still does." Cullen pulled up his shirt sleeve revealing a dark bruise. "Wanna see for evidence?"

Feinberg took a picture with his phone and finished his notes. "We have a hearing this afternoon before Judge Beckman. I will try to get you released. Your clothes are fine, but can you do something with your hair? The shave on the sides and back are also fine, but get the long hair on the top out of your face?"

"Why?"

"Judge Beckman is old and conservative. We want to present you as the wronged party, a young man trying to get a job who was taken advantage of by an unscrupulous ad man. We need you neat and clean. If you need hair clips or rubber bands, I'll get them for you."

§

Gramm downed his to-go cup of Everybody's House coffee, leaned his head back, and closed his eyes, waiting for an answer from Ivan Babin's office. White's phone startled him awake. She had a brief conversation before turning to Gramm. The interview was a go. Gramm rubbed his jowly face. If the caffeine hadn't kick in by now, he feared it never would.

White told Milo to follow them.

The Babin Group building was a refurbished brick affair with arched windows, and its own pay-as-you-go parking deck. On the way to the fourth floor, Milo informed Gramm that he was going to expense the parking charge.

"Why would you even say that?" Gramm questioned. "Now I won't sleep all night."

"What is with you and parking?" White demanded.

"It used to be I couldn't afford it. Now I'm just a whiner," Milo explained.

"In the future, we will only interview subjects that have free parking," Gramm offered.

"I like that," Milo agreed.

The Babin Group looked to be prosperous. It took up most of the fourth floor, and all the offices were buzzing with people and projects. The trio was ushered into yet another conference room—no games in this one, the walls were giant video boards displaying the agency's various ads that popped up and then disappeared. Sometimes one ad spanned two walls. Other times, the ads migrated from one wall to the other—a total video immersion experience.

Milo allowed as to how they were making him dizzy and suggested going back to Gibbs' conference room.

Ivan Babin, sporting a muscle-hugging, black turtleneck against a well-groomed white beard and casually groomed white hair, strode into the room. He introduced himself with a reverberating, old-fashioned. deep radio voice.

"I assume this about Charlie Dawson," he said, sitting down at the head of the glass conference table, motioning the others to sit.

"It is," Gramm said.

"Awful business."

"How much do you know about the manner of his death?" White asked.

"I've chatted with lovely Mia, you know, Charlie's wife, and she confided he was electrocuted of all things. I assume it was some sort of outrageous accident." Babin pinched the crease in his gray slacks, moving his hand along making the crease razor sharp.

"What kind of an employee was Mr. Dawson? "Gramm asked.

"I would say good. He won a couple of regional awards for his ads. I did worry about him lately though. A week ago, Charlie asked for an advance on his commissions. He either had money trouble or was high rolling again."

"Gambling?"

"Nothing so mundane. Inventions. Charlie was always looking to invest in the next great thing. He did not have a good track record. It drove sweet Mia crazy...Charlie said."

"Did Mr. Dawson have any enemies?"

"Charlie? No more than anyone else."

"How about a young man named Xavier Cullen?"

Babin flinched. "Oh, him. He's an angry young man. He created such a fuss in here a few weeks back. I had to have him removed—exciting."

"What was the fuss about?"

"He was ranting that Charlie had stolen his ideas. We get that from time to time."

"Did Dawson steal Cullen's ideas?" Gramm asked.

"Look, in the ad game, we all have similar ideas. A tweak here and there and it's an original. Just because this young man showed Charlie a few vague ideas doesn't mean Charlie wasn't already planning to do the same thing." Babin paused to stare at their faces to gauge how his usual argument was going. He guessed not well. He changed his tack, swung around in his chair, and leaned into his audience. "Obviously, Charlie's death wasn't an accident, or you wouldn't be here. So, did this young fellow kill him over an ad?"

"We've just begun our investigation." Gramm said. "How long did Dawson work for you?"

Babin looked up as if the years were printed on the ceiling. "Let's see, I started the agency after leaving radio in the late nineties. I used to do a noon show on KDDW called Brunch with Babin. Any of you remember that?"

White looked to Gramm who shrugged.

"Well, it was a long time ago now. Adult contemporary talk and music gave way to political talk shows." He looked at White. "I so miss my 'lunch ladies' who called me on a regular basis. They were fun."

Was I even born yet? White wondered.

Milo put an end to the reminiscing. "Answer the question."

Babin was at a loss. "Which was?"

"How long did Charlie work for you?"

"I don't know, fifteen, sixteen years or there abouts." Babin swung back to the side, sharpened the crease in the other trouser leg, and brushed off some invisible lint from the arm of his turtleneck.

"Did he make a lot of money? Was he well off?"

"This business floats with the economy. There are up times and down times, but Charlie did all right. Our benefits are generous. Mia should be well taken care of. She can continue the health insurance, unless she has her own, and, of course, there's the company-provided life insurance. I think it's up to a million now."

As they left the building, White questioned, "Lovely Mia? Sweet Mia?"

"I refer to you as lovely, sweet Robin all the time," Milo snarked.

"Your point, Robin?" Gramm asked, ignoring Milo.

Milo was about to call Gramm, Sweet Ernie, but thought better of it.

"Doesn't that sound a bit familiar?" White asked. "It's not a usual description of an employee's wife."

"Babin and Mia Dawson?" Gramm asked, mulling the pairing over in his mind. "Get rid of the husband? Collect the life insurance? Both motives for murder."

9

Xavier Cullen's eyes darted around the courtroom. The judge blew his nose. Angry words were ping-ponging between his lawyer and the prosecutor. Cullen turned hoping to see his parents in the wooden spectator pews, but the audience consisted only of a young man with a black eye. a woman glued to her phone, and an old man in a back corner who appeared to be a regular escaping the cold. Cullen felt alone.

"Your honor, this was not burglary. My client was attempting to recover artistic items stolen from him by Mr. Charles Dawson when the incident with Mrs. Dawson occurred..."

"Counselor, we're not trying the case at the moment," Judge Beckman, not a Saul Feinberg fan, interrupted in exasperation. "Get to the point."

"I ask that my client be released on his own recognizance. He is a long-standing member of the community, and not a flight…"

"Yada yada counselor."

Feinberg pressed on. "Your honor, my client…"

Judge Beckman held up his hand for Feinberg to stop as he read a note handed to him by the bailiff.

"Apparently, we are not at the point of discussing bail. I have been handed a request by the Duluth police that Mr. Cullen be held as a person of interest until they can talk to him about a homicide."

Xavier Cullen went pale.

"Why am I just hearing about this?" Feinberg demanded.

Judge Beckman looked over his glasses with small, indistinct, watery eyes. "Because, counselor, I just heard about it. The defendant will be returned to custody until this matter is cleared up." The gavel came down.

Feinberg was not going to give up without a fight. "Your honor, the police have had my client in custody for two days. Why didn't they interview him in all that time?"

Judge Beckman gaveled him down. "You can ask them that question in person, counselor. Next case!"

§

Feinberg didn't have long to wait. Cullen was back in custody, and the lawyer was in his van office behind the courthouse when Gramm called. "We're about to interview your client, counselor."

"Which one?"

He heard Gramm shuffle papers, "Cullen, Xavier Cullen."

"Homicide? Lieutenant? Really?" Even though Feinberg and Gramm were friends and poker buddies, they always kept the professional business, professional.

"Exactly."

"Who died?"

"Charlie Dawson, the man your client attempted to…"

"Allegedly attempted."

"Do we really have to do this dance?"

"I'm on my way," Feinberg said.

Xavier Cullen sat in the police interview room clad in an orange jumpsuit. His hair which had been pinned back in the courtroom now freely bobbed in front of his face.

Feinberg entered the gray room with purpose. The stakes for his client had been raised. "Tell me again exactly what you did at the Dawson house that day."

"I didn't kill him," Cullen muttered, peering out from behind a wall of hair. "I just wanted my drawings back."

"Don't jump ahead. Go step-by-step."

Cullen began in a repetitive sing-song rhythm. "I thought the house was empty and I could go in, get my stuff, and get out. The door was locked. I found a rock; smashed the window so I could unlock the door."

"Then what?"

"The lock needed a key on the inside, but there was no key. I had to smash the lock, and some of the door came with it."

Feinberg waited for more. After a few seconds he sighed. "Keep going, Xavier."

"I felt bad about that, but anyway I went inside, looked around his office, his desk, but my portfolio wasn't where it was before. I couldn't find it. It was a mess in there. There were cords everywhere. I tripped on one and knocked over a couple of those weird monitors around that red bike. That's when that woman screamed and started swinging that club at me. Scared me. I tried to get her to stop, and I guess I pushed her."

Again, there was silence. "Then what?"

"I felt bad about that too. That's it. I ran out the door, down the street to my car and took off."

Feinberg nodded. "Okay, let's get this interview over with. Don't talk unless I tell you to." He opened the door and let the guard know they were ready. Gramm and White entered the room. White started the recording giving the date, time, and identities of the people in the room.

Gramm spoke first. "Mr. Cullen, we need to talk to you about the death of Charlie Dawson. I understand you broke into his house on Tuesday morning."

Feinberg smiled, "My client does not admit to that. Nice try."

"We have security camera video collected from the victim's house that clearly shows your client breaking the door with a rock," Gramm said.

"I thought we were here to talk about a homicide."

Cullen, unused to this legal game of checkers, silently twisted his hair.

"Okay, we won't discuss how he gained entry. Mr. Cullen do you have any electrical expertise?"

Feinberg stopped him from answering. "Do you want him to change a light bulb, Lieutenant?"

"I just want him to answer the question."

Feinberg nodded to Cullen who shook his head.

"I need a verbal answer," Gramm demanded.

"No, I don't. I'm an artist."

"I understand you damaged several monitors that belonged to our victims' stationary bicycle. Did you do anything else to the bike?"

Once again Feinberg stopped his client from answering. "My client does not admit to being in the house, Lieutenant, how could he possibly have done anything to the bike?"

Milo, watching behind the one-way glass, laughed. *Just like poker. It's hard to bluff Saul.*

"I think we're going to have to keep Mr. Cullen as a guest of the city until we can get this sorted out," Gramm said.

"So, you're charging him with murder?" Feinberg asked.

Cullen flipped the hair from his face and looked at his lawyer, eyes wide.

"Not at this time," Gramm said.

"Good. Then I will notify the judge that the preliminary hearing for the alleged burglary can resume, and my client will be released on bail—finally."

Gramm and White stood up, White ended the recording, while Gramm said to Cullen, "Don't leave town."

As Gramm left the room, Feinberg shouted, "You can't tell him that!" He turned to his client, "He can't tell you that, but don't leave town without telling me."

Cullen shrugged. "Where would I go?"

§

Agnes had anxiety about the dynamics of tonight's dinner—the first married meal with Milo present. This afternoon, Milo had returned to Lakesong before Sutherland. She found him in his office trading emails with the police PIO.

"Busy?" she asked, standing in the doorway.

Milo closed his laptop. "Not with anything I want to do. Come on in. What's up?"

Agnes sat down in one of the comfortable fireplace chairs. Milo joined her in the other. She sighed. "I know you and Sutherland have been dining together for more than a year now. You two have your conversations, and rhythms, and I don't want to interrupt that."

"You're over thinking it," Milo said. "We eat. Sometimes we talk. Sometimes we just eat. Oh, and sometimes we talk about what we're eating. I can see how you don't want to get in the way of our sterling conversation. It will be tough for you, but we'll work you in somewhere."

Agnes laughed. "We did spring this marriage thing on you, and I feel…"

"No, you sprung the marriage thing on you. I knew it was coming, eventually."

"What? How could you know?"

"Sutherland, who won't take time off, went to Hawaii for three weeks with Miss Remarkable, Enjoyable, and Attractive."

"You called me that the other night when we returned from Hawaii. What are you talking about?"

"A year ago, after Sutherland fed you at the Pickwick, he described you as remarkable, enjoyable, and attractive. Waaaay over the top for Sutherland."

"I did not know that." Agnes laughed.

"Here's something else you probably don't know. John McKnight's will charged me with getting Sutherland out of his dull life, providing a little excitement. He just ran off to Hawaii with Miss Remarkable, Enjoyable, and Attractive and got hitched." Milo folded his hands in his lap. "My work here is done."

"Really? I was your project."

"No, Sutherland was my project. You were a pawn in my game. In fact, last night in the library John congratulated me on a job well done."

Agnes, feeling much better, rose from the chair and said, "See you at dinner. I should warn you: I can talk for hours about radishes."

§

Agnes worked in a predinner swim after her conversation with Milo. She showered and dressed in comfortable yet, she thought, sophisticated, black jeans, and black sweater. She thought black was a nice backdrop for her reddish blond hair—the touch of red being a new experiment.

Propped up against the headboard, she watched her husband dress for dinner. Day ten as Mrs. Sutherland McKnight, or Agnes McKnight, or married Agnes Larson. Silly, but she had spent some time today signing her name as all three and was uncomfortable with all of them for varied reasons. *Perhaps a couple of sessions with my therapist might help,* Agnes thought. *Or I could decide not to decide—for the next fifty years.*

She was hungry. She loved Martha's food. After talking with Milo, she knew things would be as silly as they always were, and she was welcome to join in the foolishness. Besides, her husband thought her remarkable, enjoyable, and attractive. She had hoped it was the case, but it's always nice to be told.

Sutherland looked handsome pulling on his go-to navy V-neck, cashmere sweater, and gray slacks. Agnes was not a go-to person. Some new clothes were needed. She had three acceptable go-down-to-dinner sweaters and had already worn two of them. Agnes laughed. *Who goes down to dinner?* Maybe she should ask Milo for a raise. *Maybe I'm hysterical.*

"What's so funny?" Sutherland asked, plopping down on the side of the bed. "Did I forget to comb my hair?"

It wouldn't matter, she thought. *You would still be gorgeous.* "No, your hair is cute, cute, cute," she said, fluffing Sutherland's hair, making him duck.

He returned the fluffing.

"Just lucky for you, you married a fluff-and-go girl."

"Well, you've been fluffed and I'm hungry. Let's go."

§

Milo was already enjoying his usual predinner vodka gimlet when the newlyweds arrived in the family room. He stood.

"Oh, Milo, thank you, but please sit down," Agnes laughed.

"I was marveling, Agnes. You could have done so much better."

"What?" Sutherland objected over Agnes' laughter. He moved to the bar.

"My usual, please, bartender," Agnes joked, sitting down at the table next to Sutherland's regular chair. "I'm feeling especially remarkable, enjoyable, and attractive this evening."

Sutherland stared at Milo and narrowed his eyes. "She didn't question it when you said before. Clearly, you've said it again."

"I didn't think it was a secret."

"Doesn't that violate a bro-code or something."

"Bro-code? Really? What are you? Fifteen?" Milo chided. "You know Agnes, I was kidding before, but you really could have done so much better."

Sutherland sat down. Agnes accepted her drink, leaned over, and hugged Sutherland. "No, Milo, I think he's remarkable, enjoyable, and attractive too."

"Aww, isn't that sweet," Milo mocked.

"I house-managed today. Sutherland, I presume, sold real estate. So, Milo, what did you do today?" Agnes asked, getting the conversation going.

"Let's see. I went to lunch. I talked with Mary Alice Bonner. Oh, yeah, and I went to work. It appears that when people kill other people, I get called in to come look, but, Agnes, you're my personal assistant. Shouldn't you know what I do?"

Martha brought in the salads—three beet salad with orange yogurt dressing for Agnes and Sutherland, a blue cheese, iceberg lettuce wedge for Milo.

"This work thing that I should know about," Agnes continued, "anything interesting?"

"Funny you should ask," Milo said, maneuvering his fork through his iceberg lettuce. "There was a murder in a house in Hunters Park. Lieutenant Gramm thought I should take a look."

"Charlie was murdered?" Sutherland blurted. "I really thought it would be health related or an accident."

Milo blinked. "Yet I was on the scene. Are you thinking I'm an insurance adjuster?"

Agnes laughed.

"Who would want to kill Charlie?" Sutherland asked.

"I can't talk to you about this until Gramm gets a chance to interview you," Milo advised.

"Gramm and I already talked, this morning, on the phone. You were there."

"I think he'll want to have a more formal, sit-down chat."

Agnes looked at Sutherland. "He looks so honest."

Sutherland grinned. "Gramm always wants to talk to me. It's becoming a habit,"

"Stop looking so innocent. It's a dead giveaway," Milo advised. They ceased conversing long enough to finish their salads.

Martha cleared the salad plates and returned with three plates of bone-in, thick-cut, sundried tomato, spinach, and gorgonzola cheese stuffed pork chops, along with Italian parmesan roasted potatoes. Martha began to pour an August Kesseler 2017 Riesling.

While Milo suspiciously inspected the stuffing for signs of green, Agnes looked wide-eyed at the plate. "Do you two each this much food every night?" she asked.

"Pretty much," Sutherland said. "Why?"

"I may ask for the child's portion."

Milo accepted Martha's blending of the spinach into his food but still yelled, "I see green, Martha."

Martha came to the family room door. "Good. If you're looking for green, you should check your hash browns for parsley and green onion."

Milo just shook his head. "Is nothing sacred?"

§

After dinner, Agnes and Sutherland said goodnight to Milo and retired to their second-floor rooms. Settling in on the couch, Agnes asked Sutherland if he was ready to continue the renovation conversation. Sutherland jumped up. "Yes! Give me a second." He dashed out of the room, into the upstairs library, and came back with several large tubes and started unrolling them on the floor.

Agnes stared. "What are those?"

"Lakesong's blueprints. Milo and I found these when we were in the vault last year. It shows the upstairs before I…"

"Vault? What vault?"

"The large room in the basement filled with old, weird stuff."

"Would any of that weird stuff be in the form of books or artwork?"

"Oh yeah, there are shelves of books throughout and paintings in the back of the vault. In fact, the room has drawers and shelves all decorated with intricate carvings. The whole room is probably artwork. It needs to be researched. I'll show it to you…" Sutherland noticed Agnes was staring at him. It wasn't a loving stare. "What?"

"I thought I finished cataloguing all of the books and paintings in this house. No one mentioned a vault to me."

"Sorry. I will show you the vault, but first let's get back to the blueprints and the remodeling conversation."

"Before we begin, exactly why are we going to see Creedence Durant tomorrow morning?"

"He's our financial advisor."

Agnes laughed. "Yes, but Sutherland, I don't have money to invest. I have a car payment, a house payment, and a 401K to which Milo generously contributes."

"I just want you to be familiar with everything and have access to what you need."

"So, you're saying I can borrow a hundred bucks if I'm short on my car payment?"

"Sure, it won't break me."

Agnes gave him a playful look. "Two hundred?"

"Okay, now you're pushing it," Sutherland joked.

10

The next morning, Milo had finished sating Annie with a bit of bacon when the intercom alerted the breakfasting trio that their calm Thursday morning was about to be interrupted. Questioning looks exchanged between them communicated that no one was expected. Sutherland checked the live video app on his phone and broke the suspense, "It's Lt. Gramm and Sgt. White." Sutherland pushed the *gate open* button.

"I told you, they'd want a formal interview," Milo said to Sutherland, taking a bite of toast.

"Here? So early?"

"My guess is Amy's on the night shift in the ER, and Gramm wants breakfast."

Sutherland rose from the table to greet them at the door while Milo let Martha know that Gramm and White were unexpected, probably hungry, guests.

"I know Lt. Gramm's usual, but we're out of Ilene's pastries for Sergeant White. Ask her what she would like," Martha said.

After removing their winter gear, Gramm and White followed Sutherland to the morning room. Surprised to see Agnes Larson at the table, White joked, "Ms. Larson, no murder investigation would be complete without you."

"I'm here for the smoothies," Agnes said, holding up her raspberry, blueberry smoothie.

Gramm grabbed some coffee from the urn and sat down opposite Sutherland. "According to my wife, congratulations are in order."

White poured herself some coffee and listened for more information, expecting to understand her boss' comment eventually. When no explanation came, she asked Sutherland why the congrats.

"He got married." Gramm announced.

"Congratulations!" White echoed. "To whom?"

Agnes held up her smoothie. "That would be me."

Of course. White smiled. "Oh, congratulations to you both."

"If you people are done," Milo complained, "I have been deputized to discover Robin's breakfast wants. Apparently, today being Thursday, we have nothing from Ilene's."

Martha, thinking Milo forgot to ask White for her breakfast order, walked into the morning room just as she was saying, "That smoothie looks good."

"One berry smoothie coming up," Martha said. "I may need a new blender."

"So, Sutherland," Gramm began, "if you admit to killing Charlie Dawson, I can eat my breakfast without having to grill you."

Martha reappeared with Gramm's eggs, bacon, hash browns, and toast otherwise known as Milo's half-lumberjack.

"Unfortunately, I was on my bike here in Lakesong when Charlie was stricken."

"Tell me what you saw and heard," Gramm said, pouring a large glob of ketchup next to his hashbrowns.

"We were riding the bikes. Charlie was behind me…"

"Wait were you and Dawson in the same place?"

"No. I was here. I guess Charlie was at his house. Gibbs' new bike lets you see riders on all sides including behind you. That's what the monitors are for."

"I've heard that before. So, you saw Charlie behind you in a monitor." Gramm said. "Then what?"

"I was in the process of passing Gibbs up in front, so I was looking ahead when I heard a loud pop or a crack and a cry. Everyone heard it and there was confusion with most of us asking what we had just heard. Then everybody noticed that Charlie was missing. That's all I know. After we stopped the ride, I called him and left a voice mail. When he didn't reply by the next morning, I called again. That's when Milo answered."

"How well did you know Charlie?" Gramm asked.

"Not well. I ran into him and his wife Mia at functions, and we rode together. Milo probably remembers he was one of the Zenith City Riders during Milo's brief foray into the two-wheeled world. In fact, Charlie was there for the Twin

Ponds shooting." Sutherland said, referring to a different murder investigation last summer.

"Do you know anyone who would want to hurt him?" White asked, accepting her smoothie from Martha.

"Can't believe it." Sutherland mumbled to himself.

Gramm took a bite of his eggs, before continuing. "Once again, what we tell you goes no further. Right?"

"Right," Sutherland agreed.

Gramm turned to Agnes, "And that goes for you too Ms....er Mrs...."

"Call me Agnes, and yes, I agree it goes no further."

"We're waiting on forensics but the preliminary report from Doc Smith indicates Dawson was electrocuted. He was riding that bike when he died. At this point we're doing the math and surmising the bike was the weapon."

"Weapon?" Sutherland repeated.

"Right now, we're going on the expertise of an EMT at the scene who told us ordinary exercise bikes do not have enough voltage to kill. But if that bike killed, someone made it do that."

"You're saying someone rigged Charlie's bike to kill him." Sutherland charged. "Who would or could do such a thing?"

"We're just starting to ask that question. Tell me about the bike riders."

Sutherland remembered Milo's admonishment more than a year ago to only answer the question. Don't go down the rabbit hole. This, however, was an open-ended question. Sutherland was less a suspect, more an informer. He was uncomfortable with that position too. "Well, there's Gibbs, obviously."

"Let's start there," Gramm said. "What do you know about Gibbs?"

"He's one of our Zenith City Riders. He's in decent shape, rides hard…"

"Did he dislike Charlie Dawson?"

"More like he was annoyed with Charlie."

"How so?"

"Charlie kept wanting the ad account."

"And Gibbs said no?"

"No, with an insult chaser."

Gramm cocked his head waiting for more.

Sutherland realized he may have said too much.

"Well?" Gramm asked, prodding Sutherland to continue.

"Well, he said Charlie was small potatoes," Sutherland hoped that did it.

"Was Gibbs often that 'direct?'"

"If you asked me that a week ago, I'd have said no, but lately he's been…um…nasty. I think it's the pressure of getting this bike through these trials and making it perfect. The Gibbs I know is competitive, but a nice guy, friendly, smiling—that sort of thing."

"But now?"

"Now he's uptight, shouting a lot, belittling the people who are helping him."

"In your opinion, does Gibbs have electrical expertise?"

Sutherland put down his smoothie. "Interesting question. I don't know. It's hard to tell how much is Gibbs and how much are his technicians."

"Fair enough." Gramm stopped to take several bites of eggs and potatoes, while trying to remember the names of the others on the ride.

Sergeant White chimed in, "Leah Davis. Tell us about her."

"Leah works for the power company..."

"Power company?" interrupted White. "Doing what?"

"General counsel. She's a lawyer."

White's enthusiasm waned.

"Did Davis dislike Dawson?" Gramm asked.

"Not that I noticed," Sutherland took a sip of his smoothie. "I think they got along. You must understand, we're not great pals. We just ride together."

"I figure working for the power company, if she wanted to rig a bike, she'd have plenty of people to ask how to do it," White suggested.

Sutherland shrugged.

"Who's next on our bike list, Robin?" Gramm asked.

"Ethan Marsden."

"I don't know him at all—chatted with him when he set up the bike last Sunday—pleasant, extremely efficient. I think he and Gibbs are related somehow."

Gramm, who was smearing jam on his toast, barked, "Next."

"Nora Swenson," White responded.

"Nora works for the nonprofit that runs all the bike trails. That's how I know her. I think she has a couple of other jobs," Sutherland said.

"Did she have a beef with the deceased?"

"No, just the opposite. On our virtual rides, the two of them have become quite chatty."

"About what?"

"Don't know. They were never close enough for me to hear."

"Any electrical know-how?"

"Well, Nora did set up the electric eye that took a picture of the finish line in one of our races last year. After the power company dropped a line from a nearby pole, she seemed to know what she was doing with it."

"Who's *our*?" White asked.

"The Zenith City Riders," Sutherland said again, proudly. "We have some fun charity races during the summer. You should join."

"Given your group's history with shootings, I'll pass," White joked. "Let's circle back to Charlie Dawson. You stated you didn't know him well, yet you knew him well enough to call and check on him."

"I didn't think anyone else would, and he is part of our group."

"Who was he besides a bike rider?" Gramm asked.

"As I said, he was in advertising and his wife's name is Mia. They're members of my country club. Also, I think he said he went to school in Moorhead or Mankato. He told me once, but I can't remember. He really liked biking. That's all I know about the man, and we've been biking together for several years. That's kind of sad."

"How about you? Do you have electrical knowledge?" Gramm asked.

Agnes laughed.

Sutherland sat up straight, "I will have you all know that I can change a lightbulb, and I have, on occasion, called an electrician all by myself."

§

115

Judge Beckman blew his nose and started coughing as he nodded to the bailiff to call the next case. "Xavier Cullen, initial appearance."

Xavier, with his hair pulled back and fastened, was brought into the courtroom by the bailiff and took his seat at the defendant's table. Feinberg stood at the table and addressed the court. "Your honor, my client has been interviewed by the police and is no longer a person of interest in the matter previously brought to the court's attention. Mr. Cullen waives his right to a preliminary hearing and asks the court to enter a plea of not guilty. I ask that he be released on his own recognizance."

The prosecutor objected noting the seriousness of the attack.

Feinberg rolled his eyes. "My client was being attacked with a golf club. He simply tried to block the weapon from assaulting him."

"The attacker was the homeowner, your honor. She was defending herself and her property," said the prosecutor.

"Are we trying the case, now?" Feinberg asked with full sarcasm.

"I take your point, counselor," Judge Beckman agreed, tossing a tissue into a waste basket. "Does your client have a place to stay?"

"He lives with his parents. His mother is in the courtroom today your honor."

Xavier's mother, not knowing what to do, raised her hand and then lowered it again.

"Young man," Judge Beckman began, grabbing another tissue before sneezing.

Feinberg motioned for his client to stand up.

"I am releasing you on your own recognizance. Do you know what that means?"

Xavier looked at Feinberg.

Judge Beckman continued without waiting for a reply, "It means you are being released without posting bail. You must sign an agreement to appear in court. If you don't appear, you go to jail. Understood?"

Xavier nodded.

"I need words, sir. Say yes or no."

Xavier managed to squeak a yes.

The judge pounded his gavel and demanded, "Next case."

§

On the way to his NPR interview, Milo's phone erupted with the Bee Gee's 'Stayin' Alive,' the ringtone reserved for Medical Examiner, Doc Smith. Milo congratulated himself on that bit of irony. "Doc. How can I help you?"

"I looked at your finger. Without running several expensive tests, I can tell you the owner's age was late teens or early twenties."

"When he died, right?"

"I don't know if it's a *he*, and there is nothing to tell me he or she is dead, just that they're missing a finger."

"Good point."

"Actually, the fact that the finger shows no sign of trauma, I think we would be safe to say, it disarticulated after death. Got any more bones?"

"Not yet. I'm going to check in with Chester later this afternoon."

"Who's Chester?"

"A small horse. What are the expensive tests and what will they tell you?" Milo asked.

"Radiocarbon dating and DNA."

"Don't you do that radiocarbon thing on ancient bones. I think these are more modern."

"You can thank atomic bomb testing. Want to know any more?"

"Nope. How much are we talking?"

"I think about fifteen-hundred for both tests. Of course, if you find the rest of the body, the city may pay the tab." The phone went dead.

§

White turned the heater to full blast in Gramm's new unmarked Ford Police Interceptor Utility vehicle as they left Lakesong. Gramm watched her do it. "I'm glad you know how to do that. There are no switches, or buttons, or dials," he said to White. "It's all on that screen I haven't figure out yet."

"While you were driving here, I read some of the manual," White advised.

"That works. We're a team. Don't get sick or I'll freeze to death."

A light snow began to fall from the gray overcast sky when they arrived at the power company's red brick building on East Superior Street. "Is it warming up?" White asked. She was a firm believer in the myth that it doesn't snow when it's bitter cold.

"It's a fooler—a lake affect snow. It's still frigid." Gramm advised.

For once, their interview subject was waiting for them in the lobby. The basketball-lanky, buttoned-up woman in the dark Chanel suit introduced herself as Leah Davis, and said, "I thought it would be easier to meet you down here. Follow me. I reserved a conference room."

I think half my life is spent in conference rooms, White thought. This one had huge photos on the wall. They showed various power facilities and vehicles—all in black and white and shades of gray—nothing fun. Otherwise, the room had the usual conference table and chairs—this time the acrylic table was small surrounded by only six chairs.

Leah sat down at the head of the small table, folded one long leg over the other, and asked, "What do you need to know from me?" She secured an imaginary wisp of hair that had not escaped her French twist.

Very corporate and confident, White thought.

"As we told you on the phone, we're investigating the death of Charlie Dawson," Gramm said.

Leah folded her hands in front of her, her face creasing with concern. "I'm curious. We all assumed it was a heart attack," Leah said, "something natural."

"Who's we?" Gramm asked.

"Let's see," Leah uncrossed her legs, pulled herself closer to the table, and refolded her hands in front of her. "Nora Swenson and I talked yesterday, and, of course, Gabriel and I had a conversation. I haven't talked to Sutherland McKnight yet."

"Tell us what happened on the ride Tuesday night."

"Not much to tell. We were riding through the virtual countryside, birds tweeting, rushing river water, all that. Then I heard a noise that didn't belong. It startled me. I looked around. I saw everyone but Charlie. Gabriel asked his people to check the bike. They said it was unplugged. That's all I know."

"How well did you know Mr. Dawson?" Gramm continued.

"It's like anything. I know how everyone rides, and what they ride. We talk equipment and the sport. I'm not aware of many personal details."

§

Milo and police PIO Kevin Richards stomped their feet on the matt and brushed the snow from their jackets. A technician hurried them along into the empty radio studio and ordered Milo to sit down at one of three microphones. Richards was left standing in a corner.

The same technician rushed into another room separated from the studio by a large, rectangular window, threw himself into a chair, and pointed to his ears. Milo, tossing his jacket on the next chair, figured the pointing was about the headphones lying on the table in front of him. He was annoyed at having no offer of coffee, or even a hello-how-are-you, so he looked around and played dumb.

Exasperated, the man flipped a switch and pronounced over a speaker, "Headphones! Put 'em on...please!"

Milo sighed and complied. After a minute he heard the show's host in his headphones, a woman named Naomi Burjer welcoming him to the show. She made mundane small talk with him for about two-point-five seconds before announcing, "We'll be live in ten."

Milo was in a mood. He resisted the urge to count to ten aloud. The opening theme music began to play, and a male announcer said, "Live from Boston, Book Beats." That was followed by Burjer's smiling voice. "I'm your host, Naomi Burjer. Welcome to Book Beats. We have such a treat for you today—bestselling author, Ron Bello, is with us. His latest book, *The Life and Death and Death Again of Harper Gain,* has quickly risen to number one on every best seller list. Good morning, Ron."

"Good morning, Naomi."

Milo was blindsided. He glared at Richards, still standing in the corner, who shrugged. Big help he was. No one told him Bello would also be in on the interview.

Burjer continued. "And a special surprise for our listeners who have already read your book, Ron, we have in our Duluth studios the man responsible for solving this complex web of intrigue, Duluth Police Consultant, Milo Rathkey. Welcome to the program, Milo."

"Thank you, and hello, Ron."

"Hello, Milo," Bello responded.

"After this is over, Ron, I'm going to choke you like a chicken."

Richards' eyes widened.

"That's going to be tough," Bello laughed. "I'm in Chicago."

"I have long arms," Milo said.

Sensing a bigger story, Burjer egged them on. "You two have an interesting relationship. Care to tell us, Milo, why you're going to, in your words, choke Mr. Bello like a chicken?"

"He told me I was barely mentioned in this book. "

"I lied," Bello admitted.

"Have you read the book, Mr. Rathkey?"

"No. I already know the ending."

"Well, Mr. Bello refers to you as 'unorthodox yet brilliant,' and your Poirot-inspired, again, Mr. Bello's words, reveal of the killer as, and I'm quoting, 'effective absurdist theatre.' He goes on to say, 'I don't know of another single person who could have figured this all out.' High praise, don't you think, Mr. Rathkey?"

"Okay, I'll only slightly choke him like a chicken. And I'd like to add that none of this would have been figured out without Lieutenant Ernie Gramm, Sergeant Robin White, and others in the Duluth Police Department. They did all the leg work. Also, Deputy Chief Sanders, who went out on limb letting us do the 'absurdist theatre,' deserves a lot of credit." Milo thought that pretty much covered his part of it, but the interview went on for another hour. Thank God, Bello was asked to read excerpts from the book which took up most of time. Unfortunately, Milo kept hearing his name in Bello's text.

§

After the Leah Davis interview, Gramm and White rushed to the car to catch Milo on NPR. As they still had a few minutes to spare, Gramm suggested they drive down to Canal Street, and park in a municipal lot by the Aerial Lift Bridge, Duluth's most famous landmark.

"You can't get near this place in the summer," Gramm grumbled, looking at the trendy restaurants and bars. "Too many tourists. I like it when it's quiet."

As they listened, Gramm relaxed. Milo was handling it. When Milo praised Gramm and White for doing most of the work, White joked about needing an agent. As the interview ended, Deputy Chief Sanders called Gramm. "Our consultant did okay. The PIO says he's a natural. The Chief loved it when he mentioned the department and, of course, you and Sergeant White."

Gramm thanked him for the call and hung up.

"What did he say?" White asked.

"Milo didn't screw up."

§

Gramm decided lunch was in order. He was a little stuffy and wanted the Chinese Dragon's egg drop soup. After texting Milo with the lunch location, White braced herself for the oral chess match. The Chinese Dragon was owned by Milo's good friend, Henry Hun whom everyone called Hank. The banter between Milo and Hank could go on for an entire meal.

Gramm and White arrived first and were seated at Gramm's favorite table in the back. "Are you going to be joined by he who's name we do not mention?" Hank asked.

"Officer Preston?" Gramm asked.

"Don't be Milo," Hank admonished.

"Unfortunately, here comes the name we do not mention," White said, watching Milo serpentine his way to the back.

"You can't give me crap, Hank. I'm a star." Milo said.

White shook her head, "A star?" she asked.

Hank held up his hand, "Don't, Robin! Don't play his game!"

It was too late. "I was just interviewed on some radio show. They called me brilliant."

Hank pulled out a piece of paper from his pocket. "I didn't know. Could you autograph this?"

Milo complied.

Hank rolled it up, told them to wait while he threw it away, and left the table.

"You did it again," White said.

"Did what?" Milo demanded.

"Delayed our order with your nonsense."

"Not my fault. How come you never blame Hank?"

"We like Hank," Gramm said.

Officer Kate Preston arrived and sat down. "Have you ordered?"

"What do you think?" White asked.

Preston laughed. "While we wait for the Hank and Milo Show to be over, I have the backgrounds on the suspects."

"Great," Gramm said, as the hot tea was served. "Go," he barked at Preston.

Preston pulled out her pad and turned it on. "Let's start with Gabriel Gibbs. Really cute! Like an older Chris

Hemsworth, but the blond scruff beard looks silly on him because it disappears."

White nodded in agreement. Gramm and Milo were silent. Neither wanted to admit they had no clue who Chris Hemsworth was.

"Okay. Not a lot of Hemsworth fans. Moving on. Gibbs is forty-two, owner of Gibbs' industries which he inherited from his father. Recently, his company designed several of the self-driving sensors for autonomous vehicles, and a better battery for solar power storage. He's described in articles as driven, singularly focused, and determined to win—totally alpha."

Hank reappeared. "Sorry," he said, handing out menus. He even included one for Milo so as to not delay ordering any further.

"Did you really throw Milo's autograph away?" White asked.

Milo whispered to Preston, "I'm a star."

Preston laughed.

Hank shook his head. "I was going to, but I realized it was on the back of an order list for one of my suppliers. The special today is Tonkotsu Ramen. It's a Japanese Ramen with pork, corn, bean sprouts, dried seaweed, pickled gingers, seasoned bamboo, scallions, wood ear mushrooms, and an egg in a bone broth. It's made for gray days like this."

"I need your Chinese penicillin…double order of egg drop soup and steamed dumplings," Gramm said.

Both Preston and White opted for the special. All eyes turned to Milo. "How do I know the seaweed is dried?" Milo asked.

"For you I will personally soak it in gasoline and light it on fire," Hank said with a grin. "You're gonna get the chicken egg foo yung. You know it. I know it. Everyone in the restaurant knows it."

Milo said in a loud voice, "They don't treat stars very well here." People turned to look.

"So sorry, Mr. Star," Hank said, walking away.

"I haven't ordered!" Milo insisted.

Hank came back.

Gramm interrupted. "I'm hungry, sick, and armed. Give Milo chicken egg foo yung!"

Hank nodded and left for a second time.

"Don't skimp on the gravy!" Milo yelled after him.

Gramm drained his hot tea and began to pour some more. "Preston, what did you find out about the victim."

Scrolling down her pad she found Charlie Dawson. "Married seven years, no children. Works for the Babin Agency. From all accounts, he's successful. His credit rating seems to take a hit every couple of years, but he always recovers. He and his wife belong to the Northlake Country Club."

"If his credit rating keeps taking a hit, how can he afford it?" White asked.

"His wife makes good money."

"She must," White said. "She drives one of those expensive electric cars."

"Back to Dawson," Gramm grumbled. "Any mention of enemies?"

"Nothing public," Preston said.

"Continue."

"Nora Swenson's an odd duck. She's younger than the rest—twenty-five, single, has several part-time jobs. Doesn't seem to belong with the others."

"How so?" Gramm asked.

"The others are all corporate—well off. Swenson rents a room."

"We know she works at Hawk Ridge," White interrupted, "and for the bike trail people. Is there anything in her background that shows electrical knowledge, or a connection to Charlie Dawson other than biking?"

"Not yet. She grew up in Moorhead, Minnesota and graduated from Moorhead State, other side of the state so she's not from around here."

White did a double take. "That sounds familiar. Didn't Sutherland say he thought Charlie went to school in Moorhead or Mankato? We need to check that out."

"Maybe that's why Swenson and our victim were so chatty on the ride?" Gramm suggested.

"Maybe they were singing the old school song," Milo offered.

"Continuing, we interviewed Leah Davis this morning," Gramm said. "What do you know about her?"

"She's general counsel for the power company. She's forty-two, married..."

"What does her husband do?" Gramm asked.

"He is a salesman for Murphy Guidance Systems, they make missile guidance systems apparently."

"In Duluth?" White asked.

"I thought that was odd too. Murphy is headquartered in Denver. In my search, I ran into an ad they placed for salespeople. It stated they could live anywhere, but to expect a lot of travel."

Hank returned with their food as a woman came up to the table clutching Ron Bello's book. "Mr. Rathkey?" she asked, looking at Milo.

What holy hell is this? Milo wondered. He nodded.

"Oh! I knew it was you. My husband said I was crazy. Could you sign my book?"

"How did you know it was me?" Milo asked.

The woman was surprised. "The pictures."

"Pictures?"

She opened the book to several pages of pictures, including a large head shot of Milo. "Please sign there on your picture. 'To Doris.'"

Hank left, shaking his head. Milo took the book and signed, *To Doris. Book Clubs are dangerous. Milo Rathkey.*

She looked at the autograph and giggled, "Wonderful! Thank you so much!" She was going to say more, but Hank reappeared with a camera and took Milo's picture.

"Is that for your wall?" Milo asked. "Famous people who ate here. I'll be the only one, but you have to start somewhere."

"No wall," Hank said. "The kitchen staff always wonders what idiot would always order the egg foo yung with all the great dishes we make. I can hang this up in the kitchen so they can have a good laugh. It helps morale."

"Glad to be of service," Milo said.

Hank picked up the menus. "I saw Jen before Christmas. She stopped in. She looks good,"

"Yeah, she does," Milo agreed.

"How do you know Milo's ex?" White asked Hank.

"Best man at their wedding," Hank said, walking away.

White stared at Milo.

"What?" he asked.

"Hank was your best man? I know he's a friend, but he's your *best* friend?"

Milo shrugged. "I never denied that."

11

After lunch, Milo drove to the Northshore Bookstore located in the old Fitgers Brewery building. He was chagrined to see a huge display of *The Life, Death and Death Again of Harper Gain*. A large authorish portrait of Ron Bello loomed over the mountain of books. Milo snatched one from the top and rushed to a cashier.

Waiting in line, Milo noticed the person ahead of him buying the same book. "I understand all this happened right here in our city!" a woman gushed as she handed her book to the clerk for scanning. "I can't wait to read it!"

As the woman left with her purchase, Milo moved up to the same young clerk, dropping the book on the counter. The man looked at Milo, cocking his head to the side. "Excuse me, sir, but you look familiar."

"I get that all the time," Milo said. "People say I look like Chris Helmsworth."

"Hemsworth?"

"Exactly."

The clerk laughed, took Milo's purchase to bag it. "I just finished reading this book. It's popular."

Milo slid his card into the reader.

Glancing at the name on his card reader, the clerk said, "Mr. Rathkey, do you want a paper or email receipt?"

"Paper," Milo muttered, hoping it would be faster.

Placing the receipt and book in a bag, the clerk asked, "Wait. Rathkey? Are you the detective in this book?"

The people behind Milo began to murmur. Two of them tried to talk to him, but Milo grabbed his purchase and bolted from the counter. He had almost escaped through the front door, only to be blocked by the store manager.

"Mr. Rathkey, I couldn't help but overhear. Would you consider a book signing in the store sometime soon?"

"You should get Bello. It's not my book."

"Oh, we've got him, but to get both of you would be special."

Milo said he would think about it and took the man's card. He fled the bookstore and vowed never to shop in person again. Once in the car, he called Mille Greysolon, but Robert, the butler, answered. "Greysolon residence."

"Robert, it's Milo. I'd like to talk to Mrs. Greysolon."

"Mrs. Greysolon is outside plinking pigeons, sir."

"Plinking?"

"Shooting, sir."

"Shooting pigeons? In the winter?" Milo asked.

"That's what she says. I wouldn't know, sir, she's never hit one."

"What is she shooting with?"

"A rook gun, sir. A single shot British small game rifle."

"Never heard of it."

"Nor had I, but she goes out into the fresh air, shoots up into the sky for about a half hour, and feels much better for it."

"I would like to run some tests on the finger bone, but it will cost about fifteen hundred."

"I will consider the tests part of household expenses, sir, go ahead."

"Of course, if we can find the rest of the skeleton, the city might pick up the cost as part of an investigation."

"*We* didn't find it originally, sir. Chester found it."

"You're right. Let's get Chester up there again, and see if he finds the rest of the bones. I'm coming over."

"I would suggest you not come dressed as a pigeon, sir."

Milo laughed. Robert had a sense of humor.

§

After a series of phone calls, Sgt. White managed to contact Nora Swenson's landlady, Mrs. Flynn, who told her that Swenson turns her phone off when working. "She told me Swenson will be up at the Hawk Ridge Observatory this afternoon," White said to Gramm.

"Outside in this cold? Is she nuts?" Gramm asked.

"I guess we'll find out. Glad I wore my snuggies today."

"Saul Feinberg lives up there on Hawk Ridge. I play poker there sometimes."

"Those houses on Hawk Ridge are fancy and expensive," White said.

"Pastrami," Gramm said.

"Are you naming deli meats?"

"That's how Saul got his money, from pastrami."

"I love pastrami, but I can't afford a house up there."

"Apparently the money is in the making and selling not the eating."

The paved portion of East Skyline Parkway gave way to gravel as Gramm pulled off to a small parking area. Before leaving the car, both Gramm and White bundled up: collars flipped, scarfs over the mouth and nose, and hats pulled down to cover the ears. The weather bureau had issued an exposed skin warning that morning, and both were taking it seriously.

By the time they finished the short uphill walk to the observatory platform, the cold had creeped through the layers and into their bodies. A short, masked woman in an Air Force parka was pounding a nail into a wooden railing on the observation platform.

"Nora Swenson?" White asked.

The woman didn't stop pounding. "Yes."

"I'm Sgt. White. This is Lt. Gramm, Duluth Police. I tried to call you earlier."

"I'm working."

"So are we," Gramm objected. "You need to talk to us."

Swenson turned and lowered the hammer. "I'm trying to fix this railing. I'm on the clock for fifteen more minutes."

Gramm looked at White who shrugged. "We'll wait," Gramm said, looking at his watch. White turned her back to the wind and looked out at the large expanse of ice on Lake Superior. She could barely discern where the lake ended, and the gray sky began. This time of year, the lake slept alone, lacking ore boats, salties, pleasure boats—crafts of any kind.

White loved sailing on the big lake and she wondered when her handsome sailing instructor would return to Duluth from the Gulf of Mexico. The thought of him kept her warm.

Gramm sneezed.

Nora Swenson's timer buzzed. She gathered her tools and said she was ready.

"We'd like to ask you a few questions about Charlie Dawson," Gramm began.

Nora nodded.

"Is there somewhere inside we can go?"

Nora looked at him quizzically. "There is no inside out here. It's an outside job."

"Let's go into our car," Gramm offered. "It's warm."

"Maybe we can talk while you drop me home. I don't live far. I had to walk. My car wouldn't start. I forgot to plug it in."

They didn't talk again until they reached the car. Gramm fired up the police interceptor's engine, and the heat flowed out immediately. Gramm's jaw was stiff from the cold. He moved it around so he could talk. Below zero with wind chill on the hill was a killer. He didn't know how Nora could walk. Youth.

To keep Nora comfortable, they had her sit in the front seat with White in the back. "Why would you walk in this bitter cold," White asked.

"I need the hours. I've got rent and student loans due."

As Gramm unbundled himself and blew his nose, White asked, "How well did you know Charlie Dawson?"

"Not well."

"So, you were just riding buddies?" White asked.

"Yes."

"Tell us about the ride Tuesday."

"It was like the other two rides except the guys had a race going on. Charlie and Sutherland were trying to catch up to Gibbs."

"And?"

"Well, at some point Charlie just disappeared. Gibbs blew up as he does these days when things go wrong. I didn't think anything of it."

"What did you hear?"

"Leah said she heard a crackle, but I didn't hear anything. I noticed the program stopped, the virtual background disappeared, and I could see everyone's room. That sucked."

"Sucked? Why?" White asked.

"They all have separate exercise rooms. I sleep, live, and exercise in one room. I had to move my dresser out into the hall to make room for the bike. My landlady is pissed—fire code. I told her the test was only for a week. If Gibbs doesn't restart the test soon, I'm going to have to pull out. I can't afford to lose my room."

"Do you have any electrical knowledge?"

"No more than most. Why?"

"I'm told you set up electric eye photo devices for bike races."

"Yes, one-time last summer. The device came with instructions. The person who did it before me drew pictures on how to do it."

"But you needed a power line, correct?"

"Yes, but somebody else ordered that." Swenson leaned back in the seat. "This heat feels so good. I want to loosen my parka, but I'm afraid to because I'll have to get out into the cold again to get into the house."

"Let's get back to the electrical thing," White said.

"All I know is I connected something blue to something white like in the drawing. Everything worked; nothing blew up. After the race, I disconnected the same things. I wouldn't call that electrical expertise."

White's phone buzzed. She looked at the text and said to Gramm, "Forensics wants to show us something."

Gramm reached Swenson's house and watched as she ran up the stairs and disappeared inside. White took her place in the front seat.

"Tell Milo about forensics," Gramm said.

White hit Milo's speed dial number on her phone, put it on speaker, and relayed the message.

"I'm on my way to Wardline, you know, the finger bone place," Milo said.

"Do it tomorrow. This could be important," Gramm shouted, and then coughed.

§

Gramm and White were surprised to see Ethan Marsden from Gibbs' office in the forensic warehouse. "I thought he was just dropping off the bike," White whispered.

The forensic team leader, Michelle Holden, introduced Marsden.

"Mr. Marsden has just finished setting up one of his company's bikes. He's going to explain how it should work," Holden said, pointing to the bike with the monitors. "We've asked him to stay and explain the differences between this bike and the bike ridden by our victim."

Marsden motioned the group to come nearer. "I've taken the cover off of our electronics box," he began. "As you can see, the white wire from the main cord comes into this box and connects to this device." He pointed to a black rectangular plastic box. "That's a transformer. It reduces the voltage from 120 to a safe twelve volts to power the speed and mileage counters, pulse sensors, and the display screen."

"What about those monitors around the bike?" Milo asked.

"Those have their own cords. Eventually, all of those cords and monitors will be gone."

Milo pointed to another series of wires that connected to a block outside the bike. "What about those wires."

"They're video lines—no power. Ignore them."

"It's hard to ignore them. It adds to the mess," Gramm said. "I'd trip on all those wires."

Marsden smiled. "Once again, Lieutenant, this is a prototype. Prototypes are messy. We don't want to spend money hiding wires until we know what needs fixing."

Holden pointed to the burnt bike. "Let's go over the victim's bike. We found traces of wires on the 120 line before the transformer box, leading up to the handlebars."

"There's no reason to have wires tied into that 120-volt line! Someone tampered with this bike." Marsden said.

"We can see that," Holden said.

"So, if someone ran extra wires up to the handlebars, exactly, how does that kill Charlie Dawson?" White asked.

"Our guess is the wires were connected to the pulse sensors built into the handlebars," Holden explained. "If that's the case, the current went up through the victim's left arm, crossed the heart, and coursed down through the right arm. Doc Smith tells us that would stop his heart."

"Why not just let go," Gramm suggested.

"He probably couldn't," Holden explained. "In many cases, once current flows through a body, the muscles contract."

"Our victim rode on his bike a number of times and didn't die. Then two days ago, he rides and dies," Milo questioned. "Why? Why then? Was it always on, and Dawson just happened to touch the right spots on the handlebars?"

"I doubt that," Holden said. "I think something was added to the electronics. Maybe a remote-control switch."

"If it's wired to the pulse sensors did Charlie Dawson's pulse rate set off this switch?" White asked. "Leah Davis said he was racing Sutherland and Gibbs for the lead."

"Possibly," Holden said, pointing to a blob of melted plastic. "All the bike electronics are in that melted blob. We are about to begin the delicate task of taking that blob apart, to follow the wires and find out what triggered the victim's electrocution. It's painstaking work with no guarantee of answers."

§

"I'm going up to exercise," Sutherland said to Agnes as he grabbed two small carrots from Martha's crudité plate. "Care to join me?"

"I just finished swimming," Agnes said.

"You can come watch me."

"I've seen people ride bikes before. It's extremely uninteresting," Agnes chided.

Not deterred, Sutherland popped a black olive. "I'm on my old bike since Gibbs has put a moratorium on riding the new one. Uninteresting or not, I'm going up. I'll be all alone, sigh."

"So, you want me up there because you're lonely."

"Yes," Sutherland beamed.

"Aww. So sweet, but still boring. I suggest your usual earbud party. Maybe a new playlist."

"Okay. I'm getting no sympathy from the love of my life." Sutherland looked back to see if Agnes changed her mind. She hadn't. Sutherland took a blue cheese stuffed green olive and headed for the stairs. "My olive and I are gone."

As he was leaving, Milo was coming into the hallway by the kitchen. "Where's Sutherland?" he asked.

"Heading upstairs for a lonely bike ride—a boy, his bike, and his thoughts. Oh, and his green olive," Agnes joked.

Milo went upstairs and knocked on the door to Sutherland's suite of rooms.

"It's open," Sutherland shouted from behind the door.

"I'm here to talk to you about your car warranty!" Rathkey shouted back.

Sutherland opened the door. "I need a no soliciting sign."

"I need to watch you get on that bike," Rathkey said.

"Which bike?"

"The killer bike."

"I can't. Gibbs has called a halt to…"

"I don't want you to do anything, just get on it."

Sutherland led the way to his exercise room. Milo looked around at the various steppers, bikes, and treadmills, glad he was a swimmer. "This looks like a torture chamber."

"You came up here to insult my devices?"

"No, just watch you get on that contraption," Milo said, pointing to the Gibbs bike.

Sutherland shrugged. He stood up, took careful steps sideways through the monitors and cords, put his left hand on the handlebars, slipped his left shoe onto the pedal and pulled himself up on the bike. He then placed his right shoe on the right pedal and stared at Milo.

"Now get ready to ride."

Sutherland put both hands on the lower part of the handlebars and leaned forward.

Milo noticed his hands were on the pulse devices. "Do you use those pulse things all the time?"

Sutherland looked at his hands. "I guess I do. This is just where I put my hands on any bike. It's comfortable for me."

"Do most riders in your group put their hands down there?"

Sutherland thought about it. "I think they do."

"Thanks." Milo turned to leave.

Sutherland dismounted. "You're not leaving until you tell me what this was all about," he demanded.

"Somebody rigged Dawson's bike to kill him."

"Through the pulse sensors?"

"We think so."

"Why didn't that kill him when we first started?" Sutherland asked.

"Good question. I'll make a detective out of you yet. Forensics thinks it was more complicated. There was a remote-control switch."

"I don't think that answered my question."

"It didn't." Milo was impressed. "It leaves your question unanswered. Why kill him on Tuesday? Why not Monday or Wednesday?"

"And the answer is?"

"Don't know, but once I do, I'll know why Dawson had to die."

§

"This weekend is Frosted Fatty," Sutherland said to Agnes after dinner.

Sutherland was relaxing on his couch. Agnes sat down and leaned back on him. "Are you saying that with or without a comma?" she joked.

"A comma?"

"Well, it could be *This weekend is Frosted Fatty* or *This weekend is Frosted* comma *fatty.*"

Sutherland started laughing. "That's just awful. I'd never say that. That's mean."

Agnes looked up at him. "Says the man who called my tennis playing gravy."

"You're not going to forget that are you?"

"Never."

"May I remind you that both you and Mary Alice knew about Milo's skill on the tennis court and kept it from me, leading to my utter humiliation."

"And your point is?"

"This weekend is Frosted Fatty, no comma."

"Are you asking me out on a date?"

"I'm sorry, my dear, I'm a married man!" Sutherland protested.

"Okay, so tell me, what is Frosted Fatty."

Sutherland called up the website on his phone and handed it to Agnes. "It's a timed bike race at Spirit Mountain. I thought we could watch the racers in the morning, have lunch, and then do a little skiing."

"Skiing? I'm not particularly good at skiing," Agnes said.

Sutherland took his phone back. "Oh no you don't. I've been bagged before. I know we'll get on that hill, and you'll get that look in your eye just before you say, 'Race you.' The next thing I know, you're flying down the hill and I'm trying to catch up to you."

Agnes smiled. "Seriously, I'm not great on skis. I am, however, a shred Betty on a snowboard!"

"A shred Betty?" Sutherland questioned.

"I can bomb without much chatter." Agnes smiled.

"You're making that stuff up."

Agnes shrugged.

"So, my shred Betty wife, do you want to go to Frosted Fatty?"

"I wouldn't miss it for the world."

12

Creedence Durant's cherubic face beamed as he stood up to greet Agnes and Sutherland. Agnes had never seen Durant's office before, and took a minute to admire the modern, industrial-looking blend of exposed brick set off by original oak woodwork. She thought it was a nice look. Creedence offered his hand first to Agnes then to Sutherland, motioning for them to sit down. Lowering his chubby self into his comfy padded office chair, Durant pushed his glasses up on the bridge of his nose and began. "First, my complete and total congratulations to you both."

Sutherland and Agnes grinned at each other. This was their first appointment as a married couple, and their first congratulations together outside of Lakesong.

"It always makes me happy when my clients are happy," Creedence said. "Now, I know this is more than a social visit. Where would you like to begin?"

"Thank you, Mr. Durant." Agnes smiled at Sutherland again. "I have a question,"

Creedence nodded.

"I own a house in Lakeside. I would like to keep it, maybe rent it out. Would that negatively affect Sutherland's taxes—our taxes?"

Creedence blinked, smiled, and looked quizzically at Sutherland who looked at Agnes, then back to Creedence. Sutherland gave him a full-shoulder shrug. Creedence continued, unsure of his footing. "That's a good question, Mrs. McKnight."

"Please call me Agnes."

"Agnes it is. Since you brought it up let's begin with taxes. Now that you're married, I would advise you to file jointly. Who does your taxes…Agnes?"

"My sister Barbara used to do them. She died two years ago. Since then, I've been going to one of those tax places."

"I see. I'm sorry for your loss."

"Thank you. Do you need to see my taxes?"

"It would be helpful if you have the last seven years of your tax returns."

"I do. Barbara was a stickler on keeping financial records." Agnes smiled, remembering her sister's voice.

"Now, as to your house in Lakeside." Creedence began to chuckle.

Agnes tilted her head, wondering what was amusing about her house.

"Sorry," Creedence apologized. "I made a silly joke in my head. You've gone from Lakeside to Lakesong. It's not that funny. I must keep myself amused. Money can be boring sometimes. Getting back to what you pay me for. Do you have a mortgage?"

"Yes, but I thought I could rent it out and then I could double my payments and pay it off sooner," Agnes said.

Creedence suppressed a smile, pushed his glasses up one more time and made a note. *Quick payoff?* "Get me those particulars. Perhaps we pay it off now."

"Now?" Agnes questioned. "No Mr. Durant, I can't afford that."

Creedence looked again at Sutherland.

Sutherland jumped in. "I think what Creedence is saying is that it might be advantageous for us, you and me together, to pay off the mortgage."

"I don't want you to have to do that. We just got married, and already, I'm going to stretch our finances? No!"

Sutherland looked at his bride to see if she was kidding. She was serious. He took a deep breath. "We need a moment, Creedence."

Creedence smiled, stood up, and said, "I'll be back in fifteen."

Now alone, Sutherland apologized.

"For what?"

"I thought you knew. I'm, as they say, well off."

"Of course, you are. I know you have a good business, but you inherited that house. You didn't pay for it, and remember, I know how much money it takes to maintain Lakesong. I pay the bills each month."

"The inheritance from my dad covers all possible Lakesong costs. It doesn't come out of my salary, so, don't worry about the house. I make a good living, and I have some other money.

If Creedence thinks paying off your mortgage makes sense, that works for me."

"If that's what you want, then shouldn't you be added to the deed or something?"

Sutherland began to protest.

Agnes held up her hand. "Let's see what Mr. Durant thinks."

Creedence stuck his head around the door. "So, are we all on the same page?"

"Not totally but we're getting there. Let's continue," Sutherland said.

"Wonderful!"

"We've decided that my name will also go on the deed when we pay off the Lakeside house if you think it's a good idea."

"That would be fine." The glasses moved up again. "Let's move on to the foundation."

"Is there something wrong with Lakesong's foundation? No one told me that! That can be costly."

"What?" Creedence asked.

"No, Lakesong's foundation is solid," Sutherland said.

"Then why would Mr. Durant bring it up?" Agnes asked.

"Creedence is talking about The Laura and John McKnight Foundation. It was set up by my mother to fund causes she was interested in."

"Oh," Agnes looked at Sutherland. "Do I know anything about that? I don't think so."

Sutherland felt fear. Had he messed up again, this time by omission. *Did Agnes really not know about the foundation?* What if she didn't know about the rest of his wealth. His last fiancée, Miss Petite, as Agnes called her, knew about it down to the last penny.

Creedence had continued while Sutherland's mind went blank with panic. "You don't have to decide this now, but you have options—continue the foundation as it is, continue it and possibly rename it, and or create a new one with your names and different purposes?"

Agnes shot Sutherland a look. "I have no way to respond to that. We need to talk."

Sutherland formed a weak smile. "I messed up. I thought you knew that my mother created a charitable foundation with money she had from her family."

"Your mother? I thought your money came from your dad."

"It did for the house—money he made in a business initially funded by my mother."

"Oh, I didn't know anything about that," Agnes said. "So, some of that money is still left to fund charities? That's nice."

Creedence looked at Sutherland. "Shall I continue?"

Sutherland gave an unsure nod.

Creedence handed Agnes a folder. "This might be helpful. Not knowing your preference, I made a hard copy for you. Sutherland prefers a digital copy. The first page is the money Sutherland makes from his current real estate business plus some minor investments."

Agnes looked at it and smiled in surprise. Turning to Sutherland she said, "You do better than I thought."

Sutherland laughed, pleased, yet unsure if Agnes' last comment was a compliment or not.

Creedence glanced at Sutherland, pushed his glasses, and blinked twice. Sutherland was not providing any clues. *Does she really not know?* Creedence wondered. "Turning to page two. This is the money Sutherland received from his father."

Agnes turned the page. "So, this is for the care and feeding of Lakesong? Quite substantial. I see where renovations to Lakesong will not be a problem."

Creedence continued. "Now, let's go to the next section, the next fourteen pages will be the various investments Sutherland, well, I have made with the money left to him by his mother."

"Is this the money for the foundation?" Agnes asked.

Sutherland braced for the answer.

"No," Creedence explained, "this was personal money that Laura McKnight left to Sutherland upon her death."

"You have money from your mother too?" Agnes asked Sutherland.

"A bit. I was only ten. I really haven't touched it."

Agnes thumbed through page upon page of stocks, bonds, and real estate holdings. Getting to the bottom line on the last page, her eyes grew wide. She looked at Sutherland.

Creedence didn't know if it was confusion or shock, but he thought it best to leave the room—again.

§

The early morning sun streamed straight off the lake into Gramm's office. "We all have coffee. We've finished the initial interviews. What do we know?" Gramm questioned as he closed the blinds on his office windows.

"You don't like winter sun?" White asked.

"Not in my eyes," Gramm said.

"Where's our murder board?" Milo asked. "Every TV crime drama has a murder board..."

"With eight by ten glossy pictures of the suspects," White added.

"Where do they get those from?" Milo questioned. "Do they bring in a professional photographer to take head shots of the suspects?"

"All I got is the camera on my phone," White lamented.

"We're not doing a murder board!" Gramm insisted. "Let's go over the suspects."

"Mia Dawson has motive. She didn't seem to like her husband—called him a louse and a thief, plus she's the beneficiary of her husband's life insurance policy. She was in the house, could have rigged the bike—opportunity. The only question is would she know how to rig the bike?"

"Have Preston check her background," Gramm ordered.

"Leah Davis—I don't see a motive or anything. Nora Swenson denies electrical knowledge and no motive or means. So, they're a wash, for now. Sutherland McKnight..."

"Can't screw in a light bulb," Milo interrupted, "and no motive or opportunity."

"Gabriel Gibbs. He's a business guy," White said. "We don't know about his electrical know-how."

"Another one for Preston to check," Gramm said. "Motive?"

"Maybe. Dawson was ruining his bike test."

"So, he killed him?" Gramm questioned. "Kind of severe."

White shrugged and moved on. "This guy Marsden seems to have plenty of knowledge, maybe opportunity since he did install the bike and the monitors, but no known motive. Don't forget Mr. Young and Dumb, Xavier Cullen. No electrical knowledge that we know of but hates Dawson for stealing his ideas. He broke into the house. Opportunity and motive. That's the group so far."

Gramm turned to Rathkey. "Thoughts?"

"Looking at opportunity plus motive, two people pop out, Mia and Xavier. We can also add Gibbs."

"Weak motive," Gramm said.

"I disagree." White checked her notes. "I think a guy who is 'driven and singularly focused' might be enraged enough if someone was derailing his pet project."

"Okay, the widow, the mogul, and the young, dumb kid are in play."

"We don't know if Gibbs has the means, the knowledge, to rig that bike," White protested.

"He could have hired someone," Gramm countered. "Get Preston digging deeper into the widow and Gibbs, while we go see the kid and rule him in or out. Does anyone really think he did it?"

Neither White nor Milo responded.

"Milo, any thoughts?" White asked.

"The ever present 'why now,' but I've got a date with a skeleton."

Gramm groaned. "Of course."

Milo put on his coat and left the office.

Gramm rushed out of his office, shouting, "I don't want a skeleton getting in the way of serious mind lint!"

Several people in the bullpen area turned to stare at Gramm.

"Don't you people have something to do?" he barked as he retreated to his desk.

"Good job," White said. "Amy has more witnesses for that commitment hearing."

§

As Gramm drove toward the west end of town, White asked if Gramm really thought Cullen killed Dawson over some drawings?

Gramm shook his head. "Motive is weak. Maybe we can rule him out. I'd like to thin the suspect pool for once."

White agreed.

"What the hell happened to Lincoln Park?" Gramm demanded. The industrial, railroad community—once simply called the West End—was in the process of morphing into a millennial haven. Corner bars had given way to trendy breweries, hardware stores to craft shops.

"Been a while since you've been here?" White asked.

"Yeah, it's been forever," Gramm said as he left West Superior Street and drove into the neighborhood. "Well, the houses haven't changed," he said looking at the small, prewar bungalows. "I bet you can still get in here for under a hundred thousand."

"Looking to downsize?"

"Not yet. I like my harbor view from Observation Hill." Gramm pulled in front of Xavier Cullen's address, a holdout against trendy, a dull-green asphalt-sided two-story house flanked on the right and left by renovated, brightly painted structures, one baby blue, the other bright yellow.

"When the realtors call these homes prewar, exactly which war are they talking about?" White asked, approaching the front porch.

"In this case, World War One." Gramm knocked on the door. A short, paunchy, older man with a slightly stooped back opened the door. Dark, deep-set eyes, stared at the two cops. The stare was far from friendly. "Yeah?"

Gramm showed his badge, introduced himself and his partner. "We're here to see Xavier Cullen. Are you his father?"

The man turned his back on the two and walked into the house. White and Gramm followed him. White closed the door behind her. "Yeah. I'm Frank Cullen. Call me Duffy," the man said without turning around. "What's my idiot son done now?"

"We have a few questions about his attempted burglary several days ago," Gramm said.

Duffy stopped and finally turned to face Gramm and White. "Geezus, save me from that kid! He quit a real job to become an 'arteest.' Can you believe that? He breaks into a house to chase scribbles. Who the hell does that? Stupid, stupid, stupid. I'm surrounded by stupid."

"Where is Xavier?" Gramm asked.

"Basement." Duffy shrugged. "He works and sleeps down there, so I don't have to look at him. He just riles me up. He's not good for me." Duffy led the way into the kitchen, introducing the cops to his wife Bunny, a woman who did not respond and continued to punch her bread dough. "Down there," Duffy gruffed, pointing to the heavily grained, closed door to the left of the kitchen table.

"Cops are here to talk to stupid," Duffy mumbled.

Hearing those words, Bunny slugged the dough harder.

With care, Gramm and White navigated the uneven, narrow-tread basement stairs into a large, wood-paneled room with a deteriorating drop ceiling. The walls were covered in bright, multicolored, neon artwork and a snake pit of extension cords.

Tracing all the cords to a single outlet, White murmured, "Looks like a fire waiting to happen,"

Gramm was looking at the small, rectangular black boxes connected to each sign by black wires. "If he made these, this kid's got some electrical knowledge."

Xavier was working at a far tool bench, using a torch on glass. Gramm shouted his name. He startled and turned around, pointing the torch in their direction. Seeing his mistake, Xavier turned the torch off. "Sorry, I didn't expect anyone."

"We have a problem, and we hoped you could help us," Gramm said.

Xavier nodded. "Do I need my lawyer?"

"Your choice, but then we have to do this at the station."

Xavier shook his head.

"We think Charlie Dawson's bike was rewired to kill him sometime on Tuesday."

"I didn't do it. I told you that."

White looked around the room. "Do you sell much of your work?"

"Some locally. Neon is getting popular. I'm working on a web page to advertise my stuff."

"Well, Xavier," Gramm began, "looking at everything displayed on the wall, I see small black boxes and wires and I'm thinking you've got the knowledge and the tools to rig that bike."

"But I didn't. I just wanted my portfolio back. I didn't hurt him."

Gramm pointed to a black box below one of Xavier's pieces. "Is this a transformer?"

"Sort of. These are the old neon signs. Those black boxes are transformers and exciters. The modern stuff uses LED technology. I don't do LED unless a customer asks for it."

"You see, Xavier, that's a problem. We need to find someone who knows about transformers who was in Charlie Dawson's house sometime on Tuesday. So far, you're it."

Xavier looked like a scared rabbit in search of an exit. "Are you going to arrest me again?"

"Not yet, but you're moving up on our suspects list."

"I just wanted my stuff back! Geez!"

"Where do you get the money for all these supplies?" White asked.

"When I sell, I use the money to buy supplies. I was hoping to get some extra money from work at that ad agency—build my business."

"Convince us you didn't kill him."

Cullen's dull expression didn't change. "I didn't know anything about that bike and those monitors before I went into the house. Besides, rewiring that bike is probably a lot of work. Running him over with my car would be easier."

"Did you think about running him over?"

"Yeah, I kinda did," Cullen hunched his shoulders. "I felt really bad about that. I'm nonviolent."

On the way back up the stairs Gramm said, "I've never had a suspect use laziness as an alibi before."

"Well, so much for ruling him out."

Gramm sighed.

"I like his designs though. Kinda fun," White said.

§

Milo was settled into Mille's great room, in what had become his usual wingback chair next to the fireplace. Mille was complaining to Robert about her sugarless coffee before turning to Milo and asking what he had learned.

"We know the finger belongs to someone in their late teens, early twenties. More extensive tests are being performed now as approved by Robert."

Mille gave Robert a side glance. "You're spending my money?"

"Someone has to, Madam."

Mille tried to hide a smile by taking a sip of coffee. "Early twenties you say. That would add weight to my family's Leif Björklund story." Mille said no more.

"What is the Leif Björklund story?" Milo was forced to ask.

"The facts are: Leif was a boyhood friend to my father, mother, and my uncle—mother's brother. Björklund disappeared at the beginning of World War Two."

"How does disappearing at the beginning of a war become dead in your attic?"

"That's your job, Mr. Rathkey."

"So far you've given me one finger bone and a possible name. I'd like a little more of that story if you have it."

Mille pursed her lips. "It may not be true. It may lead you astray."

"Take a chance. I don't stray often."

"You're being sarcastic, Milo Rathkey, but you haven't proven your worth yet." Mille sniffed for no reason, and began, "It seems that Björklund and my Uncle Leonard were rivals for the same young lady. Björklund won, but then disappeared around the end of 1941."

"And the young lady?" Milo asked.

"Don't know. She didn't marry my uncle; I do know that. He died in the Pacific. All this happened before I was born you understand, so I'm just telling you what was told to me. Don't take it as fact."

"Did your parents believe your uncle had something to do with Björklund's disappearance?"

"My father joked about it. My mother said my uncle did something horrible to Leif. She didn't say what, but there is a skeleton in my attic. I'm thinking murder."

"What did the police say?"

"Police?" Mille jerked forward in her seat. "Why would the police say anything?"

"A dead Leif?" Milo said, pronouncing the name as if it was a part of a tree.

"That's Layf, not Leaf, Mr. Rathkey. It's Scandinavian." Mille corrected. "I don't know if the police ever knew. Leif just disappeared within days of Pearl Harbor. All his buddies, including my uncle joined up. I guess he got lost in the moment."

Milo stood up. "I think it's time to see if the rest of him got lost in your attic."

Robert called for Chester who bounded into the room with unexpected energy.

The humans and Chester mounted the stairs to the third floor; Milo popped his head into the four rooms that bordered the long hallway. "What were these rooms again?" he asked.

"Servants sleeping quarters, sir," Robert said, "back when this house had servants."

"And the big room at the end of the hall?"

"I surmise a dining hall and general area for what little relaxation servants obtained."

"So, there's a kitchen?" Milo asked.

"No. There's a closed off dumbwaiter that comes from the downstairs kitchen. And before you ask, the body was not in there. I removed the boards and checked."

"How did you know about the dumb waiter if it's boarded up?"

"It still functions between the kitchen and the master bedroom on the second floor. I use it for Mrs. Greysolon when she's under the weather. When I saw the boards nailed over the wall on the third floor, I figured it was covering the same dumbwaiter."

Milo told Mille to let Chester roam. She turned him loose and the three humans watched for ten minutes as Chester galloped everywhere, bounding around the old furniture, knocking some of it to the floor. Tiring himself out, he slowed to a walk, exploring the hallway and smaller rooms. He didn't notice—or didn't care—that the three humans were playing follow the leader. Going into the first of the smaller rooms on the left, Chester began whining.

Milo, Mille, and Robert followed him in. He was nose down in front of what appeared to be a closet door. After pacing back and forth in front of the door, Chester lay down and began whining again.

Milo walked over to the door, turned the knob, and pulled it open. Robert grabbed Chester by the collar before he could pounce. On the floor, wrapped in a green, wool blanket lay a skeleton. Patches of mummified skin still clung to the skull in places.

Mille gasped.

Milo suggested they close the door and go back downstairs. Milo's gaze moved from Chester to the closet door. *Something is off.*

13

"It's almost noon. I thought we could run over to the La Monde Café down the block for lunch," Sutherland said as he and Agnes left the Algood Building that housed Creedence Durant's third floor office. Looking across the street, he spied Gustafson's and started to explain its connection to Milo and the police.

"Aren't those the people who catered your party last December?" Agnes interrupted.

"They are."

"Let's go there," Agnes said, speeding to the crosswalk. "I loved their food,"

Sutherland caught up. "It's quite noisy, we'll have to shout, not really conducive to quiet discussion," Sutherland advised.

"Good, nobody will hear me when I yell."

"Yell? About what?"

The walk signal began blinking and the two crossed the street. Agnes stopped in front of the restaurant and said, "Confusion at the lack of complete disclosure."

"I'm not understanding."

Agnes stepped to the side of the entrance to let other patrons enter. She grabbed Sutherland's sleeve to pull him with her. "Sutherland, we just got married. Let's say I want a new couch. We decide we can afford a new couch. That's normal. After this morning's revelations, if I say I want a new couch, you could say 'no problem, I can buy a couch factory.'"

"I don't want to buy a couch factory."

"But you can, and now I know you can. You can buy twelve couch factories," Agnes said, jerking open the door into Gustafson's.

Sutherland was sure he was missing something, still wondering why he was in trouble, and now buying multiple couch factories. The clatter, clang, and commotion of Gustafson's assaulted his senses. He lost track.

"Agnes Larson! And Sutherland!" Nick Christos shouted. "Welcome to our quiet, intimate, little cafe."

His wife Nicola looked up from the cash register and smiled.

Agnes stood for a moment, taking it all in. "Perfect!" she proclaimed.

Trying to do something right, Sutherland led her to one of the back booths. "This is where Milo, Gramm, and White eat all the time!" he shouted as if it needed a historical marker.

Agnes, removed her coat, folded it, and put it on the seat alongside of her. She sat down facing the restaurant so she could see the hectic comings and goings. Sutherland moved into the booth across from her. He had a view of the back wall with one faded picture of a Greek harbor and the rest-room traffic.

She parked the portfolio of Sutherland's assets on the bench beside her.

"I know you two," Pat, the waitress, said, handing them menus. "Welcome to our quiet little corner of Superior Street."

Agnes laughed.

"We have one special today, a spit roast beef and lamb gyro with a side of fries, rice pilaf, or fresh fruit." Pat said. "What to drink?"

"What I need is a glass of wine," Agnes said.

"Don't we all," Pat cracked, "but no alcohol license."

"Then I'll take strong coffee."

"Same for me," Sutherland said.

"So cute," Pat said, before leaving for a customer who had been trying to attract her attention.

"I've had their hummus and Greek salad. Both are delicious," Sutherland said.

Agnes scanned the dessert menu. "I'm going healthy with two pieces of Baklava. I'm in the mood for honey, nuts, and buttered dough."

Assuming the large grin on Agnes' face was a good sign, Sutherland plunged ahead. "So, can we talk why I need to buy a couch factory?"

Agnes tilted her head in bewilderment, wondering if her new husband was from a different planet. "What?"

"The couch factory."

Agnes, not knowing what to say, said nothing. Luckily, Pat returned with their coffee and took their orders.

Sutherland felt a large hand on his shoulder and looked up to see Ernie Gramm. "You're in our booth," he said sternly, but then smiled.

Sutherland moved over, "Sit down, Lieutenant."

White raised an eyebrow. "Maybe they would like to be alone," she said to Gramm.

"Alone?" Agnes shouted, looking around at the hustle and bustle of Gustafson's.

"Alone?" Agnes shouted, looking around at the hustle and bustle of Gustafson's. White slipped in next to Agnes. As she did, the portfolio slid off Agnes' coat and unto the floor under the table. Agnes put her foot out tapping the floor trying to find it. She located it and kept her foot on it deciding what to do next.

"Where's Milo?" Sutherland asked.

"Off chasing finger bones," Gramm said. "You live in a bad neighborhood."

Pat returned, admonished the group for not arriving together, and took the newcomer's drink orders.

"Anything new on the Charlie Dawson front?" Sutherland asked, sitting back, stretching out his legs, absently kicking the portfolio closer to Agnes.

"Early days yet," Gramm said.

Without looking down, Agnes kicked the portfolio across to Sutherland. Startled, Sutherland caught the playful sparkle in Agnes' eyes and engaged in a game he never played before—KTP, kick the portfolio.

Agnes immediately kicked it back.

"We haven't ruled you out as a suspect," White joked.

Sutherland nonchalantly slid the folder back toward Agnes as he unfolded his napkin with great flourish. She tried to stifle a giggle at their game. To hide it, she joked, "Oh, he's guilty of many things, but maybe not murder."

"I don't know," Gramm said. "He has electrical knowledge—his extensive light bulb changing abilities which he has admitted to."

Agnes pushed the portfolio to Sutherland's side again. Sutherland, noticing that Gramm and White were beginning to get wise to the game, placed his foot on the portfolio where it remained for the rest of the lunch.

Agnes fleetingly stuck out her lower lip in a false pout.

§

Waiting on coffee from Robert, Milo looked at his phone which had been vibrating for ten seconds. Ron Bello was calling him. He sent it to voice mail. At the same time, he noticed two previous calls from the PIO Kevin Richards. A look of aggravation swept across his face.

"Problem, Mr. Rathkey?" Mille asked as she sat down in her favorite chair.

"Some guy wrote a book about a case I solved, and now I'm being chased for interviews. It's a pain."

"Oh, I'm reading that book!" Mille said. "Do you get a cut of the profits?"

"Not that I know of."

Mille shook her head. "You need a business agent."

"People are recognizing me. It's creepy."

Robert handed Mille a glass of water with lemon, and a cup of coffee to Milo. He then sat down to hear how they should proceed.

"I think I need to bring in the police," Milo said.

Mille immediately began to spout about *her* privacy. When she finished, Milo stated the obvious, "I understand completely, but you do have a dead body in your attic…"

"It's not fresh," Mille corrected.

"Doesn't matter. It's dead. However…" Milo raised his hand to delay the next onslaught of Mille's protest. "The cops are busy. An eighty-year-old skeleton isn't going to get much attention. I think they'll be happy to let me investigate like I'm doing now."

Mille sat back and seemed content with Milo's solution. After a few moments of false calm, Milo stirred the pot. "Are you ready to come clean with me."

"Me?" Mille looked at Robert who shrugged. "I didn't kill the man. I wasn't even born yet."

"I know you didn't kill him, but I also know either you or Robert found him—all of him, not just his finger. Blaming it on Chester doesn't wash."

Hearing his name, Chester stood up on his front legs, the hind quarters remained on the ground. He looked around to see if there was a treat coming his way. After a few seconds, he laid back down with a huff.

Mille gave Milo her best, "how dare you question me" stare for several seconds, but Milo was not impressed. After several Chester-like huffs, she caved. "Oh, all right. I was looking for that stupid stethoscope in the closet when I found the skeleton. Scared the hell out of me. I slammed the door and came downstairs for a double brandy. I half thought about just leaving him there."

"Madam!" Robert intoned, suggesting to Milo that Robert was not in on the ruse.

"So, instead you created a bogus story involving Chester, a finger bone, and called me. Why?" Milo asked.

Mille took a sip of her water. "I didn't give Chester the bone. He took it, and I pretended he found it. Robert took it from him, and everything fell into place. I called you because I don't want the police traipsing all over my house."

"Well, that body will require one interruption to your privacy. The medical examiner will have to remove it and confirm the identity. Other than that, if I have the whole truth this time, I don't see anyone else needing to be here. Like I said earlier, the police will probably be happy to let me investigate."

"So, tell me, Mr. Rathkey, how did you see through my ruse of the bone detaching and moving under the door?"

"Chester is not a chihuahua. In fact, he's more of a horse. His paws would never fit under that door to grab the bone. They would only push the bone back under."

Mille folded her arms. "So, I shouldn't underestimate you, Mr. Rathkey?"

"No. My time is valuable to me and expensive to you."

"Clever and humble too," Mille said with sarcasm.

Milo called Gramm, but the call went to voice mail.

§

The din at Gustafson's was subsiding as the lunch crowd began to thin out. Finishing his humus, Sutherland was worried that Gramm and White had taken over the conversation, and that maybe Agnes was feeling left out. Sutherland was wrong again. Agnes was glad to be talking murder and not money.

"Can I ask a question?"

"Sure, Ms. Lar…McKnight, go ahead," Gramm said.

"Agnes."

"Okay, Agnes, what's your question?"

"Why electrocute Mr. Dawson? Isn't that a lot of work?"

White nodded. "You're the second person to say that this morning. It's a good question. It screams major premeditation…"

"And it sends a message," Gramm interrupted. "We just don't know what the message is…yet."

"It certainly has put a halt to our beta test," Sutherland said, "which is too bad. I was enjoying Gibbs' bike."

"So, no more test?" Gramm asked.

"Gibbs messaged us saying we were taking a brief break. It had something to do with analytics."

"How so?" Gramm asked.

"He had a long explanation. The test was designed for six bikes, but Gibbs said they're reconfiguring something or other, and we'll begin again early next week."

"Who's they?"

Sutherland shrugged. "The people Gibbs screams at all the time."

Gramm's phone began to vibrate. He looked at the screen. "It's Milo," he said, putting the phone back in his pocket.

"Aren't you going to answer it?" Sutherland asked.

"It's Milo's bone thing. It can wait."

Looking at Agnes begin her second honey-oozing entree, White asked, "Two desserts for lunch?"

"Yeah, it's a two-desserts-for-lunch kind of day." She stared at Sutherland who half smiled and pushed the portfolio toward her on the floor. This time Agnes put her foot firmly on it and didn't push it back.

§

Milo left Wardline and headed up the hill to the cop shop. On the way he returned Bello's call.

"Milo!" Bello sounded cheery.

"You sound too happy," Milo complained.

"I'm coming back to Duluth to work on my next book."

"And you're telling me? Why?"

"Because it's all about you. That case with the dead couple. Bows, arrows, exploding airplanes, you…it's a guaranteed best seller."

"I'll feed you to the carp."

"Maybe I shouldn't tell you about my conversation this morning."

Milo turned into the police parking lot. "No, don't tell me."

"Well, if you insist. There is great interest in the movie rights to *The Life, Death, and Death Again of Harper Gain.*"

"I'm thinking after I feed you to the fish, I will chop you into little pieces."

"Don't you have to chop me up first, then feed me to the fish? As an author I would have to get that right. Meanwhile, I figure you could be a consultant. It will pay well."

"Ron, have I ever told you, I have money, a lot of money?"

"Yeah, but I don't—yet."

"Who's going to play me?"

Bello bit his tongue, not wanting to further provoke Rathkey. "I need a place to stay."

"You can stay at Lakesong. That way I can take my time and not overfeed the carp."

"I'm going to be in town for at least a month, maybe more. I was thinking of renting something."

Milo's phone buzzed. "I gotta go," he said and hung up. Gramm was calling.

"You called. Whaddaya want?" Gramm asked.

"I found a body."

"Good for you."

"The body that belongs to the finger."

"Do I have to care?"

"Yes and no."

"Meet me in the office. White and I are on the way up."

"I'm already here."

14

"The kid plays with neon signs," Gramm said to Milo, stuffing his scarf, hat, and gloves into the sleeve of his coat. "By the way, Robin and I had a pleasant lunch with Mrs. and Mrs. McKnight at Gustafson's. You weren't missed."

"What kid?" Milo asked.

"What?"

"You said the kid plays with something or other. What kid?"

"You're not interested in Mr. and Mrs. McKnight?"

"I see them all the time, every morning for breakfast, and most nights at dinner. What kid?"

"Xavier Cullen." White sat down in her usual chair. "He's a neon artist."

"My turn to ask why we care," Milo said.

"Neon takes electricity," Gramm said, "and one of those transformer thingies. In other words, the kid could make that bike go zap."

"Ahh, means, opportunity, and motive."

"Zooms up on our list," White said.

"Except he brought up a good point," Gramm argued. "He didn't know the bike was there."

"Yes, he did," Milo countered.

"He did?"

"He broke into the study. How did he know where to go in that house if he hadn't, as they say, cased the joint previously?"

"Good point," Gramm said, begrudgingly.

"I got a body to go with the bone," Milo said.

Gramm sighed. "Okay tell us what's going on in your other life."

"Up in Mille Greysolon's attic—although it's not really an attic, it's a third…"

"Get to the point!" Gramm yelled.

"There's a skeleton in her closet. It may be the remains of some guy named Leif Björklund. Mille thinks he disappeared at the beginning of World War Two. Maybe murdered by her uncle."

"Is the uncle still alive?"

"Nope. He died in World War Two."

Gramm stared at Milo. "I may be having a seizure, but I could swear you're wasting my time with an eighty-year-dead guy in the attic who was murdered by another dead guy."

"I need you to send Doc Smith out there to collect the skeleton. If it's murder, I'll investigate and fill out the paperwork. No need to interfere with your love of neon beer signs."

"They're not beer signs," White corrected. "They're art pieces."

Gramm's phone buzzed. He looked at the caller ID and his eyebrows shot up. "The Widow Dawson," he said as he answered the call. "Good afternoon Mrs. Dawson. What can I do for you?"

Gramm listened for several minutes before saying, "Don't touch it anymore. I'll send someone out for it." He hung up and told White to send Preston out to the Dawson house. "Charlie had a second phone—discovered by the widow."

White texted Preston.

"Where'd she find the phone?" Milo asked.

"In the pocket of a suit. Apparently, she's already giving away her husband's clothes."

"Already? That's cold," White said.

"I see your cold and raise you Artic. She also said she's selling the house. Plus, I got more. Ask me what the widow said she found on the phone."

"I refuse," Milo quipped.

"Texts from Nora Swenson asking Charlie for money."

Preston entered the office in time to hear Gramm's last point.

"Why would Swenson ask anything from Dawson?" White asked.

"There has to be a connection beyond bike riding," Gramm guessed.

"Married man plus burner phone equals affair in my world," Milo said.

"Swenson and Dawson? Kinda a big age gap, isn't it?" Gramm grumbled.

"Did you find out which college Dawson attended?" White asked Preston.

"Moorhead State."

"Interesting coincidence," White said. "Dawson and Nora Swenson attending the same college."

"Yeah, but years apart," Milo added.

Gramm nodded. "Second interview—inside this time!"

§

The ride home from Gustafson's was quiet. Agnes was reading the portfolio. Once they arrived home, she begged off any further discussion saying she had work to do in her office and a portfolio to finish reading. Sutherland left her alone and went up to the second floor to check his emails. Still unclear about why he might be purchasing a couch factory, he worked out on his old bike and tried not to worry. In the late afternoon, Sutherland went in search of Martha's crudités and spotted Agnes in the gallery.

"I will never tire of this wonderful room!" Agnes said as she looked around Lakesong's gallery with its living trees, three-storied, glass-domed ceiling, and calico cat sleeping in her favorite Giana tree. "Your mother had wonderful ideas."

Sutherland was pleased Agnes was sharing her love of Lakesong and wasn't upset as she had been before lunch. "I agree." He sat down next to her.

She slid her arm through his and snuggled into his sweater. "When we renovate upstairs, we should continue with your mother's idea of bringing the outside in."

Relieved to hear her talking about their future, yet not being able to help himself, Sutherland charged ahead. "Can we talk about this morning?"

Agnes shook her head. "Nope. Not in the mood. What's your hurry? Does the money disappear?"

Sutherland winced. "No, it doesn't. Sometimes I tend to be too efficient."

Agnes laughed.

"Can I say I think the love of my life is terrific, and I need her help?"

Agnes was pleased. "Oh, how nice. How may I help you, Mr. Too Efficient?"

"The money doesn't disappear, but rather than buy a couch factory, I really want to expand the foundation's reach. Make it more relevant to this time. I'm hoping you have new ideas."

"So, you married me for my new ideas?"

"Oh, no. I married you for your wit, beauty, and ability to play foot hockey with a multimillion-dollar portfolio under the lunch table."

"Nice save." Agnes sat up and faced Sutherland. "Please understand, I love you, but this morning I learned that I, Little Orphan Agnes, married Daddy Warbucks. It was a shock. Luckily, I got some time to process it while eating double Baklava for lunch. When we came home to this lovely house, I was ready to read the fourteen pages of investments, plus the twelve pages of the Laura and John McKnight Foundation where, by the way, I learned I am now on the board of trustees." Agnes put her fingers up to Sutherland's lips stopping the beginning of a Sutherland explanation. "Let me finish. I realize life has changed for me. I just don't want it to change for us."

Sutherland stared at Agnes in wonder. How could he be so lucky, so smart, so...something. Other ladies in his life had researched his bank balance then made reservations on the Riviera. Agnes got mad and ordered double Baklava. "So, has this morning been a *good* morning?"

Agnes debated how to answer. "Certainly, a different morning. My plan for today was to see if I could rent out my house, catalogue the paintings and books in the vault, and make sure I had enough in checking account for my car payment."

Sutherland grimaced. "I still hope that payment doesn't break us."

Agnes put her arms around her handsome, well-intentioned—if sometimes oblivious—husband, and suggested they discuss further foundation business upstairs, in private.

§

Officer Preston made good time driving over to the Dawson house. She rang the bell and waited. She rang again, knocking as well.

"I'm coming!" a muffled voice called from inside the house.

Preston heard the turning of a deadbolt and finally the door opened. Mia Dawson looked surprised to see a uniformed officer at her door.

"What do you want?" she asked curtly.

"I'm officer Kate Preston, ma'am. I am here to collect the phone you called about."

"Oh yeah, that. Wait here and I'll get it."

Preston pushed against the door to keep it from closing. "I would prefer to get it myself, to prevent it from getting any more fingerprints."

"Oh, okay." Mia said, pointing to the stairs. "It's on the night table, third door on the left. Be careful, there are a lot of packing boxes up there."

Preston mounted the steps. Mia followed close behind. "Have they figured out what happened to Charlie yet?" She asked.

"All I know is he was electrocuted," Preston said.

"Yeah, that's what's funny. I think you people are looking at the wrong thing. The bike had a step-down transformer. That voltage wouldn't kill anyone."

"I wouldn't know, ma'am," Preston said as she entered the third door on the left, gloved up, and bagged the phone. "Did you know your husband had this phone?"

"I already told the Lieutenant that I didn't. I looked through it, so my fingerprints are already on it."

"I understand," Preston said.

§

Preston found Gramm, White, and Rathkey in Gramm's office discussing a recent call from Deputy Chief Sanders. Gramm looked up as Preston entered. "Deputy Chief Sanders called. He wanted to know why you haven't solved this case yet."

Preston smiled. "Deputy Chief Sanders doesn't know I exist, Lieutenant."

"Oh, maybe he was wondering why I haven't solved this case yet. Is that Charlie Dawson's second phone in your hand?"

"It is," she said, handing it to White.

"Did the widow say anything interesting?" Gramm asked.

"She thinks we're looking at the wrong thing."

"What does that mean?"

"She said something about there wasn't enough voltage because it was stepped down." Preston checked her pad for the notes that she had compiled once she returned to her patrol car. "She said, the bike has a step-down transformer, so it couldn't have killed her anyone."

"Does she know what did?"

"She didn't say."

"Maybe he put a fork in the outlet. My young nephew tries to do that all the time," White joked.

"I think he got hit by lightning," Milo added.

Gramm shook his head. "You take the next Sanders call, Milo. He likes you."

White gloved up and began to scroll through the texts. After a few minutes, she announced, "There's chatter about a fireplace invention and some heat-retaining wallpaper. Apparently, our victim invested thousands and lost it all. More recently, he's even been texting Gibbs about investing in that bike. Gibbs has not responded. Then there's Nora Swenson."

"Keep us in suspense," Gramm said, "because patience is my strong suit."

"Nora is asking him for money. A couple hundred bucks a month. She doesn't say why."

"And his response?"

"He says he's broke. She doesn't believe him."

"Is she blackmailing him?" Milo asked.

White shook her head and continued to scroll the conversation. "It's hard to tell. Her texts say that he owes her."

Gramm gloved up and held out his hand. White gave him the phone. Gramm began looking at the texts. Meanwhile, Milo asked Preston if she had Nora Swenson's financial statements.

"Only preliminary stuff. She lives paycheck to paycheck."

"Don't we all," White said. "No offense, Milo."

"None taken. Been there, done that."

"I'll do a deeper dive," Preston offered.

"Swenson says our victim owes her," Gramm said as he continued read through Dawson's message thread with Nora. "Maybe she gave him money in the past—one of his failed investments?"

"What about the financials for Leah Davis, the Dawsons, Gabriel Gibbs, and that guy Marsden?" White asked Preston.

"Waiting on those. I should have them on Monday."

"I think we interview Swenson this afternoon, and because we're waiting on financials and forensics, we take the weekend off," Gramm said.

"A free weekend during a murder case? I love it!" White cheered.

§

Milo left Gramm's office to take a call from Doc Smith and was pleasantly surprised with Doc Smith's giddy enthusiasm for the eighty-year-old skeleton.

"I'm on my way to Wardline. Join me." he urged Milo, clicking off with saying goodbye—as usual.

Gramm had reluctantly delayed the second Nora Swenson interview to allow Milo enough time to meet the good doctor. Milo had not been present at the first Swenson interview, and Gramm wanted him there for this one to be sure Milo didn't miss any opportunity for mind lint to surface.

Milo thought Doc Smith would bag up the skeleton, pat Chester on the head, and leave—a quick and dirty body grab. His shoulders slumped as he pulled into the Wardline estate behind two medical examiner cars and a body transport vehicle affectionately termed the body bus. "The whole damn circus is in town," he muttered.

Milo had barely knocked when Robert opened the door with a sour look on his face. "Oh, sir, I am sorry to say that Madam is upset. She wanted to avoid all these people traipsing throughout her house."

"Couldn't be helped, Robert. Where's Doc Smith?"

"Upstairs with the late Mr. Björklund."

Milo brushed past Robert and hurried up the steps to the third floor. Doc Smith was smiling as his two associates were easing the skeleton into the body bag. "Easy does it, people," Smith was cautioning. "I don't want any damage to the bones."

Smith looked up to see Milo. "Milo, what a find! Thank you for a great weekend."

"We aim to please. Mille Greysolon thinks the guy who was in the closet may have been murdered by her uncle."

"Even better."

"To add to your fun, the dead guy's name might be Leif Björklund."

"I'll let you know if this is the late Mr. Björklund, and if he was murdered." Smith smiled again.

"You're enjoying this." Milo said.

Smith clapped Milo on the shoulder. "Milo, I get dead bodies that have been stabbed, beaten, shot and just plain died. This guy, assuming it's a guy, has spent eighty years in the closet. You gotta admit, this is kinda fun."

Milo wanted only unusual cases for his re-opened PI business and had to admit this one was, different, but fun?

Smith's associates carefully placed the body bag on their gurney and began the arduous journey down two flights of stairs. Robert arrived in time to see the gurney wheeled out of the old servant's quarters.

"Is there an elevator in this house?" Milo asked.

Robert looked surprised. "An elevator, sir? Why would we have an elevator?"

"To help remove dead bodies?"

"Drole, sir, but the people who built this house did not have that foresight. Does Lakesong have an elevator?"

"Of course," Milo said.

"Pity the body wasn't stored there, sir," Robert allowed.

Milo was beginning to like Robert. He followed the body down the stairs and out to the body bus, avoiding a scene with Mille. Doc Smith said he was going to work on this case over the weekend and should have results by Monday.

Milo called Gramm to tell him he was now free for the Nora Swenson interview.

§

Sutherland pressed the code to open the vault door expecting Agnes to follow him into the large room. She didn't. He poked his head back out and found her examining one of the electric train engines of his childhood. Sutherland and Darian had taken most of Sutherland's old toys out of the vault and placed them in the anteroom where Darian had enough space to play with them.

The dust on the model train layout that had accumulated from twenty years of disuse was long gone; a sign ten-year-old Darian was making good use of the toys.

"Do you like electric trains?" Sutherland asked Agnes.

"I don't know. I never thought about it." Looking at the vast array of tracks, trestles, and switches, Agnes added, "I assume *you* do. This looks like the train museum."

"That's Darian. He's been busy," Sutherland said. "A lot of the pieces had come loose, and it looks like he's glued them back onto the plywood. He's also added a few new items to the set, such as that log roller there. It puts logs on a long car when you push that button." Sutherland pointed to a black box with a red button, one in a series of red-buttoned black boxes.

Agnes smiled. "Oh, I see, ten-year-old Darian put all of those pieces in all by himself."

Sutherland nodded. "Bright young man."

"And then used his piggy bank fortune to buy a new log rolling thing and car which seems to fit in with all of the other things on this board."

"Maybe." Sutherland smirked.

"Maybe the log roller is either a modern facsimile or an original antique, neither of which ten-year-old Darian can afford on his allowance for feeding the cats."

"You underestimate Darian's business skills, but I take your point. He may have had help...on an odd Saturday... now and then when you were busy. If I can pull you away from the toys, I'd like you to see inside the actual vault."

Agnes followed Sutherland into the massive room, with racks of books, paintings, and boxes. She spun around looking at the walls of drawers and cupboards, all with elaborate carvings. Agnes walked over to one, tracing two intertwined snakes above a winged dragon. "I've never seen anything like this anywhere else in Lakesong. Who carved it?"

"I don't know," Sutherland said. "My father didn't know. In fact, Bella Bixby, who lived in Lakesong before us, didn't know."

"I can tell you, the people who carved in this room, were not the same people who did the furniture and woodwork in the rest of the house," Agnes explained.

"Do you know about carvings?"

"It was part of my art history courses," Agnes said. "Each carver's work is distinctive, just like each painter's brush strokes are distinctive. I know of several experts who could tell us more. This is interesting."

§

183

Nora Swenson's second-hand Civic started this morning because she remembered to plug in the car's block heater last night. Nora agreed to come up to the heated police station for the second interview. Milo made the trip up the hill from Wardline in record time.

Gramm and White joined Swenson in the interview room while Milo went into the anteroom to watch the interview through the one-way mirror.

"Why am I here? I told you all I know in your car."

Gramm shook his head. "Not quite all. I don't think you were completely forthcoming in our first interview."

Swenson cocked her head to one side as if she didn't know what he meant.

"Since we talked last, we have received information that you were asking Charlie Dawson for money."

Swenson remained quiet.

"In fact, you texted Charlie Dawson that he 'owed' you. Why would a man you hardly knew *owe* you money?"

"I didn't know him, and he did owe me," Swenson said.

"Explain," White said.

"Charles Dawson was my biological father. He never acknowledged me and never gave my mother a dime to help support me—ever. He owed both of us."

"So, you hunted for him?" White asked.

Swenson laughed. "Nothing quite that malevolent. I had a nice childhood. My mother became a nurse and married a nice guy. We didn't need Charles Dawson. But now I'm on my own, working three jobs, and living in a rented room trying to finish my advanced degree. I could sure use a little money. I wasn't asking for much."

"What did he say?"

She raised her chin and pursed her lips before exploding. "He had the nerve to say he was broke! He lived in that big yellow house plus he was a DINK!"

"Dink?" Gramm looked at White for clarification.

"Dual income, no kids."

Gramm sighed. "Getting back to Charlie Dawson—how did you know where to find him?"

"It wasn't hard."

"How was it not hard?"

"I wasn't looking for him. I ride bikes. My main job is working on the bike trails. When I moved here, I joined the Zenith City Riders. I was looking at the on-line directory to see if I knew anyone. I stumbled onto a Charles Dawson. Once I found the name, I checked him out with Mom. He was the right Charles Dawson—nice house, no kids, two incomes. I figured a couple hundred bucks a month would have been coffee money to him."

"What did you do after he said he was broke?" White asked.

"I called him a bastard. My mom was right to close the door on him."

"So, you killed him out of revenge for you and your mother?" Gramm was hopeful she'd say yes.

"No, but I was going to tell his wife I existed hopefully to cause him some grief. I told him that on our ride the night he got fried."

"What did he say?" White asked.

"He just laughed and told me to go ahead and tell her."

"Of course, dead he could be worth more to you," White said. "You now have a claim on his estate."

Swenson paused. "I never thought of that. How long would that take?"

"We're cops, not lawyers," Gramm said. "Why didn't you tell us this the first time we talked?"

"You didn't ask."

"Are you hiding anything else?" White asked. "Is Leah Davis your mother?"

"As I'm short with black hair, and she's an Amazonian blond, and would have had to have given birth to me when she was still in elementary school, I don't think so."

Gramm told her she could go, but they would need to know if she was leaving town. Swenson rolled her eyes.

Gramm, White, and Rathkey formed up in Gramm's office. "I think she's lying," White said. "I think she knew Dawson was worth more dead than alive."

"Everyone lies," Milo said, "but only one person lies because they are the murderer."

"You say that all the time," White said.

"Because it's true."

"We all know that," Gramm interjected. "But what I want to know is does that woman have the expertise to do whatever to that bike?"

"Well, that's the problem," Milo smiled. "We have to know more *about* the whatever, before we can know who *did* the whatever to that bike."

15

Milo sat alone drinking his coffee in the morning room when Martha served his brioche French toast and bacon and stated the obvious, "Our newlyweds seemed to have skipped breakfast."

"That happens."

"I'll clean up and leave if that's alright."

"Sure," he said, breaking off pieces of bacon, dropping them for Annie. Jet, who didn't eat bacon, received one small piece to use as a hockey puck.

Milo's phone rang with 'Stayin' Alive' by the Bee Gees.

Martha reappeared in the morning room. "Please, whose ringtone is 'Stayin' Alive?'"

"Doc Smith, the medical examiner," Milo said as if it should have been immediately obvious.

Martha walked back into the kitchen shaking her head. "The death doctor gets 'Stayin' Alive.' Why should I be surprised?"

"Whacha got Doc?" Milo asked.

"I don't think our skinny friend is Leif Björklund."

"What? Why?"

"I had one of my associates look up any records they could find on Leif. Guess what they found."

"No clue."

"A death certificate. Leif Björklund died in 1941 of leukemia."

"So, who's our guy?"

"Don't know, but I've stopped calling him Leif."

"What happens next?" Milo asked.

"I found a relative of Björklund who is willing to provide a DNA sample. We will test him against the skeleton just to make sure it's not Leif."

"How do you find a relative of a hundred-year-old dead guy?" Milo was impressed.

"I called Mrs. Greysolon, and she gave me several names. It seems her family and the Björklund family were close."

"Close? Mille's family gossip says her uncle might have killed Leif."

"Maybe the Björklunds just didn't like him."

§

Agnes roused but did not open her eyes—a habit from her former life before Sutherland and his blackout shades entered her regular morning routine. Today was the one-week anniversary of her being the Agnes part of Agnes and Sutherland living at Lakesong, a dynamic, lovely week to be sure, nothing dull or ordinary.

She tapped her foot on the floor which caused the shades to open. Winter sunlight streamed through the floor-to-ceiling windows. Her towheaded husband roused. The morning light worked better than an alarm.

Sutherland squinted one eye and turned toward her. "So much light. So early. Why?"

"Early? By the sun's angle I'd say late morning," Agnes laughed.

Both his eyes opened as he fumbled for his phone. "It's after eleven. Good grief, I never sleep this late!"

"I'm a bad influence."

"Yeah," Sutherland smiled, "you sure are. We missed breakfast."

"Yup. We can grab lunch at Spirit Mountain."

"Absolutely."

§

Sitting down across from Mille, sharing a cup of coffee, Robert said, "Mr. Rathkey called, Madam."

"What did he want?" Mille sipped her morning coffee.

"He had somewhat disturbing news. The unfortunate person that dwelled in your attic may not have been Leif Bj…"

"I know!" Mille cut him off. "The medical examiner called me yesterday looking for a Björklund relative—testing DNA or some such thing. He told me that Leif had a death certificate—died of leukemia."

"If they don't think the body is that of Leif Björklund, Madam, why do they need a DNA test?" Robert asked.

"To make sure." Mille sipped her coffee. "This is disturbing. If the skeleton isn't Björklund who did my uncle murder? This is getting out of hand."

"I see your point, Madam."

"If gawkers come on our property, I'll shoot them." Mille smiled. "People make bigger targets than pigeons."

"Indeed, Madam. And they move more slowly."

§

Milo was about to ease into Lakesong's indoor, saltwater pool when his phone did the da dunk sound from 'Law and Order' indicating a call from Gramm. *It's Saturday! We have the weekend off,* Milo thought. Stepping back to the pool coffee bar, he picked up his phone. "What?" he demanded.

"Late Friday email from Holden. Read it!"

"Who the hell is Holden?" Milo asked, but Gramm was already gone. Milo checked his email, finding the most recent one to be from Michelle Holden, head of forensics. He hated reading emails on his phone but sat down and scrolled through it. After a lot of blah blah, the last two paragraphs caught his attention.

Approximately sixty percent of the control box was melted beyond recognition, however, we separated that which we could. Checking the separated parts against the control device provided by Gibbs Industries, a partially melted three by six inch device was found that did not have a corresponding unit in the control bike. Because bits of two wires were still connected to the device, we believe that these two wires were the ones leading to the pulse monitors—the wires that Mr. Marsden said didn't belong there.

We conclude that the stationary bike had been wired by person or persons unknown to electrocute the victim.

Milo's phone rang again with the *da dunk* ringtone. "What now, Ernie?"

"I've got White and Preston on here," Gramm said.

"*You're* making a conference call?" Milo was shocked.

"Amy did it," Gramm said, giving his wife the credit.

"We were shocked too," White said.

"So, boys and girls, what do we think?" Gramm asked.

"Definitely murder," Preston said, a sentiment echoed by White.

Milo rolled his eyes. "I would hope it's murder since we've been working on that premise since early Wednesday morning. However, that's not the point I found interesting."

"Okay, I'll bite. What's interesting to you?" Gramm asked.

"The device, the box, that forensics cannot identify has got to be the switch. You know I always ask, 'why now.' What made the bike kill Dawson Tuesday night, not the Monday or Wednesday? That switch was wired into the bike to kill when the killer wanted to kill."

"A lot of kills in that sentence, Milo," White joked.

"That switch talks to the mind of the killer. This was a premeditated and painful death," Milo said.

Gramm agreed. "Somebody really hated Charlie Dawson."

§

Sutherland draped his arm around Agnes as they sat in the Spirit Mountain ski chalet supporting the six members of the Zenith City Riders. The couple arrived late, missing all the stage-one runs of the Frosted Fatty, the downhill slalom bike race on fat winter tires. They ordered brunch and watched the riders take their individual runs down the tree ladened hill.

"I bailed three times on my first run," Jeff Spangler told Sutherland. "I hope my second run was the best. Last year I hit a tree. That pretty well took me out for the day."

"A tree?" Agnes questioned.

"Yeah. The runs begin parallel to the ski lifts, then cut through the trees. The blue guidelines get pretty narrow in there—it's dicey."

Nora Swenson came up to the couple and introduced herself to Agnes. "I got a little first aid after a hard fall. The bike's fine, thank goodness. I borrowed it. I gotta do my second stage-two run."

Agnes wished her luck. "I've lived here all my life. How has this race escaped me? I thought this was a race, like all the riders go together."

"No, they go off individually," Sutherland explained. "The judges count their best time in each stage then average them together."

At the end of the second stage, the winners were announced. None of the Zenith City people made it in the top three. "You've got to get those people into training, coach."

"Wait, I'm the coach?" Sutherland asked.

Agnes laughed. "If you don't know, that could be the problem."

Sutherland congratulated the Zenith City group before he and Agnes stepped outside and put on their equipment for a little downhill racing of their own—Sutherland on his skis and Agnes on her snowboard. They stood at the top of an intermediate hill and assessed snow conditions and terrain.

Sutherland noticed several jumps had been built into one side of the hill. "Are you going to jump those?" Sutherland asked, smiling.

"You mean like go airborne over those mounds? No way. A person could get seriously hurt."

"Good. I'm glad we agree."

Agnes smiled at Sutherland, the daredevil smile and eye twinkle he had already learned to fear. "Race you to the bottom!" She yelled as she took off.

Sutherland sighed and began chasing her until he realized she was lining up to jump one of the biggest mounds. He stopped just in time to see her go airborne, reach down, grab the heel of the board, and take the landing with just a little wobble.

Another skier stopped next to Sutherland. "That's a great Ollie," he said.

"Her name's Agnes," Sutherland corrected.

The man laughed. "No, the jump she just did is an Ollie."

"I better catch up, or I'll never hear the end of it," Sutherland said, pushing off, racing downhill.

Agnes was at the bottom of the hill waiting for him as he brought his skis to a halt with a sideways flourish of snow that he thought was cool.

"Mr. McKnight, you're late."

"I'm glad we agreed not to take any jumps, Mrs. McKnight."

"I lied," Agnes said. "Let's go again now that we're limber."

Another trip up the ski lift later, they were once again looking down from the top of the hill. This time, however, it was Sutherland who pushed off first. Agnes followed and watched Sutherland fly over the same mound, do a spread eagle, and land it. Not to be outdone, Agnes flew over the mound landing a few feet from Sutherland.

By midafternoon after racing, jumping, and falling, they were spent and retired to the chalet for beer and a double basket of wings. "I wonder if Milo still has that big bottle of Excedrin?" Sutherland stretched his back. "I don't think the strippers are going to do it today."

Agnes looked at him. "Strippers? What are you talking about?"

"Turmeric and ginger, my anti-inflammatory duo. Milo said they sounded like strippers. Aren't you hurting?"

"Yoga. You need to try it," Agnes said.

Upon arriving back at Lakesong, Sutherland stretched out on the couch in the family room to watch some basketball. Agnes joined him was catching up on her social media when her phone began to buzz. There was no caller ID, just a number. She walked out of the family room so the call wouldn't interrupt Sutherland's game.

"Hello?" she said with some hesitation.

"Agnes? Agnes Larson?" a woman's voice said. "It's me, April Lindstrom, you know from Mrs. Pearson's house."

The name April Lindstrom sounded familiar. "April! Yes. Hi." Agnes sat on the marble steps trying to recall the face that went with the name.

"I'm calling because I just found out Mrs. Pearson is in trouble." April was never one for idle chit chat.

"Trouble? What do you mean?"

"The county is threatening to take the house away and auction it off. Mrs. Pearson and the current girls will be thrown out on the street. I'm contacting as many of us as I can find to let everyone know. I'm hoping we can raise enough money to keep the house going. Can you contribute? I'm setting up a GoFundMe page in between calls. I'll DM you the link when I'm finished."

Agnes stood up and walked into the gallery trying to make sense of what April had just dumped on her. Mrs. Pearson was the woman who fostered both her and her sister Barbara through middle and high school. "I have a few dollars, April, send me the link."

"Oh, good. Could you help find more of the girls? You were older than me and knew some of the people who left before I got there. I couldn't find your sister."

Agnes didn't want to get into her sister's death. "I'll contact some people I know. Does Mrs. Pearson have the same phone number?"

"Yes. It's still the landline."

"Good. I'll get back to you, April. Remember to text me the GoFundMe link when you finish it. Thanks for calling." Agnes hung up and went back to the family room in search of Sutherland. The basketball game was on, but Sutherland was off, asleep on the family room couch. He roused as she sat down next to him.

"I wasn't sleeping, just resting my eyes," Sutherland said, looking at the television and sitting up. "Oh crap! How did the Timberwolves get behind by that much?"

"You were sleeping on the job, point man. I'm sure the players felt your absence and couldn't cope. I need your advice."

Sutherland turned off the TV. "I'm all ears."

"Why would the county auction off someone's house?"

"You haven't paid your property taxes? We can take care of that on Mon…"

"Of course, I did! This isn't about me. I'm talking about a friend of mine. Someone I know. I got a call saying this friend was going to lose her house. You think it's about taxes?"

"What friend?"

"A person I knew from middle school and high school."

Sutherland took her hand. "I have to warn you that this is one of the ugly sides of money. People will come to you with all sorts of stories looking to scam you because you have money. Is that what's going on here?"

Agnes pulled her hand away. "No! I am talking about Mrs. Pearson not a scammer. I told you about her. She was our foster mom for seven years. Barbara and I stayed with her, and she was wonderful to us. A woman called and said Mrs. Pearson's in trouble. If that's true, I want to help her. The woman, April Lindstrom, has a GoFundMe page." Agnes checked her phone. "I don't have the link yet. I don't know long it will take to the raise the money, how much money is needed, or when it's due. I need information."

"Look, I rush ahead and sometimes jump to conclusions. Are you sure about the woman with the GoFundMe page?"

"I knew her as a girl. I don't know," Agnes said, haltingly.

"Can I make a suggestion?" Sutherland asked with caution.

"Sure."

"Rather than just take April's word for it, can you go talk to Mrs. Pearson and find out from her what's going on.?"

Agnes' eyes brightened. "Of course, I can. I was so upset and muddled by the news, I skipped over the obvious. How many years of nonpayment does it take before the county seizes the property?"

"I'm not sure. Talk to Mrs. Pearson, find out the particulars, and then talk to Creedence."

"All that's well and good, but I only have $375.46 in my checking account. I would like to add more than that to the GoFundMe account if it's legit."

"I'm sure Creedence can sort it all out."

Agnes wondered how even Creedence could make $375.46 more sizeable in only a few days.

Sutherland put his arm around her and whispered, "Don't tell anyone, but you have more than $375.46. If you don't believe me, ask Creedence."

Agnes looked at him and blinked her eyes. "That's right. I read all about it this afternoon."

§

Milo started a fire and sat down in his cozy library to read before dinner. He tucked Charlie Dawson's deliberate, premediated murder in the back of his brain to let it cook, a process that had worked in the past. He began a new book by an author he had not read before. Less than one chapter in, the intercom announced that someone was at the front gate.

Milo checked the Lakesong app on his phone and sighed. The visitor was Ron Bello. He pushed the *open gate* button.

Bello drove onto the grounds and parked at the front steps. Milo opened the door. "This is a 'no soliciting' neighborhood."

Bello charged up the steps and shook Milo's hand. "Good to see you again, Milo. May I have your autograph before tomorrow's interview?"

"Very funny, Ron. Come on in," Milo said. Despite Bello's intrusion on his privacy and peace of mind, he liked the guy.

Bello followed Milo into the library. "I was reading a book—not yours," Milo said.

"No problem. Millions of people are not making the same mistake. Are you going to offer me a drink?"

"You're annoying like family. You can get your own."

Bello walked into the family room, poured himself a healthy amount of the rare McCallan Scotch Milo and Sutherland had found in a Lakesong tunnel last year, and returned to the library.

"I don't know what I'm going to do when that bottle is empty," Bello said, sitting down and stretching out his long legs in the overstuffed club chair opposite Milo. After sipping the aged Scotch, Bello admitted, "I've asked around and can't find that exact year anywhere."

"Don't worry, we have more."

"Where are you getting it from?"

"If I told you, I'd have to kill you, but that's okay because I'm going to kill you anyway."

"For a guy who threatens me all the time, you don't have a threatening manner."

"You took me by surprise. I was going to kill you tomorrow morning on live Sunday-morning television."

Jet marched into the room and wound around Bello's legs, while squeaking softly.

"Besides, I never do my own dirty work," Milo said. "Jet is my assassin."

Jet rolled over, exposing his belly. Bello let go with his deep laugh, bent down, and scratched the purring cat. "He looks terrifying."

"Part of the effect."

"So, what are you working on now?" Bello asked.

"Someone stole a candy bar from Mr. Paulson's corner store in 1974. It might have been me. I'm looking into it."

"Tragic. Did Mr. Paulson ever recover from the financial loss?"

"He was insured. Dull story, almost as dull as the airport incident."

Looking at Jet, Bello allowed as to how Milo protested too much. Jet squeaked, wanting more tummy rubs. Bello took another sip of Scotch enjoying the flickering fire. Jet knew he was going to have to train this new human, but a fleeting shadow caught his eye, and he was off.

"My first book received fair reviews and sold about ten thousand copies. My second book did slightly better. However, my third book has been number one on all the best seller lists and looks to remain there for a long time. I ask myself, what did the third one have that the first two didn't."

"Harper Gain," Milo jumped in.

Bello smiled. "Of course, that gets the first people to buy the book, but then they have to recommend it to their family and friends for the book to keep selling. In this case, it seems the public is enthralled with a scruffy, barrel-chested detective."

Milo looked down. "Barrel-chested? Where do you get that from?"

"If I were you, I'd object to scruffy."

Milo rubbed his Saturday stubble. "Scruffy's fair, but not barrel-chested. I've worked hard to get the barrel down to a small cask."

Bello looked dubious. "Let's just agree that you're a work in progress. At any rate, my publisher thinks a second book featuring Milo Rathkey would jump off the shelves, and I agree with him."

"Sounds dangerous—all those books flying around the bookstore."

Jet, having conquered the evasive shadow, jumped up on Bello's lap for more pets. Bello set his glass down and complied. The relaxed setting could easily lead him to a nap, but that would be rude. He shook off his drowsiness and proceeded to business. "Before we get into all of the flying books, like I told you on the phone, I need to rent a place in town."

"Ask Sutherland. He deals in real estate. I do murder."

16

Milo sat in a makeup chair at the local ABC Television Affiliate. Radio was easier. No one cared what he looked like. Bello had already had his turn at beautiful and was thumbing through a magazine. The makeup person, tall, gangly, with a slight Russian accent held her gaze about a foot from Milo's face making him uncomfortable.

"Just give me what you gave Ron," Milo said.

The woman laughed. "I don't think so, Ron being African American, and you being, what?"

"Part Labrador."

The woman chose a shade of pancake makeup and applied it liberally to Milo's freshly shaved face.

"Ron says I'm scruffy," Milo said.

"I agree, but I have anti-scruff foundation."

A producer came in to inform them that they had five minutes to air. "Ken and Wendy will introduce you both. The segment will be question and answer. Just be yourselves."

"Last week on NBC, I got to be Lassie," Milo confided.

"Lassie was a collie not a Labrador," the makeup woman contested. "Keep your dogs straight."

When the makeup lady finished, Milo and Ron followed the producer out of the makeup room and into the studio where a floor person showed them to their chairs. "It's Sunday friggin' morning, Ron, and I'm in a television studio instead of my nice warm house."

"You can thank me later," Ron said. "It builds character."

"I'm already a character," Milo quipped as he and Bello shook hands with Wendy and Ken.

The robot cameras moved into place.

Wendy, a young, pretty, brunette, put down her phone, and waited for the cue that the pretaped introduction was over. "This morning we are pleased to have Ron Bello, journalist and author, in our studio, along with Duluth Detective Milo Rathkey. Both gentlemen were intimately involved in the murder investigation that led to the startling revelation concerning the famous Harper Gain."

Ken, a handsome, if toothy, man with an insincere, authoritative manner picked up the narrative. "According to Ron's book—can I call you Ron?"

Bello started to respond.

Ken continued, "Ron's book centers around the investigation into the death of former district attorney and blogger Patsy Rand. According to your book, *The Life and Death and Death Again of Harper Gain by Ron Bello,* you, yourself, were a suspect in the death of Patsy Rand, were you not?"

"I was—not a comfortable feeling."

"Milo, did you think Ron here was a viable suspect?"

"He had murderer written all over him," Milo said with a straight face.

Ken appeared shocked. Bello and Wendy laughed.

"You have to get used to Milo's humor, Ken. May I call you Ken?" Bello jibed.

"Well, instead of going to jail," Wendy began, "Ron Bello has written about his experiences in a best seller that is number one on all the best seller lists. So, Ron, toward the end of the book, you describe Milo's Agatha Christie-like gathering of the suspects to reveal the killer as 'absurdist theatre.' Why did you call it that?"

"The room was filled with action and suspense. It was a three-ring circus. We had suspects trading accusations in ring one, the murderer running in ring two, and a dog attacking in ring three. Throughout it all we politely consumed incredibly fine sherry."

"I would like to point out," Milo began his memorized shpiel, "that the actual apprehension of the murderer was expertly handled by Lieutenant Ernie Gramm and Sergeant Robin White of the Duluth Police Department, along with other officers, and a dog named Tricksie." Milo felt his job was done, again, and sat back to have Ron continue what Ron did best—promote his book.

"Speaking of that," Ken broke in, oblivious to Milo's statement, "how in the world did you figure it out. Now, we don't want to give away the entire plot, but we do want some insight into how your mind works, Mr. Rathkey."

Not wanting Ken to be eviscerated, Bello answered. "You're right, Ken, we don't want to give away the ending, but let's just say Milo's solution was extraordinary."

"But, Mr. Rathkey, how did you imagine it. What is your process?" Wendy asked.

"I notice small details."

"Such as?" Wendy asked.

"Well, take Ken here. He has two blue socks on today, but they don't match. Why? If he was a corpse on the floor, I would have to know why. If Ken was a suspect, the socks would become even more important."

"What if I just got dressed in a hurry?" Ken asked, looking at his socks.

"But why were you in a hurry?" Milo asked.

"I overslept?" Ken said, not liking his sock faux pas being outed for public consumption.

"Did you have a late night? Did your alarm not work? You do this show at this time every week. How could you oversleep?"

Ken's face was getting rosy through the makeup.

"Ken's late every week," Wendy monotoned. "No mystery there, but I must admit, I never notice his socks."

The interview moved on to Milo's latest case, an incident at the Duluth Airport. Once again, Milo gave the credit to the Duluth Police Department as instructed. It would hopefully help Gramm with Deputy Chief Sanders.

"Let's get breakfast," Bello suggested as they were leaving the television studio.

"There's a pancake restaurant near Lakesong on Superior Street," Milo advised.

"By the way, I loved your sock thing," Bello said. "It rattled Mr. Ken doll."

Milo shrugged. "Did you notice one of his socks had a small unicorn at the top. I took that to be a woman's sock."

"Meaning?"

"Meaning nothing until you realize that Wendy likes unicorns."

"How do you know that?"

"You really are not observant, Ron. Her phone was in a glitzy, unicorn adorned case."

Bello shook his head in disbelief. "It must be exhausting to be you."

"Tell me about it."

When Ron and Milo arrived at the Pancake Shop, Milo was upset to see a long line waiting to be seated. "I love their pancakes, but I hate to wait."

"I don't think we have to," Bello said. "I see Sutherland over there with Agnes Larson. They are at a table for four, but there's only two of them."

"Let's go. By the way, Agnes and Sutherland are married," Milo said, moving around the line, past the hostess to Sutherland's table.

Bello followed.

"Good of you to hold a table for us," Milo said as he sat down.

"I hope we're not intruding," Bello apologized, noticing the couple was halfway through plates of waffles with whipped cream and strawberries.

"Not at all," Agnes said. "Please sit."

"I understand congratulations are in order, Sutherland. You snapped up this lovely lady. And Agnes, what were you thinking?" Bello joked.

"I know," Agnes laughed. "I have a flaw in my decision-making capabilities."

"What brings you two out on this Sunday morning," Sutherland asked.

"We're television stars," Milo said, accepting a menu from the waitress.

"Milo is the star. I'm the sidekick."

"How long will you be in town, Ron?" Sutherland asked.

"Have I worn out my welcome already?"

"Certainly not. I was wondering if you have time to have dinner with us at Lakesong."

"Martha's cooking? I'll make time. I'm going to be in town for at least a month. I'm looking for a place to rent— tired of hotel rooms."

Agnes looked at Sutherland who shrugged. "We may have a place you can rent," Agnes offered. "I still have my place in Lakeside, and I am not using it."

"Updated kitchen, lovely fireplace, two bedrooms, two and a half baths," Sutherland added. "Cozy bungalow on a quiet street, large porch..."

"Said like a true real estate man," Milo joked.

"It is what it is. I am what I am," Sutherland said.

"I'll take it. How much?"

Agnes' eyes widened with indecision. She looked at Sutherland.

"To be determined," Sutherland said. "I'm sure you'll get the friend and family discount."

Bello waved that off. "I have a living stipend from my publisher, use it or lose it."

As they negotiated, Milo ordered buttermilk pancakes with bacon and sausage. "I get to eat my entire breakfast," he announced.

"As opposed to?" Bello asked.

"Annie the cat demands her tithe every morning or bad things will happen to Milo," Sutherland explained.

§

After breakfast, Sutherland took Bello over to tour Agnes' Lakeside bungalow. Milo began his plan of a quiet Sunday afternoon, getting past chapter one of his new book and later a swim to work off the pancakes. Agnes headed over to Wellwood for a fact-finding session with Mrs. Pearson.

Looking up the steps of the grand house, a warm, safe feeling swept over Agnes. After several bad foster situations, she and her sister Barbara were placed together with Mrs. Pearson. Agnes was in sixth grade, Barbara in eighth. Agnes last saw Mrs. Pearson at Barbara's funeral over a year ago.

The eight-bedroom, house featured three sets of steps leading to a porch with four, white ionic columns that supported a third-floor balcony. Smaller columns held up the second-floor balcony. It was ante bellum in Minnesota. A relative had given it to Mrs. Pearson, and she opened it for foster girls after her husband died.

Adult Agnes knew she could mount the steps and go through the front door, something that was not allowed when she was a young resident. Girls used the side door. Agnes decided against the front door, walked around to the side, and pressed the doorbell. A teenage girl with long brown braids over her shoulders opened it and asked, "May I help you?"

My God, was I ever that young? Agnes wondered as she informed the girl that she had an appointment to see Mrs. Pearson. The girl stepped aside, and Agnes walked into the familiar foyer. "Where would Mrs. Pearson like to see me?"

"In the left front parlor." The girl added, "If you go down this hallway and turn…oh, you seem to know where you are going."

Agnes turned and smiled. "I do." She entered the red and gold room and sat down on the edge of a crushed-velvet, Victorian chair. As she waited, she saw three girls walk by as if on an errand, trying to hide their true mission: catching a glimpse of the visitor. She knew the drill—count to ten and walk back again with a book. Their giggles gave them away.

Agnes loved this house. Coming home each afternoon from school, she pretended that the grand old house was hers. The house meant safety and comfort to both her and Barbara.

Mrs. Pearson, a tall woman with a friendly face and bad feet, padded into the room still wearing the turned-over beige orthopedic shoes that Agnes remembered fondly. Agnes stood. "Oh, for goodness sakes, Agnes, sit down," Mrs. Pearson said, sitting down opposite. "So good to see you again, Agnes. I was surprised yet pleased to get your call. What can I do for you?"

"I need some 'straightening out,'" Agnes said.

Mrs. Pearson laughed. That was her phrase when any of the girls went 'sideways,' Mrs. Pearson's term for doing something wrong or naughty.

"I got a call from April Lindstrom. She said you had a tax problem."

Mrs. Pearson morphed from friendly and welcoming to stony. Agnes recognized that face—not unfriendly, just a blank slate. It carried no judgement. "I wish she hadn't done that."

"Then it's true? She said the county is going to take away this house."

"Yes. It's my fault. I was a fool. I trusted our treasurer. He went more than sideways, Agnes. He not only ran off with our funds, but I discovered too late that he failed to pay our property taxes going back years."

Agnes nodded. "Can I see one of your tax statements?"

"What in heavens for?"

"April has started a GoFundMe account to raise money," Agnes said.

"My dear, I appreciate it, but it will be too late." Mrs. Pearson smiled. "We owe in excess of $25,000 and it is due in three days, this coming Wednesday."

Agnes sat back aghast. *This can't happen. I must solve this! Sutherland said his money is our money. Did he mean it?* Agnes clung to her purse.

Mrs. Pearson continued to talk, but Agnes was only hearing bits and pieces. "We are appealing to the county for more time, but…"

Agnes straightened her posture in the Victorian chair. "I have a solution. May I take the tax bill?" Agnes asked.

Mrs. Pearson stared at Agnes, no longer the shy, fearful, twelve-year-old girl who first came to this house to live. "Your solution is?"

"I'll pay the taxes. My gift to you for the gift you gave to both Barbara and me," Agnes said. "And I will not be talked out of it."

"How much of the debt can you afford?"

Agnes took a deep breath, hoping Sutherland meant what he said. "All of it. I know there are other problems, but as you used to tell Barbara and me, deal with the problem that is in front of you. Once that's gone, another will take its place. So, the taxes will get paid on Monday, then we'll meet to discuss replenishing the lost money. Our home must not be shut down. It must continue to help others like it helped us."

Mrs. Pearson, secretly pleased that someone had listened to her often-given advice, padded over to her secretary desk, retrieved the latest tax notice from one of the cubbies, and handed it to Agnes.

Agnes thanked her.

"Thank you, Agnes. I am going on faith that you can do this."

Agnes met her gaze and nodded. "I wouldn't offer if I couldn't."

Mrs. Pearson started to walk her to the front door. Agnes shook her head. "The side door. We girls use the side door. It's so much easier."

"Of course." They walked down the hall to the side door. "Agnes," Mrs. Person said, "thank you for even trying."

"I will succeed and call you Monday."

After Agnes had left, three of the girls crowded around Mrs. Pearson. "Who was that?"

"She once was you, just older now, and wiser, too, because she listened to me. Now, go set the table."

§

"I know I'm interrupting your Sunday so I will make this brief," Gibbs said on the conference call with the beta testers.

Leah Davis mumbled to herself, "He knows he's interrupting our Sunday and doesn't care." Nora Swenson laughed. Leah didn't realize she could be heard. Embarrassed for a second, Leah decided she just didn't care if Gibbs heard her.

Gibbs continued, "I feel it's time to resume our test. We have looked at the metrics and concluded that the test is still valid with five of us. I suggest we ride tomorrow night at six."

"I suggest we don't," Leah said. "What proof do we have that our bikes aren't a death machine, like Charlie's." *Not that you care as long as your precious test goes on.*

Gibbs was taken aback. "Death machine? Come on Leah, you don't really believe that."

"Yes, I do, Gibbs. The bike killed Charlie. How do we know our bikes won't kill us?"

"Marsden!" Gibbs yelled.

"Yeah?" Marsden said. Sutherland could tell from the background noise that Marsden and Gibbs were not in the same room. He congratulated himself on a fine piece of Milo-like awareness.

"Tell them what you told me about the police."

"The police believe that Charlie Dawson's bike was rigged by someone to kill him. The target was Charlie. The rest of the bikes should be fine," Marsden said.

"'Should be' isn't good enough," Leah said.

"Fine!" Gibbs almost shouted. "I will send Marsden to each of you to check your bikes. Does that work?"

"Mr. Marsden," Leah began, "do you know how Charlie's bike was changed?"

"I do. I was with the police forensic unit when they discovered wires that did not belong—wires that we did not put there. I can check each of your bikes. If these wires are not present, you are good to go."

"Does that work for everybody?" Gibbs asked.

All three said it did.

"Tuesday night at six," Gibbs said, leaving Marsden on the call to get a time he could check each bike.

§

The traveling Sunday night poker game had traveled to Saul Feinberg's multi-story modern house set into a cliff on Skyline Drive near Hawk Ridge. Ernie Gramm and Creedence Durant sat bundled on Saul's expansive deck watching the twinkling lights of the city and harbor below. The lights gave an outline border to the black waters of the lake. Superior could be twinkly-light friendly, or dark and foreboding depending upon the viewer's focus and mood. Creedence saw twinkly; Gramm, with his unsolved case, saw the endless darkness.

Milo and Sutherland were the last to arrive, bringing the harbor-gazing to an end. The group gathered around Saul's poker table that was set up in his living room. Gramm's mood lightened as he glanced in the kitchen at the stacks of pastrami waiting for a break in the poker game. Saul made his own pastrami from a recipe left to him by his grandfather—the one-time Pastrami King of The Upper Midwest.

Saul shuffled the cards. "Ernie, we can't talk shop tonight; I'm representing one of your suspects."

"If you know something counselor, you have to tell us," Gramm insisted.

"No, Ernie, actually, I don't," Saul retorted. "Seven card stud, nothing wild." He dealt two cards down and one up to each player.

Milo's up card was a six of spades. He checked his down cards, a seven and five of spades—a possible straight if he was lucky. Looking at two deuces down, Sutherland was trying to keep his poker face as Saul flipped him a third deuce up. Saul peaked at his king of diamonds and a ten of clubs down. A king of hearts up, was promising. Creedence pushed his glasses up on his nose as he looked at a nine of clubs and a three of hearts down, and an eight of hearts up. Garbage. The bidding was light.

"I understand congratulations are in order, Sutherland," Feinberg said as he dealt the second card up. "I read about your Hawaii elopement."

"Thank you, Saul," Sutherland said.

Feinberg looked around at the lack of congratulations by the others. "Am I last to know about it?"

"So last," Gramm said.

"So very last," Creedence added, looking at his new card. "Who dealt this mess?"

"Their first anniversary is coming up," Milo added.

"I went to Hawaii once," Creedence said. "I came back with a second-degree sunburn, and a bad choice in t-shirts, but, alas, no wife."

"You took the wrong day cruise," Sutherland joked.

The second round of bets was more vigorous than the first.

"All right, Gramm, enough, stop badgering me!" Saul exclaimed in jest. "The kid is off limits, but I'm open to spill the beans about Gabe Gibbs,"

Gramm looked up from stacking and restacking his chips. "I knew you'd crack."

"Not on the kid, but Gibbs is not my client."

"So, Gibbs is a suspect?" Sutherland asked.

"Should be," Feinberg said. "It's his bike."

Sutherland looked at Gramm who held up his hand in a gesture of "no comment." Sutherland's gaze went to Milo who was displaying his best poker face.

"As long as you insist, Saul, tell me all about Gibbs?" Gramm urged.

Saul dealt the fifth card up. Sutherland was looking at his fourth deuce, two up, two down. Milo was one card away from a straight flush. Everyone else folded. Sutherland bid a dime, a light bid, but designed to keep Milo from folding. Milo upped it to a quarter.

"A quarter? You're bluffing, Milo," Sutherland scoffed as he matched it.

Gramm shook his head. "All you millionaires throw quarters around like they were, um…"

"Quarters?" Creedence added.

"I went to school with Gibbs," Feinberg began his narrative. The sixth card up didn't help either Sutherland or Milo. "Woodland Prep, turning boys into fine men." Feinberg aped the school's moto.

Sutherland bet a quarter; Milo matched it. Gramm leaned back and crossed his arms, watching the chips hit the table.

"Was Gabriel Gibbs turned into a fine man?" Gramm asked.

"No, but it's a catchy motto. Gibbs was a snotty little kid who morphed into a full-blown snotty teen— aggressive, super competitive, and insufferable. Lucky me, Gibbs is now my neighbor. He lives next door."

"What? We were told he has an apartment at his office," Gramm said.

Feinberg dealt the final card down. Sutherland bid a quarter. Milo matched the quarter and raised another twenty-five cents. Sutherland called and turned over his cards. "Four deuces. Beat that."

Milo laid out the nine and eight of spades, added the seven and six of spades and slowly turned over the matching five of spades. "Sure, no problem," he said, smiling. "Straight flush. I do believe that beats your pathetic four-of-a-kind."

"Nooo. This is your fault," Sutherland blurted, pointing an accusatory finger at Feinberg.

"Stop! You lost," Gramm insisted. "I'm just about to get some useful information. So, Saul, why does he have a house?"

"I don't know. We're neighbors but not that close, personally, or geographically. We have a woods between us which suits me fine."

The deal went to Creedence who called five-card draw. "We're going conservative tonight," Sutherland said, noticing the lack of wild cards.

"About time!" mumbled Gramm who hated wild cards.

Feinberg won the hand with two pair, and he won the next hand of lowball, double draw, roll 'em—not a Gramm favorite.

After five more hands, with Milo and Feinberg winning two each, the group paused to construct pastrami sandwiches. "I also have the usual parting gifts—packages of sliced pastrami for all of you to take home," Feinberg said.

"Ooh goodie, party favors," Milo mocked.

The game resumed, going past midnight before the group called it quits. Gramm had managed to only win one hand as did Sutherland. Milo and Feinberg were the big winners.

Milo stalled, letting Gramm and Creedence leave before asking Feinberg more about Gibbs. "You don't seem to like this Gibbs character much—kinda unlike you."

"Not then. Not now."

"Why?"

"Gibbs was always about having to win—grades, sports, even girls…with an ugly twist. He took away other guy's girlfriends—a power thing. It led to a couple of fist fights as I remember."

"Did he date your girlfriend?" Sutherland asked.

"He tried. I was one of the fistfights. He would come to the dance with a girl, then dump her, and make moves on someone else's date. He was an ass."

"So, who was your girlfriend?"

"Claudia Beckman. You probably never heard of her."

"Beckman? As in Judge Beckman?" Milo asked.

"Yeah, his daughter. He still doesn't like me."

Milo thanked Feinberg for the pastrami as did Sutherland. On the way down to Lakesong, Milo said, "Now that was interesting."

"That Feinberg dated a judge's daughter?" Sutherland guessed.

Milo shook his head. "Gibbs has a house?"

§

"Great news: I almost won money tonight," Sutherland said to Agnes as he arrived back in his Lakesong rooms.

"Oh no, did you lose the mansion money, the foundation money, real estate money, or Mom's money?" Agnes joked.

Throwing his keys on the coffee table, he sighed. "All of it. We may need that $375.86 in your checking account."

"That was forty-six cents, Sutherland—$375.46."

Sutherland plopped down on the couch beside her. "Oh no, we're ruined."

"Speaking of ruined," Agnes took his hand, "Mrs. Pearson's back taxes will cost twenty-five thousand dollars." She waved the tax bill. "They're due on Wednesday. The GoFundMe page will not be up in time." She searched Sutherland's face looking for understanding. "I want to use some of your money, and then replace it with money from the GoFundMe."

"My money? Agnes it's our money! That's what the meeting with Creedence on Friday was all about."

"Has anybody ever told you, you're a very nice person?"

"Not recently."

"Well, I think you are, offering me your mother's money to help my friend."

"Ahh, Agnes, it's been my money since before I was a teen."

"Forgive me. I only found out about it this afternoon. Which reminds me, I have a question."

"Sure."

"Where did your mother get all that money?"

"From her father. My grandfather was in shipping. He amassed a fortune. My mother inherited. She invested and amassed even more."

"Did she have sisters or brothers?" Agnes asked.

"Actually, she has, or had a sister, Lana, who was a rebel, I guess, and was disowned and disinherited. Big scandal back in the day. My dad said Mom tried to give Lana what would have been her rightful share, but Aunt Lana always refused. At least that's the story I got."

Agnes was intrigued. "What happened to your aunt?"

Sutherland thought for a second, stunned by the realization that he didn't know.

"Have you ever met her?"

"No."

"Would you like to?"

"I don't know. I never thought about it."

"Do you know where she lives?"

"No. I don't even know if she's still living."

Agnes leaned against him. "Well, as luck would have it, I know of a person who can find out for you. He's a private investigator. He's a little quirky but quite good. I work for him."

Sutherland laughed. "Is that right? Why have you never mentioned that before?"

17

Noticing the overnight coffee had turned from toasty brown to dark sludge, Officer Kate Preston poured it down the drain and made a new pot. She was at the cop shop before the others, anxious to share the intriguing facts she had uncovered.

A yawning Lt. Gramm slogged in, poured himself a cup of the fresh brew, nodded to Preston, hung up his winter paraphernalia, and sat down at his desk. He was followed seconds later by White who brought her own coffee. She was about to say 'good morning' to Preston, but never got the chance.

"Leah Davis has a motive," Preston blurted, jumping up and following White to her desk.

"Wow, just like that, first thing Monday morning. Good morning to you too. Let's go bother Gramm." White threw her coat, scarf, and gloves on the back of her chair.

Gramm looked up; his bushy eyebrows knitted together. "Looks like we're getting started."

Preston and White sat down. "Kate has solved the case," White joked.

"Good," Gramm said, leaning his head back on his chair and closing his eyes. "Make all the appropriate arrests, do the paperwork, wake me in time for lunch."

Preston had long since learned to ignore the office banter. "Leah Davis has motive, but before I get to Leah, let me go over the nonsurprises."

"Nonsurprises bore me on Monday mornings," Gramm grumbled.

"Go ahead, Kate, bore us," White countered.

"Nora Swenson doesn't appear to be getting any money from our victim even though she said he owed her. I do admire how she makes her money stretch. Ivan Babin doesn't have anything in his bank accounts that looks suspicious. The same goes for Xavier Cullen, Ethan Marsden, and Mia Dawson. However, compared to her husband she's swimming in money."

"From what?" Gramm asked. "What does she do?"

"She's a consultant for alternative energy companies. She refers to herself as a senior technician."

Gramm sat up. "Really? Can we assume she has electrical expertise?"

"You're looking for means, I'm more interested in motive," White said. "Did Charlie and Mia have separate bank accounts?"

Preston nodded.

"You need warrants to look at bank accounts. I don't remember asking for any," Gramm said.

"Swenson, Babin, McKnight, Marsden, and Cullen gave us access. Obviously, I have access to our victim's accounts. I've used third party sources for Davis, Gibbs, and Mia Dawson to approximate their wealth. If we need to look at their actual bank transactions, I'll ask for a warrant."

"What have you found out about Gibbs?" Gramm asked, finally opening his eyes.

"He's rich, but no financial connection to the victim."

"Sutherland McKnight makes a good living, and he has two joint checking accounts, one with Agnes Larson, the other with a…" Preston pretended to look at her notes, "a Milo Rathkey."

"You checked on McKnight?" White was mildly shocked.

Preston shrugged. "He's part of the group."

Gramm took a long sip of his coffee and began to change out of his boots. "I suspect if McKnight were going to murder anybody, it would be Milo. We should grill Milo about the joint checking account just to be annoying. So, let's circle back to the interesting. Why do you think Leah Davis has a motive?"

Preston checked her notes, wanting to get this right. "Forensics went through our victim's second phone and found deleted messages between Charlie Dawson and Leah Davis. It appears that the victim was asking for money from Davis. He mentioned an investment but wasn't specific."

"Two questions," Gramm said. "Why would he think Leah Davis would give him money, and what's the investment?"

"To answer the first question—about Leah Davis, let me read you this," Preston said. *"Because you and Gabe were*

*soooo close, I thought you would join me in my little investment.
I think it's going to pay great dividends. Charlie."*

"He spelled *so* with four oes?" White laughed.

"He did. I sense an affair, and a threat to tell Leah's
husband," Preston said.

Gramm allowed as to how that was interesting, but asked
if there was proof she took the bait.

Preston held up her hand. "Yes. Look at her phone records.
She transferred $20,000 to an unknown bank account. It left her
account through one of those cash transfer apps and went into an
unknown account. I checked; it belonged to Charlie Dawson."

"Good work. We need to talk to Davis about Dawson's
inuendo and money demand," White said.

"Are we thinking Charlie's *little investment* is in Gibbs'
bike?" Gramm asked.

Milo joined them and Preston filled him in. Milo's only
response was a dejected, "I got an 'atta boy' email from the
Deputy Chief."

"What does that have to do with Charlie Dawson's murder?" White asked.

"Absolutely nothing, but the fact he knows my name
makes me uncomfortable."

"Do you think I hired you without telling him your
name?" Gramm asked.

§

Agnes left Lakesong early to pay Mrs. Pearson's tax bill.
Not knowing how long Agnes' tasks would take, Sutherland
bolted after his weekly Monday morning meeting to deal

with Marsden's bike inspection. To his relief, Marsden was a couple minutes late.

"Death machine inspector," Marsden joked, standing in the doorway after Sutherland opened the gates to let him in.

Sutherland smiled, but thought the joke was in poor taste. He let Marsden in and guided him up the stairs.

Sitting down on his weight bench, Sutherland watched Marsden remove the cover of the electronics box on Gibbs' bike, look at the wiring, and pronounce it safe. "Your bike hasn't been tampered with. It's the way it came from the warehouse."

"Of course. I thought everything would be okay," Sutherland offered.

Marsden closed the cover. "So did I, but better to be safe. You're good to go."

"How about Leah's and Nora's bikes?"

"Your bike is the first. I'm off to Nora Swenson's next. I'll do Leah Davis' tonight when she gets home from work."

"Don't forget to check your own bike," Sutherland said, walking Marsden down the stairs. Marsden turned and looked at the expansive marble and wood double staircase. "Nice house you have here," he said.

"Thanks, it's been in the family for decades."

Marsden's smile faded for a moment. "Must be nice."

As soon as he ushered Marsden out the door, Sutherland hustled to the garage. He had a busy day ahead.

§

Agnes once again found herself sitting across from Credence Durant in his Superior Street office. This time she was alone. She slipped her winter coat from her shoulders, adjusted her posture as she had done with Mrs. Pearson, and got straight to the point. "I need $25,000 today to pay the taxes on my friend's house. I have researched the problem. It is real, not a scam. I have the tax bill here," she said, and placed it on Durant's desk. "Sutherland and I have discussed it, and he approves."

Creedence pushed his glasses up on his nose and looked over the bill.

After a few minutes, Agnes asked, "How should I access the funds? Will I need a cashier's check?"

Creedence opened the decorative, wooden box that had been sitting on his desk. He removed two credit cards and handed them to Agnes. "These arrived Saturday. A personalized checkbook has also been ordered. I used the name Agnes Larson, but that can be changed if you wish."

"This is fast."

"Um…well…Sutherland might have called me from Hawaii to get the ball rolling. He's very efficient with these things."

Agnes gave him "the look." "Did he call *before* we were married or *after*? I thought our getting married was spontaneous."

Creedence waved his hands in the air. "Oh no, afterwards, definitely afterwards, the next day actually. He said you had gotten married on the yacht. The captain performed the ceremony. There was a sunset. It was all legal."

Agnes laughed. "I didn't know a sunset was required to make it legal."

Creedence laughed. "Always, in Hawaii."

Agnes looked at the credit cards. They looked normal. They had her name on them. "What, no black credit cards?" she joked.

"Sutherland never wanted one for himself, but if you…"

"I'm joking, Mr. Durant. These cards are fine."

"You can pay the tax bill by credit card, that way I pay the bill when it's due. That's part of my job."

Agnes examined the credit cards, turning them over, looking at the backs. "How do I activate them?"

"They are activated."

"Can I really charge $25,000 on this card? What's its limit?"

Creedence pushed up his glasses again and blinked. "Both are unlimited, but before you go shopping for your own yacht, I would appreciate a heads-up."

Agnes dropped the cards on the table. "I'm not comfortable carrying around unlimited cards!"

Creedence shrugged. "They're no different than cards with a credit limit. They all have theft protection insurance. By the way, do you have current credit cards I should know about."

Agnes laughed. "I have one. It has a $5000 limit. I never come close to it, and pay it off every month."

"If you wish, I can have the bill come to me, and I will pay it, along with the others."

"I don't think so. I'm just not there yet."

Creedence push his glass up again. "No problem. If I can do anything else, just ask."

Agnes sat back and took a deep breath. "My plan is to go to the tax office right now. Can you assure me there won't be a problem with these cards?"

"Absolutely."

Agnes took a moment to decide where to put the new credit cards in her purse. She chose an unused zippered compartment to keep them separate from her old card. "I'm off to put the McKnight money to good use," she said to Creedence, standing to bundle up for the freezing weather.

"And the county is grateful," Creedence joked, handing back Mrs. Pearson's tax bill.

If the county was grateful, Agnes' welcome at the tax assessor's office didn't show it. She waited twenty-five minutes for two other customers to air their grievances before stepping up to the counter. Handing the clerk Mrs. Pearson's tax bill, she said, "I'm here to pay these back taxes." Her voice not reflecting her nervous rapid heartbeat.

The clerk looked at the bill, went to her computer, clicked in far too many keystrokes for Agnes' liking, and then pronounced, "Back taxes plus interest comes to $25,436.92. I'm afraid for an amount this large we will need a certified check."

"I prefer to use my credit card," Agnes said, handing the clerk one of the new cards.

"You may not have understood the amount. It's $25,436.92."

Agnes took note of the woman's name tag. "Ms. Bronwin, I do understand. Run the card, please." Agnes' nervousness was being replaced by anger.

Ms. Bronwin called her supervisor. This woman looked friendlier. "What's the problem?"

"This woman wants to pay an overdue tax bill with her credit card," Bronwin said, huffily, as if it were a crime.

"Is there a problem with the card?" The supervisor asked.

"It's a $25,000 overdue bill!"

Agnes took a deep breath to calm herself. "I've asked Ms. Bronwin to run the card."

The supervisor looked at the clerk. "You haven't run the card?"

"No! It's $25,436.92!"

The supervisor took the card, ran it through the reader, typed in the amount, and within seconds it chirped, *approved.*

Staring at the clerk, Agnes demanded, "I will want a receipt."

Ms. Bronwin pushed a button on the card reader and waited for it to print. With a cool stare, she handed it to Agnes who gave the clerk the best resting bitch face she could muster. She admitted to herself, it needed work.

Leaving the county building, walking down the steps in the cold Duluth sunshine, Agnes thought the process went from frightening to aggravating, but the result was wonderful. Her sister Barbara would have been proud of her. She called Mrs. Pearson to report the good news and was surprised to get an invitation to join her board.

"Me?"

"The board is in disarray. We trusted our treasurer. He failed us. We need some new blood."

"I think I'm old blood."

Mrs. Pearson laughed. "Whatever you want to call it, I think we need you."

§

With the new information uncovered by Preston, Leah Davis warranted a second interview—this one came with an invitation to the police department. She was not happy. "I told you what little I know about Charlie Dawson. I'm busy. Why am I here?"

Gramm and White sat opposite her in the interview room. Milo and Preston watched from behind the one-way glass. "You failed to mention your investment," Gramm said.

"Investment? What investment?"

"With Charlie Dawson. You and he were investing in Gibbs' bike."

Leah smiled. "We were? I don't recall that."

"Let me read this to you from Charlie Dawson's cell phone," White said. *"Because you and Gabe were soooo close, I knew you would join me in my little investment. I think it's going to pay great dividends. Charlie."*

Leah was shaken. "That's private correspondence. I'm a lawyer…"

Gramm held up his hand. "Stop! Dawson has been murdered. We got this from his phone. It's all perfectly legal, as you probably already know. Let me ask you this, were you having an affair with Gabriel Gibbs?"

"I don't think that's any of your business."

"When we ask a question like that, people who are not having an affair just say no," White explained. "We now assume you and Gibbs are having an affair."

"Past tense—were. He's pretty to look at but not pretty to deal with. I can do better." Leah tightened up her signature French twist.

"You ended the relationship?"

"I discovered that I had competition. He wasn't worth it."

"Is the competition anyone we know?"

"I didn't know, and frankly, I didn't care. All I knew was that he was far less available for me."

"Maybe he was working?" Gramm suggested.

"You don't know Gabriel Gibbs. There was always a one o'clock. I was usually Tuesday and Thursday. Then I wasn't."

"Was Charlie Dawson blackmailing you over your affair with Gibbs?"

Leah laughed. "Hardly. My husband travels extensively. We have an understanding. If Charlie told my husband about Gibbs, at most, he'd be disappointed in my choice. I know I was."

"Dawson asked you to help him invest in Gibbs' bike. Why did you go along if it wasn't extortion?"

Leah folded her arms. "Well, you're wrong there too. The investment wasn't in Gibbs' bike, it was in a competitor's bike. I looked it over, and I thought the investment was sound." Leah inched up in her chair. "Now that I've straightened you out about my affairs, sexual and financial, can I return to work?"

Gramm thanked her for coming. She told them in the future to contact her lawyer. When she left, Gramm shook his head. "He always has a one o'clock? Who has time for that?"

"Gabriel Gibbs, apparently," White said as she and Gramm joined Milo in Gramm's office.

"What time is it?" Gramm asked.

"Not one o'clock, only twelve-thirty," White said, "and I'm hungry."

Gramm laughed. "I'm with you. I think we should interview Gibbs after a visit to Gustafson's."

"I'm not hungry," Milo said. "Big breakfast."

Gramm shrugged.

"See you this afternoon," Milo turned around and left the office.

"He's passing on his beloved meatloaf sandwich?" White marveled.

"Yeah, kinda suspicious."

"What does he know that we don't?"

"Hopefully, it's mind lint that will clear up this murder."

§

Knowing Gibbs was at his "one o'clock," Milo sat in the reception area of Gibbs Industries after asking to see either Gibbs or Marsden. Ethan Marsden came out to see him. "I'm afraid Gabe is tied up in meetings. Maybe I can help. Come back to my office."

Milo followed him through the labyrinth of hallways to a spare, concrete-block room in the back of the building. Marsden's office was small, containing a gun metal desk and one file cabinet. He sat down in his wheeled desk chair. The rest of the space was taken up by a Gibbs bike with its plethora of monitors.

"Kinda tight," Milo judged, sitting down in the only other available chair, a yellow molded plastic model that Milo thought belonged in a cafeteria.

"That's why I spend a lot of time at the warehouse," Marsden smiled.

"I want to ask about investors in this bike." Milo pointed in the direction of the bike, hidden in the mass of equipment and wires.

"Gibbs owns all of this. He doesn't take on investors."

"Charlie Dawson wanted to invest. We think he had twenty thousand dollars set aside," Milo said.

Marsden laughed and sat back in his chair. "Dawson was a Whack-A-Mole doll, popping up, bugging Gabe. Gabb whacked him down every time. It was amusing, yet sad to watch."

"Why would Dawson keep demanding to invest?"

Marsden picked up a pencil and absently tapped the desk. "Charlie only heard what Charlie wanted to hear. He was a pest, not only about investing, but also handling the company's advertising." Marsden stood up, maneuvered his way to the bike, and patted the seat. "When this bike is ready, the ad campaign will be international. Gabe may have eventually thrown him a side job or two, but there is no way Dawson could have handled our account."

"Would it shock you to learn that Dawson was planning to invest in a competitor's bike?"

Marsden smiled. "A competitor? Really? If Gibbs knew, he would have exploded. Something like that would set Gabe off."

Milo sat up. "I understand Gibbs disappears almost every day at one o'clock. How long has he been doing that?"

Marsden retraced his steps back to his desk and sat down. "As long as I've been here. He likes his siesta time," Marsden smiled. "Don't get me wrong, he works hard—comes back in the afternoon and works into the night, but he does like those one o'clocks."

"We're kinda dancing around it," Milo said. "Gibbs leaves, goes to his house on skyline drive, and meets…Leah Davis, or whoever took her place."

"I'm not privy to that information. He is his father's son."

"Tell me about his father."

"I've been told his old man had a large sexual appetite, mostly for married women." Marsden started tapping his pencil again. "Then one day he decided to settle down with one of them. Unfortunately for me, his choice was my mother. She left us and moved in with him."

Milo didn't react. "So, you and Gibbs are step…"

"Brothers, yup." Marsden put the pencil down.

"Are you close?"

"I've tried." Marsden put his arms on the desk and leaned forward. "I work here because my mother insisted old man Gibbs, Gabe's father, guarantee me a job. I know Gibbs keeps telling people I'm crazy, but I'm nowhere close to as crazy as Gibbs. That man's psychotic."

Milo stared at Marsden, wondering how he could say such a thing so calmly. "Why do you say that?"

"He ticks all the psychopathy boxes: he seems normal, almost friendly most of the time, but hit the right button and he goes off—he lacks remorse and empathy. He can seem charming, but trust me, he's not. Please, ask other people. I may be biased because he hates me."

"Why work for him?"

"When I was a teen, I 'acted out,' as they say. That's yesterday's news. I'm a changed man, but my employment history is terrible. I'm here until I can get my resume clean, then Gibbs and I are history."

"Why wouldn't he just fire you?"

"He can't," Marsden said, leaning back. "There's a codicil in the old man's will prohibiting him from doing that—my mother's doing."

"Do you think Gabriel Gibbs is capable of murder?"

Marsden began tapping his pencil again. "I don't like to condemn the man, but yes. When I say he's psychotic, I mean it. Nobody sees it. He's too charming most of the time. I try to stay out of his way. I can't get out of here fast enough."

18

Milo was missing his beloved Gustafson's meatloaf sandwich, but the identity of Gibbs' one o'clock guest was too intriguing. He sat down on the steps of Feinberg's front porch with his drone, his smartphone, and the instructions written out by Jamal, Martha's middle sibling, who had perfected the drone-smartphone connection last summer. Today was the first time Milo needed to use the device. He didn't plan to tell anyone that a freshman in high school was directing this evidence gathering.

Step One: turn on the drone, blue button that says on.

Milo thought Jamal's instructions were overly simple, but effective.

Step Two: press the icon on the phone's drone app. It looks like a camera eye.

You should see a button in the app that says Connect. Press it.

"I can do this," Milo said. He pressed the connect button. Stuff began to happen—something about a Bluetooth connection. Milo, beginning to panic, returned to Jamal's instructions.

Don't panic! Wait until the app finds the Bluetooth connection.

"Bluetooth?" Milo said to no one. "What the hell does that mean?"

Yes, Mr. Rathkey, it's called Bluetooth. I don't know why.

"Okay, this is freaky."

Step Three: pick up the drone controller, the thing with the small joy sticks. Look in the center for a place to put your phone. Do it.

Milo placed his phone in horizontally.

Step Four: use the joysticks on the controller to send the drone up, down, and over, just like we practiced last summer.

Milo noticed a note at the bottom of the instructions that said: *Edited for Milo by Martha.* "Well, that explains Jamal being in my head. Martha knows me."

He was about to lift the drone when his phone rang with the beginning verse of Chuck Brodsky's "Talk To My Lawyer." Milo touched the green button and put his phone on speaker. "Hello Saul."

"Why are you sitting on my porch with a drone?"

"How do you know?"

"My doorbell told me."

"I'm back to my old life, checking on wayward spouses."

"I'm not married and I'm not home."

"I know that. I'm checking on your neighbor."

"If you're talking about Gibbs, he's not married either."

"But his partners may be. I want to get an ID on them."

"You better not crash that thing. I don't want the neighbors finding a crumpled drone, thinking I'm spying on them."

"I've been practicing, and you're wasting my time. We'll talk about your Peeping Tom reputation later."

"While you're waiting for Mrs. Whomever, be useful and check my roof for ice dams."

Milo hung up, went back to the app, and launched the drone. He watched the video on his phone and remembered to push the record button. That was not in Jamal's directions. It took about fifteen minutes. The batteries, which Milo had not been warned to replace, were about depleted when he saw what he needed.

§

"Xavier Cullen, do you have anything more to say before I pass sentence?" Judge Beckman asked, wiping his nose with a tissue.

Cullen, standing with Saul Feinberg before the judge, asked, "Do I get my drawings back?"

The judge shrugged. "Not the business of this court. Talk to your attorney. I'm sure counselor Feinberg can help you in that regard. Now, if it were up to me, I would put you in prison, young man. Breaking and entering, and assault are serious crimes."

Cullen was about to speak, but Feinberg nudged him to be quiet.

"However," Judge Beckman continued, oblivious to Cullen, "the district attorney has reached a plea bargain with you in return for your guilty plea and I will honor that agreement. Xavier Cullen, I sentence you to two hundred hours of court approved community service and a one thousand dollar fine. In addition, you must make restitution, in an amount to be determined, to Mrs. Dawson for the damage you did to her house." The gavel came down. "Next case!" Beckman coughed.

Feinberg walked Cullen out of the courtroom into the large, marble hallway. Taking out his phone, Feinberg said automatically, "Get that community service out of the way as soon as possible. Judge Beckman doesn't like your plea deal and would love to have you hauled back in for violating the terms of the deal."

"I still want my drawings," Cullen said. "I wonder if that other guy took them."

Feinberg refocused from his phone to his client's face. "What other guy?"

"The guy in the study. I told you about him. He's the one that delayed me. I waited for him to finish taking that silly bike apart before I went in. That's why I got caught."

"I don't remember you mentioning any other person in the room," Feinberg said.

"Well, he was there. He delayed me and when he left, he locked the door. That's why I had to break in."

"And it wasn't Charlie Dawson?"

"No. It was a tall, skinny dude."

Feinberg mentally kicked himself for missing this. "Come on, you have to tell this to the cops."

Cullen didn't move. "No, the judge said you have to help me find my drawings."

"That's what I'm doing. This guy may know where they are."

§

"It's time to resume the beta test," Gibbs announced to the assembled group of technicians as he arrived back from his one o'clock. "Also, Marsden, get the new bikes ready. I'm going to start the second testing group—see how the servers respond to two groups biking at the same time."

A myriad of objections told Gibbs his people were not on board. "Okay, let me hear it, one at a time."

One of the lead programmers went first. "You're rushing the process. The data and fixes from the first group have not been fully implemented—you're introducing too many variables."

"Don't care," Gibbs responded.

A second tech raised his hand.

"Are we in kindergarten? If you have something to say, say it, goddamn it!" Gibbs shouted.

"I...I...Well, there are three glitches from the first group. Rider two disappeared for five seconds on the first ride, the entire program froze at mile thirty-eight on the second ride, and Gibbs, your bike did not tilt into two turns. I think we should work on those before we resume the ride, and second group is out of the question."

"We've been shut down for five goddamn days!" Gibbs shouted. "I expected you to solve those glitches by now. If you can't make this work, you are all gone, and I will hire competent people."

If anyone else had an objection, they kept it to themselves, except for Marsden. "One of your friends died on the bike," he said, stepping forward. "Or did you forget that?"

Gibbs' face contorted into a nasty smile. "Marsden, did you check the remaining bikes like I told you?"

"I did…"

"And?"

"They were not tampered with."

Gibbs walked up to Marsden, stopping millimeters from his face. "Then shut up, you crazy, glorified, errand boy."

Marsden smiled but didn't move. "But not an immoral son of a bitch like you and your old man!"

Gibbs lashed out, his fist connecting with Marsden's right eye. Marsden fell back a step but managed a jab that caught Gibbs on the jaw. Gibbs growled in anger, tackling him around the waist, slamming him against the wall. The five technicians stood watching this train wreck, not wanting to get between the combatants.

Trying to get out of Gibbs' grasp, Marsden fell to the ground. Gibbs pounced, and they traded blows. Two security guards, alerted by one of the technicians, stormed into the room, grabbed the two, and pulled them apart.

Gibbs' mouth was bleeding. He didn't seem to notice. Breathing heavily, he shouted at Marsden, "You can rot in hell."

A dark purple welt was beginning to grow under Marsden's left eye, a cut was dripping blood under his right eye. "Admit you killed Charlie Dawson," Marsden yelled.

"Get him out of here!" Gibbs shouted.

One of the security guards walked Marsden out of the room "You should update your resume. He'll probably fire you."

Marsden laughed.

§

Agnes Larson, emboldened by her successful morning at the tax office, brought Lakesong's blueprints down from Sutherland's quarters, and spread them out on the massive dining room table.

She needed to search this whole house before embarking on her second phase of cataloging books and art. As Sutherland kept saying, it was hers now too. She had two sets of blueprints: the original ones Sutherland and Milo found last summer with no gallery, plus the newer blueprints that showed the gallery. She noticed neither set showed Sutherland's renovations to his second-floor space. What else was not recorded?

Almost immediately, her eye was drawn to a small wing on the north side of the building labeled *bedroom suite*. The long-lost elevator opened there on the second floor. Agnes realized that beyond the elevator were a cluster of two bedrooms, a sitting room, and a bathroom. She had never checked these rooms for art and books.

She grabbed a magnifying glass to examine the fine detail in the blueprints, and discovered this area also contained a stairway that led up to a third floor. *What's up there?* she wondered. Looking at the newer blueprints, she noticed that the gallery with its glass dome cut the third floor into two separate areas. *How do I get to the third floor on the south side?* she wondered. The third floor upstairs above the library, Sutherland's rooms, and the guest rooms didn't seem to have a staircase—something to ask Sutherland about. She had a legal pad with project notes. She added *third floor south access* to her list.

Agnes' eyes began to blur after several hours of pouring over the blueprints. "Time for coffee," she said to no one, and marched from her office to the kitchen.

Martha, who was checking a beef tenderloin marinading in the refrigerator, overheard Agnes grind coffee beans for the French press. As Agnes came over to heat the water in the microwave, Martha questioned, "Afternoon pick me up?"

"Vitally needed. I have just discovered Lakesong has rooms and a third floor I never knew about."

"I think Milo told me that he and his mother lived in a suite of rooms on the second floor," Martha said. "He told me they were like a separate apartment. I haven't heard about a third floor, but I guess there is one now that you mention it. I see it from the cottage on both sides of the glass dome."

Agnes added the hot water to the French press, and began stirring the grounds, taking note of the time—four minutes to steep. "It looks to me like the third floor ran the length of the house, but the gallery dome cut it into two sections. Here's the puzzle: there are steps on the north side, but I don't see how to get up to the part that's above Sutherland's room on the south side."

Martha smiled. "Sutherland's rooms? Don't you live there too?"

Agnes eyes rolled. "Yes, Martha, but, until we renovate, they really are his rooms with my shower gel added."

"Why do you care about the third floor?" Martha continued, handing Agnes the half-and-half.

"I didn't complete my cataloguing job," said Agnes. "I catalogued the artwork and books only in the places that were public. I didn't know about the vault in the basement, the suite on the second floor, the whole third floor, and who knows what else."

"More secret rooms?" Martha asked, referring to the staircase between the two libraries that Agnes found last fall.

"That would be fun, but right now, I'm hoping there is some way to get to that cutoff portion of the third floor. If not, when we expand, we will have to add a staircase. That's my problem for the day. How is your day going?"

"Quite well. Ron's in town to write again."

"I know. He's renting my house. Are things heating up between you two?"

"Heating up? Really? No. We're friends only. He's in the middle of a writing frenzy and I have two sibs to raise."

"Two? What happened to Breanna?"

Martha laughed. "She's still my sister. She's just in Chile."

"Chile? What are you talking about? When did that happen?"

"Next week actually. She's not there yet. It's part of her Lind Scholarship. She gets telescope time in the Atacama Desert. A group of university students have been invited to spend two weeks there working on…" Martha paused.

"Working on what?"

"She explained it to me, but I have no idea. The only thing I remember is 'standard candle supernovas'—whatever they are."

"Oh, standard candle supernovas. I have two lavender scented ones on the big tub in the guest bathroom I use." Agnes laughed. "Well, the candle part anyway."

"You bathe in a guest room?"

"Yeah. Sutherland doesn't have a tub. I trudge down the hall like I live in a dorm. So much for mansion life."

"That's a long way to go just to take a bath."

"A bathtub is number one on my remodel list. Speaking of a long way to go, isn't Chile a long way for Breanna to go? She's kind of young."

"Almost nineteen years old." Martha returned the tenderloin to the refrigerator and turned to face Agnes. "Am I worried? Yes. But remember, she's my sister, not my daughter. She's an adult and doesn't have to ask my permission. I was on my own at eighteen."

"Me too."

§

Feinberg and Cullen arrived unannounced at the police station. Feinberg exchanged pleasantries with the desk sergeant while he and Cullen waited for Gramm to escort them back to his office. When Gramm arrived, Feinberg said, "My client has an interesting piece of information for you."

Gramm nodded. "Let's go back."

The duo followed Gramm back to his office. White saw the procession and joined them. Gramm sat back in his chair and motioned for Feinberg and Cullen to sit. White listened from the doorway.

Gramm stretched his back and folded his arms, "So, talk."

"There was another guy in Charlie Dawson's study," Cullen said.

"Are you talking about the day you broke in?"

"Yeah, I had to wait for him to leave before I could go in. That's why I got caught."

"What was he doing?"

"Something with that bike. He had the black box open…"

"And you didn't think to mention that?" Gramm yelled.

"Stop, Ernie. I gotta take the blame on this one," Feinberg said. "Xavier says he told me about another person in the room. I completely missed it,"

Gramm took a deep breath. "Okay, let's move on. So, you saw the guy open the electronics box and then what?"

"I was in the bushes, waiting for him to come out. I peaked in a couple of times. After about a half hour he came outside, locked the door, and took off down the alley."

"He locked the door!" White repeated.

Cullen turned. "Yeah, that's why I had to break the window to get in."

"He had a key?" Gramm questioned, trying to get it straight in his mind.

"Well, yeah," Cullen said, turning back to Gramm.

"Who the hell was he?" Gramm blustered.

Xavier looked at Feinberg.

"Tell him!"

"I don't know. He was wearing a baseball cap."

"What team?" White asked.

"I don't watch sports. It was red."

Milo who had returned joined White in the doorway. "I suppose you're wondering why I called you all here," he joked.

Feinberg stood up as did Cullen. "We were just leaving."

"Thank you, Mr. Cullen." Gramm said.

As the attorney and his client left, Milo sat down, looking at Gramm. "So?"

Gramm filled him in on Xavier Cullen's revelation. "Why didn't we see the other guy on the security camera?" he asked White.

"Remember Burglary obtained the clip. All they cared about was the break-in. We need to get more of that video."

Gramm nodded and turned back to Milo. "So, where did you go?"

White sat down next to Milo.

"I talked to Marsden. He thinks Gibbs is capable of murder. Can you get me a meeting with the police psychologist?"

White stifled the urge to say it was about time.

"Okay, I'll bite," Gramm said. "Why?"

"Marsden mentioned something about Gibbs. I need to check it out."

"Something? What?"

"Too early." Milo asked if they knew Gibbs and Marsden were stepbrothers.

"No, I didn't." White looked at Gramm who shook his head.

"I have more," Milo said.

"You have been busy, what else?" Gramm asked.

"I have a drone."

"We know that."

"While you were eating lunch, I used it to spy on Gibbs' house up on Skyline Drive."

"And?"

Milo held out his phone. "Watch." He played the video. "A woman leaves Gibbs' house, gets into a green car, and drives away."

"Your drone is too high, I can't make out her face," Gramm said.

White laughed. "That's a green Tesla. I can tell by the shape. There was a green Tesla in the Dawson garage."

"Mr. Gibbs' current one o'clock, Mia Dawson." Milo said.

19

Before going to bed, Milo left a sticky note on the kitchen island for Martha saying he would miss breakfast. He added that she shouldn't grieve too long over his absence and to please feed Annie her bacon. Before dawn, Milo swam, showered, dressed, and headed out to Ilene's bakery. He was craving cream puffs, and only Ilene's would do.

"Milo! Early morning?" Ilene said as he entered the bakery. Milo noticed her winter hair was white with fire engine red tips for Valentine's Day. Ilene's hair color changed by the season.

"I need cream puffs," he said as he sat down at his favorite table by the counter. Most of the other tables were occupied, and Ilene was busy, so Milo went behind the counter, poured himself a cup of coffee, and sat back down at his table.

After about five minutes, Ilene came over to him. Noticing the coffee she said, "Why didn't you get yourself a cream puff?"

"I didn't want to overstep my bounds."

"So considerate, but it's busy. Get yourself a cream puff."

Once again Milo wandered behind the counter, grabbed a plate and two cream puffs, passing Ilene who was returning the coffee pot to the warmer. "Do you want me to ring it up too?" Milo asked.

"Only if you leave me a big tip."

Milo returned to his table, took a bite of the cream puff, and closed his eyes, savoring it. His phone *da dunked*, the ringtone for Ernie Gramm. Upset that his cream puff moment had been interrupted, he answered. "I'm fueling my brain, Ernie," he said.

"Cream puffs?"

"Of course."

"At Ilene's?"

"Yup."

"Hold that thought. We'll be right there." The phone went dead. Milo returned to savoring his cream puff.

Fifteen minutes later, Gramm and White walked into Ilene's. White complimented Ilene on her matching hair color and ruby nose stud.

Milo asked for another cream puff. Ilene told him to get it himself. "I get no respect," Milo said rising to go behind the counter once again.

White laughed.

As Milo reached into the display for his cream puff, a patron at the counter asked if he could get a coffee refill. Milo grabbed the pot and filled not only the patron's coffee, but every cup along the counter. Ilene crossed the room, to join Milo behind the counter.

"I need an apron, Ilene."

"I'll take it under advisement. Now take your ass back to your table. You're wasting my coffee."

Milo smiled, pleased that nothing in their relationship had really changed even though he was no longer a struggling private detective, and Ilene was no longer his landlady.

"If you're done with your waiter's job, can we get down to business?" Gramm asked.

"The man asked for coffee," Milo said. "There is a universal law: if someone asks for coffee, you are obligated to deliver."

"Let's talk the Widow Dawson and Gibbs. I think we should interview them together to get their interaction. White thinks it's too soon."

"We're still gathering information. I don't think we want them sharing their answers," White argued.

"That Gibbs-Dawson thing didn't seem to surprise you, Milo. Why not?"

"Step-down transformers," Milo said, taking another bite of cream puff.

"Oh, of course," White laughed. "I thought the same thing."

"Care to explain, Milo?" Gramm asked.

"Both Mrs. Dawson and Mr. Gibbs used the same term, step-down. No one else did. They just said 'transformers.'" Not enough to convict, but curious. I suspected one heard it from the other. In this case I think Mia is the one who uses that term in her work, and Gabe got it from her."

"An affair moves them up on the suspect list—get rid of the husband," White said.

"Like I said before, collect the insurance," added Gramm. "Babin's out. Gibbs is in."

Milo disagreed. "I think their affair takes a back seat to the mystery guy Cullen says was fooling around with the bike. We need to know who that guy is and what he was doing."

"And who hired him to rig the bike?" White questioned.

"I'm thinking it could have been either the widow, Gibbs, or both in cahoots." Gramm said.

"Cahoots?" White questioned.

"It's a town in Michigan," Milo joked.

"For that matter," Gramm added, "it could have been a Nora Swenson-Leah Davis duo who hired that guy."

"I doubt it. The mystery guy had a key." Milo said.

"It's got to be Mia, unless you're thinking Charlie Dawson paid the guy to electrocute himself," White argued.

Milo shook his head. "Maybe the mystery man wasn't rigging the bike. Maybe he was doing something else."

"This is making my head hurt," Gramm complained. "I want to see Mia Dawson's reaction to what we know."

The three finished their breakfast, and Milo paid the bill, something Gramm thought he could get used to. White had contacted Mia Dawson to inform her they had more questions and would be arriving at her house shortly.

Meeting the police at the door, Mia immediately informed them that she had already told them everything she knew. Gramm sighed. *Why do they always say that?* Gramm and

White sat down on Mia's living room couch. Mia picked a large, comfortable chair. Milo stood.

"So, what more do you think I can help you with?" Mia asked.

"Are you aware there was a man in your house the day your husband died? We were wondering if you know what he was doing here," Gramm said.

Mia looked dismissive. "That Xavier kid. We've been over that. You arrested him."

"Not Cullen. Somebody else," Gramm said.

"What do you mean somebody else? How many people were in my house?"

"We want to check your surveillance video."

"I already provided that."

"Only the burglary," White jumped in. "We want to see the entire afternoon."

Mia stood up. "My computer is in the kitchen."

Gramm, White, and Rathkey followed her. When they were all sitting around the kitchen table, Mia opened her computer and downloaded the video. "Here it is," she said, backing away from the computer. "Have at it."

In handing the computer over, Mia accidentally caused the video program to close, leaving White looking at her computer desktop. The background graphic was an ad for Mia's consulting business, "Alternative Sources of Energy for Businesses."

White looked up. "Your business looks interesting. What do you do?"

"Businesses have rooftops and parking lots—space for solar panels. It's a growing industry," Mia said. "The companies I work for sell solar panel systems. When a salesman makes a pitch, They bring me, the techy, to answer the widget questions."

"I don't understand," Gramm said.

"Okay, the salesman says we can save you X amount a year in electrical costs if you install solar panels, and then someone asks how. They pay me to answer the how, what to install, where to run the wires, and how it interfaces with the power they currently get from the electric company."

"Does your system need transformers?" Gramm asked.

"Yes, of course, we use step down transformers all the time. And I did not kill Charlie."

Milo looked at Mia and asked, "How long have you and Gabriel Gibbs been having an affair?"

Gramm got comfortable. *This works well. I can just sit back and see what happens.*

Mia laughed. "You people are like my late husband… accusing me of having affairs. You should be accusing me of having an affair with Ivan Babin. That's what Charlie did."

"Babin denied having an affair with you," Gramm said.

Mia pursed her lips. "Why would you even ask him that?"

"He referred to you as sweet Mia."

"He was just having fun."

"Too old for you?" Milo asked.

"Too gay!"

Gramm's bushy eyebrows knitted together. "If your husband thought you were having an affair with his boss, he obviously didn't know Babin was gay."

Mia shifted in her seat. "Charlie was oblivious to most everything."

"I found the guy with the red hat," White blurted, looking at the outside camera video. Gramm, Milo, and Mia Dawson crowded around the computer. A man wearing a Boston Red Sox baseball cap could been seen using a key to enter the study. The camera showed only the door, so there was no video of what the man was doing once he entered. There was video of Xavier Cullen arriving and looking in the window and then disappearing from the doorway. The unidentified man left and locked up, just as Cullen said he did.

"Do you recognize him?" White asked Mia.

"Not at all."

"According to Cullen, the man was doing something to the bike, the same bike that killed your husband," Gramm said. "Did you hire him?"

"No!"

"He had a key," Milo said.

"Wait, wait, you have it all wrong."

"Enlighten us," Gramm demanded.

"I didn't give anybody a key to the house. Charlie must have. I told you guys he was a louse. Charlie was working with one of Gibbs' competitors. That guy was probably hired by Charlie or that other company to get info on the bike. You know—industrial espionage."

"How do you know that?"

"Charlie was also a moron. He bragged about it to me. Gibbs wouldn't let him invest in the Gibbs bike, so he went out and found someone making a competing product."

"Did you tell Gibbs about this? After all, you two are still a couple."

"It might have slipped out."

"Get it right, Mrs. Dawson. This is getting serious," Gramm warned.

"Okay, sure, Charlie was trying to ruin Gibbs' work from day one. He started riding the bike off-program, skewing the data. Of course I told Gibbs about it."

"When did you tell Gibbs?" Gramm asked.

"Last Monday."

"And Charlie Dawson died on Tuesday," Gramm said.

White transferred the surveillance video to a thumb drive, and the three left, knowing Mia would probably call Gibbs. Mia Dawson did exactly that.

"What?" Gibbs answered in a gruff voice—not his usual smooth demeanor.

"We have a problem," Mia said.

§

Gramm and White drove to Gibbs industries. Milo had asked White for a still of the unidentified man, one that showed most of his face. He waited for about ten minutes and the picture showed up in an email. Milo saved it to his phone and emailed it to his friend and fellow private detective, Joe Ripkowski. He waited a few seconds and then called.

"Milo! Good to hear from you," Joe answered.

"I just sent you a picture of a guy. I want you to find out who he is."

"Give me a second," Joe said, looking at the email. "Well, I can't see all of his face, so it's gonna take some time."

"Let me know when you get it, Joe."

Ripkowski laughed. "I'm joking, Milo. I know the guy. He's a low life—thinks he's James Bond or something. His name is Hammer."

"Are you sure?"

"He's the only Red Sox fan I know in Duluth."

"How come I don't know him?" Milo asked.

"He's new. Sometimes he takes PI jobs that skirt the law."

Milo asked Joe for Hammer's address. "Good work Joe. Send me the bill."

"Will do, Milo."

Milo hung up and mused over the fact that Joe used to argue about charging Milo, but that sensibility seems to have gone away. Milo fired up the Honda and proceeded to Gibbs Industries, arriving fifteen minutes after Gramm and White.

Milo found them waiting in the reception area. "Gibbs is in a meeting," Gramm said.

"It's too early for his one o'clock," Milo said.

"I think this might be a real meeting," Gramm said.

"Mr. Gibbs has asked that you join him in the conference room," the receptionist said.

"We know the way," Gramm grumbled.

"It's almost as if he knew we were coming," Milo joked as he, Gramm, and White walked down the corridor to the pinball ladened conference room.

Gibbs was waiting for them. "Before we begin," he said, "let me say once again, I did not kill Charlie Dawson."

"Did you pay someone else to kill him?" Gramm asked as he sat down.

Gibbs laughed. "You say that like it's an easy thing to do. How would I go about doing that? Do I put an ad on Craigs

List, or just make a Facebook request? 'To all my Facebook friends who may be killers for hire, I need…'"

"Stop!" Gramm cut him off. "Why didn't you tell us you were having an affair with Charlie Dawson's wife? Your good friend."

"Friend? I hardly knew him."

"He was riding your bike," White said.

"He was part of our riding group. I barely know Sutherland McKnight and Nora Swenson, but they're part of the group. I have five other people I barely know in the second group," Gibbs stated as if he was talking to children.

"Answer the question," Gramm insisted.

"Which is?"

"Why didn't you tell us about you and Mia Dawson?"

"It was, and is, none of your business. It has nothing to do with Charlie."

"What?" White asked. "You're having an affair with his wife, but it has nothing to do with him? Try that again."

"Look, I didn't kill him. I borrowed his wife. I could have borrowed his lawnmower. I wouldn't kill him over either one," Gibbs insisted.

White did a quick shake of head as if clearing some unwanted bits from her ears. "Are you really equating a lawnmower with a wife?"

"For the purpose of explaining how stupid your argument is, yes."

"Did Charlie know you were borrowing his…lawnmower?" Milo asked.

"I have no idea. He never mentioned it. I didn't care."

"Let's say Charlie didn't mind you borrowing his wife," Milo said. "Did you mind Charlie selling out your bike?"

Gibbs set his jaw, his hands balled into fists, then he walked to the other side of the room and turned with a smile. "The physical bike is not the important part of the system. It's the software and the speed at which the servers talk to each other. None of that is in the damn bike. Was I pissed? Yeah, I was going to take immense pleasure in calling him out as a traitor, and kicking him out of the group, but he died first."

"Convenient," Gramm said.

Gibbs smiled, "It was just that, convenient."

"Do you know a guy named Hammer?" Milo asked. White and Gramm stared at him.

"Doesn't ring any bells," Gibbs said. "Who is he?"

"He's this guy," Milo held up his phone showing a picture of the guy who broke into Dawson's home.

Gibbs looked at it. "I don't know him. Who is he?"

"Not important," Milo said.

Gibbs stood up. "I have work to do, so, if that's all, I have to go." Hearing no objections, Gibbs strode out of the room.

"I still think he did it," White said.

"Maybe he and Mia Dawson," Gramm added. He turned to Milo. "Hammer? Our mystery man's name is Hammer? When were you going to tell us?"

"Does he have a first name?" White asked.

"Mister. I have an address."

Gramm stood and flexed his back. "Let's go and ask *Mr.* Hammer what he was doing to Charlie Dawson's bike."

§

Henry Hammer lived in a small apartment above a laundromat in the central hillside. "I admire his choice of apartments," Milo said as they stood outside Hammer's door. "Convenient for washing clothes. I used to have to haul mine six blocks when I lived above Ilene's."

Gramm gave him a sideway glance. "If you're done reminiscing, we can get on with this."

"Yeah."

Gramm knocked on the door. There was no answer.

"Shouldn't one of us yell 'police, open up?'" Milo asked. "That's what they do on TV shows."

"You're in a mood, aren't you?" Gramm said, knocking again.

"I want to be authentic."

Gramm shrugged. "Police, open up!" he yelled, knocking on the door harder—still no answer. "Well, thank you, Milo, I feel so authentic."

20

Agnes knew how to be a resident at Wellwood—Mrs. Pearson's foster home—not a board member. But if this was the next problem, she was ready to tackle it for Mrs. Pearson. She rang the bell at the side door and waited. The girls should be in school. To her surprise, the same girl in braids answered the door. "Oh, I thought you would be in class." Agnes told the girl. "I'm here for the board meeting."

The girl smiled, "Teacher workday. The board meeting is being held in the dining room." The girl stepped aside and let Agnes enter. Agnes walked straight ahead and entered the dining room. Mrs. Pearson had always worn a blue dress for important occasions. Some things don't change. Today's dress was royal blue with a gold butterfly pin.

"Agnes, welcome to our little board," Mrs. Pearson said, pointing to an empty chair on her left. Agnes was feeling a wave of nostalgia, seeing in her mind the girls that occupied these chairs in her time. She wanted to sit down in her familiar chair, the one she had claimed during most of the six years of dinners in this room, but it currently hosted an older gentleman reading a newspaper. Agnes sat down in what was once April Lindstrom's chair. *April won't mind.*

Mrs. Pearson began with introductions. "Agnes, this is Mr. Hardgood Shaw, and Mrs. Sunny Upton. Hardgood, Sunny, may I present Agnes Larson, a former Wellwood resident, and our rescuing angel. Thanks to Agnes, the tax problem has been solved."

"What?" Mr. Shaw exclaimed, bothering to look up from his newspaper for the first time. "How did you do that, little lady?"

Little lady? Agnes felt her ire rise. "Mr. Shaw, I haven't been called little since I hit five-eleven in tenth grade."

Shaw glanced at Upton who shook her head. "'Little Lady' used to be an enduring term in my day," he complained.

"In your day, you had witch trials," Sunny Upton joked. Shaw laughed at himself. "Hardgood, just call her by her name, which is Agnes, and let's get down to business. Now that the tax problem is in the past, my group's problem needs to be addressed. Agnes, I belong to The Women's League. For years, with Emma Worthington's help we have provided dresses and suits for foster children who are going to the prom; maybe even for you, Agnes. However, Emma has died, and we aren't able to buy as many items as in previous years. I'm afraid some children will go without."

Agnes remembered the racks of used prom dresses, all of them dazzling to a girl who never had a fancy dress. "We must fix this!" she exclaimed.

"Well said," Shaw agreed, "but how? Our former treasurer absconded with our funds."

"I am new to all of this. How does this board work?" Agnes asked.

Mrs. Pearson answered. "I formed a nonprofit corporation a number of years ago to deal with our various sources of income. The board oversees the nonprofit. We get money from the state for each child in our care, and we get donations from generous people such as yourself. I thought the board was the best way to be transparent as they say these days. However, after Mr. Evans did what he did, I think perhaps we weren't paying enough attention."

"Has someone notified the police?" Agnes asked.

Shaw harumphed. "They have a warrant out for his arrest, for all the good that will do."

"Let's get back to the point," Sunny said. "The lack of dresses and suits not only affects the residents of Wellwood, but many other foster children in the area as well."

"Several other women who once lived here have started a GoFundMe page," Agnes said. "It was initially formed to pay the taxes, but I'm sure we can put that money toward dresses, at least for Wellwood residents."

"That's hopeful. We also have two fund raisers planned," Sunny added, "but we usually have it covered by this time."

"What's a go and fund me page?" Shaw asked.

"GoFundMe is an internet fund raiser. People contribute," Sunny explained.

"Aren't there charitable foundations that could provide us with money. Isn't that what they do?" Agnes asked.

Shaw harrumphed again. "It's not as easy as that, young… er…Agnes. We have applied to several charitable foundations in the past only to be turned down. Applying takes a lot of time, and we never make the cut."

"Hardgood isn't wrong," Sunny said. "We assess what we need for the year, and then I usually fill out the paperwork. We have yet to be accepted."

"Let me see if I can help," Agnes said. "I might have an in with the Laura and John McKnight Foundation."

"I knew John McKnight quite well," Shaw said. "His son Sutherland seems like a good fellow, but young, wet behind the ears. I think the foundation only meets once or twice a year to decide on their money distribution. Most of their money goes for the arts."

Sunny Upton leaned her head on her hand. "Oh, Hardgood."

"What?" Shaw asked.

"I think we should let Ms. Larson use her *in* with the McKnight Foundation," Sunny urged. "What's the harm?"

Shaw shrugged. "No offense, but she's a foster kid. How would she have an in with the McKnights?"

"She paid the taxes, Hardgood," Sunny said slowly, as if speaking to a child. "Are you not getting it?"

Hardgood sat up straight, not used to being berated twice in fifteen minutes. "No. I am not getting it. I asked her how she came to do that, but I was cast in with the Salem lot for calling her little lady."

Agnes felt like Milo, being talked about in the third person. *Hello? I'm right here,* she thought.

"So sorry, Agnes," Sunny said. "Anything you can do will be appreciated."

"I still don't get it!" Hardgood blustered. "And I'm still a member of this board. I demand to know what I don't know."

Agnes folded her hands in front of her and smiled. "Mr. Shaw, I'm afraid you lack some vital information. I am Sutherland McKnight's wife."

Shaw began to blink. "I was told your name is Larson."

"And McKnight if I choose to use it."

"It would help if people clued me in," Shaw muttered.

Mrs. Pearson smiled at Agnes. "Mr. Shaw isn't the only one who was not clued in. I see now how you managed the magic of the tax bill."

"So sorry. I'm still getting comfortable with my new status as a married person."

Mrs. Pearson then brought up other business and the meeting moved on. After adjournment, Agnes was about to leave by the side door when Sunny pulled her aside. "Please excuse Hardgood. He means well and has done much to help Mrs. Pearson and the children. He's just from a different time."

"I'll keep that in mind."

"Will you tell your husband that he's wet behind the ears?" Sunny laughed and Agnes joined in. "I saw Mary Alice Bonner's notice in the paper. I wondered who you were."

"I imagine there's a lot of that going around in some circles," Agnes said.

"Oh yes, but don't worry, unless you're oblivious, like Hardgood, Mary Alice has made it clear you are a friend of hers."

"Is that important?"

Sunny smiled. "No one wants to disappoint Mary Alice."

§

Leaving the elusive Henry Hammer for another time, Milo was driving back to the police station when Doc Smith called. "Whacha got Doc?" he asked of the medical examiner.

"Remember when I said this skeleton couldn't be Leif Björklund?"

"As if it was yesterday."

"Well, I was wrong. This is Leif Björklund."

"Matched the DNA?"

"Matched it to a Nils Karlsson, a great nephew of Björklund, but that just proved they were close relatives, it didn't prove the skeleton is Björklund. However, as if this case couldn't get any better, we've hit forensic gold, Björklund's dental records from 1940."

"From 1940? You're kidding?"

"I'm not a kidder, Milo. When sons follow fathers into dentistry, and nobody throws out records, miracles happen. There are only two dental families in Duluth that go back that far, and we lucked out. I'm having so much fun with this! Our skeleton is definitely Leif Björklund who died of leukemia in December of 1941."

"So, somebody buried him in a closet?" Milo asked. "Is that legal?"

"No, of course it's not legal. Even in 1941, bodies went to funeral homes. The question is who took him, stuffed him in the closet, and why."

"Okay, so dead Leif was stolen."

"Yes! His body was awaiting the funeral at the Edleman Funeral Home when it walked out the door. So fun! Luckily, the body had been embalmed or someone would have noticed the odor of decay back then."

"How do you know the body was stolen?"

"Leif has his own police report. I had one of my interns go through the police files for December 1941. Somebody stole this chap, an actual body snatching. It was never solved. The cops didn't find the body or the thieves. I sent the file back to Gramm. You can get it from him."

"Wait, you have interns?"

"Yes. It's a growing field. We never get sued, and we have puzzles to solve, such as this one."

"Okay, Leif Björklund dies of leukemia, awaits burial, gets up, walks over to Wardline, and settles into a third-floor closet for eighty years." Milo summed up Doc Smith's information.

"Well Milo, it's been my experience that the dead do not need much to amuse themselves."

Milo was seeing a side of Doc Smith he had never seen before. "So, who helped the late Leif crawl into the closet?"

"That's where my investigation ends and yours begins." The phone went dead.

§

"I need some food!" Gramm said, walking from the parking lot to the cop shop.

"Too late for the lunch menu." White checked her phone for the time. "Past two o'clock."

"It's time for vending machine burritos!" Milo shouted, rushing toward the front door.

Gramm agreed but didn't rush anywhere.

White phoned-in a roast beef sandwich delivery from the car.

Gramm joined Milo in the empty police station cafeteria where the Lieutenant popped a couple of antacids in preparation for the burritos.

By the time the two returned to Gramm's office, White was dipping her sandwich into the au jus. "You know those things will kill you," she said, waving her dripping French dip sandwich at the burritos.

"Don't care," Gramm said. He bit into his first burrito. "Yum."

Milo did the same.

Gramm wiped his mouth with a cafeteria napkin. "My nuked burrito-filled gut tells me Hammer could be our guy. He was in Dawson's study. He could have rigged the bike. He had all afternoon."

"Motive?" White asked.

"The classic: money," Gramm guessed.

"He's just a PI. How does he know how to rig a bike to electrocute someone?"

Just a PI? Milo thought.

Gramm shrugged. "You give him step-by-step instructions."

"I suppose. Nora Swenson was able to follow detailed instructions to set up that electric eye," White conceded.

"We need to talk to this Hammer guy, now," Gramm said.

"Maybe I should. You know, PI to PI," Milo offered.

"Good idea. Take Preston as backup. If I remember, you got the crap kicked out of you the last time you staked someone out."

"That was more than a year ago."

"Don't argue. Just do it!"

§

Milo checked Henry Hammer's driver's license and gun permit on one of the police bullpen computers and printed a copy of both. Hammer was tall, dark haired, and appeared to be exceptionally thin with an acne scared face.

"Not a pretty man," Milo said to Preston.

Together they scoped out Hammers' place. Preston drove the unmarked police car to a large parking lot in the back of the building where they could view the door to the laundromat, and the door that provided access to the upstairs apartments. Hammer's registered vehicle wasn't in the parking lot.

Milo and Preston waited for more than an hour with no Hammer sighting. Milo called Gramm to see if someone could bring them coffee. Gramm said he would see what he could do but added that a real cop would have brought his own coffee.

Fifteen minutes later, Henry Hammer drove his salt-encrusted, black Dodge Charger into the parking lot, and entered the door to the upstairs apartments. Preston and Milo exited their cruiser and followed the suspect up the stairs, hoping to get to him before he reached his apartment.

"Mr. Hammer?" Milo yelled. "we need to talk to you."

Hammer didn't hesitate. He turned, pushed Milo into Preston, and ran to the stairs taking them two at a time. Preston pushed Milo away and chased Hammer down the stairs. Milo followed.

By the time Milo reached the door, Hammer was at his car in the parking lot with Preston still in pursuit. Milo saw the man bounce off the side of the car and onto the ground. Milo walked over in time to see Preston read the handcuffed man his rights.

"Nice work," Milo said.

Preston nodded, handing Milo Hammer's nine-millimeter.

White, Gramm, and two cups of store-bought coffee pulled into the parking lot just as Preston was bringing Hammer to his feet.

"What's this about?" Hammer demanded.

"Why did you run?" Milo asked.

"I thought you were a mugger."

Preston pointed out she was wearing a uniform.

"Who are you people?"

"I'm Officer Preston, and your mugger is Police Consultant, Milo Rathkey."

Hammer was wide eyed. "*The* Milo Rathkey? You're a friggin' legend in this town. I'm gonna read your book when it comes to the library."

"Not my book," Milo began, but was cut off by the arrival of Lieutenant Gramm. Who introduced himself and asked, "What's your full name?"

"Henry, Henry Hammer. What's this all about?"

"We have a picture of you breaking into Charlie Dawson's study in Hunter's Park."

"Whoa! I didn't break in anywhere. Dawson gave me a key. He hired me."

"To do what?"

"Take pictures of that weird bike. It was a mess with those TVs everywhere."

White noticed they were drawing a crowd, and she suggested they take the interview inside to Hammer's apartment. Hammer didn't object but asked Preston if she would take off the cuffs. "It's not a good look in front of the neighbors."

Hammer's apartment was small. They walked into a disheveled room strewn with empty beer cans and old pizza boxes still containing left-over pizza slices. An ashtray full of cigarette butts overflowed on a beverage-stained coffee table. Milo wondered if his old life had looked like this.

"Do you mind if I smoke?" Hammer asked as he picked up a pack of Marlboros from the coffee table.

"Yes," White said.

He threw the pack down and flopped unto a dirty, orange-plaid couch. Milo, White, and Gramm remained standing.

"Why did Dawson want the pictures?" Gramm asked, looking down on his new prime suspect.

"Don't know. Don't care. You can tell Dawson that he isn't getting them until I get paid. He was supposed to transfer the money on Tuesday. I haven't seen squat."

"Bad news, Hammer, Dawson's dead," Gramm said, "but we'll take those pictures."

Hammer looked at him. "Are you gonna pay me?"

"How about I don't arrest you for industrial espionage, and you give me the pictures."

Hammer scratched his head. "I was taking pictures of a dumb-ass bike, how is that…what you said."

"You opened the bike and took pictures of its electronics. That's what I call espionage."

"It was his bike."

"It wasn't his bike."

"I didn't know that."

"Didn't you wonder why Dawson wanted you to take pictures of his own bike? Why not take them himself?" Milo asked.

"You know how this PI stuff works. I don't question people. I get asked to do crazy shit, and I do it. Usually I get paid."

"Give me the pictures now," Gramm barked, "or we take you up to the station, and charge you with murder. You were screwing around with the bike that killed Dawson. Get it?"

Hammer held up his hands. "I get it." He went into his bedroom and came out with a thumb drive. "I transferred them for Dawson, but I guess he won't be needing them."

Hammer passed the thumb drive to Gramm who handed to White. "Get these pictures to Holden ASAP. She needs to see them."

White stepped into the hallway and had a brief phone conversation with Holden to alert her that pictures of the Dawson's bike would be on the server within the hour.

As they were leaving the apartment, Milo turned back to Hammer. "You're new at this."

"Yeah?"

"Always get payment up front." Milo said, returning Hammer's gun.

§

Agnes was still in the kitchen talking to Martha when Sutherland burst through the garage door into the hallway adjacent to the kitchen. "Hello, beautiful!"

Martha patted her hair. "Why, Mr. McKnight, I don't think we've known each other long enough."

Agnes laughed.

Sutherland shook his head. "I think this whole house has caught Milo's humor. I hate to compliment and run, but I have a bike ride scheduled in ten minutes."

"Wait!" Agnes shouted. She chased after Sutherland and asked him if he was sure the bike was safe. He assured her that it had been checked out by one of Gibbs' people. Agnes insisted on going up with him just to make sure. Sutherland didn't know what good that would do but thought the company would be great.

Sutherland quickly changed into his riding gear and was the second one to log onto the server. He was looking at Gibbs in front of him, and Nora alongside on his right. Seconds later Leah appeared on his left, and then Marsden behind him.

"Hey, I was on the other side last week," Nora said.

"The software chooses your initial position, Nora," Gibbs said. "It's random. Let's have a moment of silence for Charlie Dawson."

Leah thought that was out of character for Gibbs, and she was right. The moment was just that, a moment. "Okay, people, let's ride," Gibbs said after a few seconds. The program turned him around and he began to disappear in the distance. The four riders all looked at each other. Sutherland shrugged and began to pedal. Nora, Leah, and Marsden followed. Agnes walked around looking at the Loire Valley in all the monitors.

21

Milo's phone played two stanzas of "Uptown Girl" before he was awake enough to realize he was getting a call from Mary Alice. "Kinda early, isn't it?" Milo asked, noticing it was just a little before seven.

"This is an invitation to breakfast, and you need time to warn Martha you won't be needing that heartstopper breakfast."

"When did lumberjack become heartstopper?"

"When the person eating it realizes he's not a lumberjack. You must accept my invitation. The dogs miss you."

"Well, we can't have sad dogs on our hands. I'll be over in a bit."

"I have Ilene's creampuffs in the refrigerator—picked them up last night."

"Make that a faster bit," Milo said, patting his stomach which was going to start growing again if he kept eating all these creampuffs. He didn't care. He'd swim more.

"Is it sad dogs or creampuffs that put a sprint in your step?"

"Blue eyes." Milo hung up, shaved, showered, dressed, and left a sticky note for Martha. He jumped in the Mercedes and drove the short distance to the Bonner estate.

When Mary Alice opened the front door, Phoenix and Flash darted out to jump on Milo, almost pushing him off the steps. Luna, the female of the group, stayed back as usual, not being silly like the boys.

"Do you need an engraved invitation to come inside? You're letting in the cold, and Luna and I don't appreciate it."

Milo inched his way through the dogs. "The dogs…it's not my fault."

"Your protests are so endearing."

Milo, Phoenix, and Flash moved as one into the warm house. Luna led the way to breakfast.

Milo and Mary Alice sat down in the dining room and waited for cook—Mary Alice's cook demanded she be called 'cook'—to bring out the breakfast. Milo smiled at the serving dishes of scrambled eggs, brioche toast, and roasted potatoes.

"I'm so glad you are teaching me to eat healthy," he snarked.

"Eat your cream puffs," Mary Alice commanded.

Milo moved his fork to the plate of creampuffs. Spearing one, he felt Luna's head land in his lap. She looked up at him with soft, brown eyes and was rewarded.

"She loves you," Mary Alice laughed.

"She loves my creampuffs," Milo stated.

"It gives you two something in common. So, how are the newlyweds doing? Has Agnes figured out who she married yet?"

"Sutherland, I think, unless you have other information."
Mary Alice smiled. "You don't get it either, do you?"

"Get what?" Milo asked, reaching for a second creampuff.

"She has married money and money is a force, my dear, naïve Milo."

"You have money. Wait a minute, I have money."

Mary Alice laughed. "We have funds. Sutherland has money. Agnes and Sutherland will be fun to watch."

"You're making my bank account feel bad about itself."

"Ahh, poor baby. Have some eggs."

§

"Good morning, oh husband of mine," Agnes said as she joined Sutherland in the morning room.

Sutherland put down his paper and smiled. "Good morning, sleeping beauty."

Agnes poured herself a cup of coffee. "Thanks for letting me sleep. Where's Milo?"

"Martha said he left a note. He's breakfasting with Mary Alice," Sutherland said.

"Oh."

"Problem?"

"Not really, maybe a delay. I'm going exploring today on the second floor, starting with the suite of rooms that he and his mother lived in. I wanted to talk to him about it."

Sutherland cocked his head, looking much like a beagle. "How do you know those used to be his rooms?"

"I mentioned to Martha the rooms were on the blueprints, and she told me that Milo told her that's where they lived when he was a child. I hope he still has a key in case the doors are locked."

"It's probably placed above the door. I was never privy to that household secret, but apparently Milo was. That's where the key to the elevator door was safely kept."

"Maybe the key was placed above the door to elevator to keep out a young, inquisitive Milo, or a young, inquisitive Sutherland?"

Sutherland laughed. "Young Milo! Now there's a thought for the day. Because you have conjured up the vision of a young Milo, I am forced to share a deep family secret. There exists a skeleton key for all of the locks in this house."

"Where, oh, where might this deep family secret be kept?" Agnes asked.

Sutherland looked around in mock fear that someone could overhear. "I need you to promise never to reveal this secret."

Agnes put her hand over her heart. "I do solemnly swear never to reveal the secret of the Lakesong skeleton key."

Sutherland took a sip of his smoothie. "It's in the exercise room closet where I stashed my dad's papers. I found it and hung it from a hook on the wall. I screwed the hook in myself."

"That's it? The deep family secret is hanging from a hook in the exercise room?"

"Closet."

"Exercise room closet?"

"Pretty much."

"I was hoping for a secret panel with a puzzle that had to be solved."

"Well, you have to get around the treadmill and open the closet door…oh and turn on the light. It's behind the door."

Martha came in from the kitchen. "Smoothie?" she asked Agnes who shook her head.

"No, I feel like eggs today, but not Milo's plate of eggs. One egg over easy and two pieces of toast."

Martha turned to go back to the kitchen.

"Oh, you better give me some bacon," Agnes called after her.

"For you or the cats?" Martha asked.

"The cats."

"Already fed them their bacon."

Annie rubbed up against Agnes' leg and meowed as if to say, "I could always use more." Jet sat down near her chair and blinked, his yellow eyes turning his facial features on and off, the effect a black cat has when it closes its eyes.

"That reminds me," Sutherland said, "Martha is due a raise this month." He whispered a substantial percentage in Agnes' ear.

She laughed. "I should have married Milo and worked for you."

§

"These pictures are great. Where did you get them?" Michelle Holden asked.

"As luck would have it, someone was paid to take those pictures of Dawson's bike the day Dawson died," Gramm said. He noticed Charlie Dawson's bike had been stripped down with most of it laid out on three work benches along one wall of the forensic warehouse.

"Let's go to my office," Holden said, leading the way through the warehouse with its large noisy heaters hanging from the ceiling, blowing hot air into the cavernous space. The office was tight, barely holding Gramm and White. Milo stood in the doorway.

Holden sat at her desk, opened a drawer, and pulled out a large magnifying glass. She moved it over four of the pictures before picking up the phone and calling a colleague. "Tanya, come into my office for a second. I need your opinion." To the cops she said, "Tanya Pritchett is heading up the investigation."

White stepped out, giving Tanya room to sit down. "You need a bigger office," Gramm said.

"I'm lucky I've got one at all," Holden grumbled.

Tanya Pritchett, a young, tall woman with box braids pulled back into a bun, sat down in the chair vacated by White. "What do you need?"

Holden handed her the pictures and the magnifying glass. "I need your young eyes to look at these pictures and tell me what you see."

Pritchett looked at the pictures. "What am I looking at here?"

"Charlie Dawson's bike before it melted."

"How much before?"

"Hours."

"Interesting," Pritchett said, as she scanned the pictures. "I see our mystery device."

"So did I," Holden agreed.

"It's not melted in these pictures. We need to compare the pictures to the control bike the Gibbs people provided."

"Go. Do it," Holden said.

Pritchett left, followed by Holden, White, Gramm, and Rathkey. Several technicians turned to watch the procession to the Gibbs Bike. The cover was off the electronics portion of the bike and group gathered around it.

"Just as I thought. As you can see here," Pritchett began, "this white box we see in these pictures is not in the control bike. It was clearly added to the victim's bike. Without getting all technical, it appears the device bypasses the transformer and sends lethal current to the pulse meters on the handlebars."

"What made it fry our victim Tuesday night. Why not Monday night, or Wednesday night?" Milo asked.

"Something in the electronics on this bike triggered it—switched on the killer current."

"Something? What something?" Gramm asked.

"We don't know yet. These pictures will help in answering that."

§

Knowing what thirty years of neglect brings—dust, dirt, and spiderwebs—Agnes changed into her work jeans, a sweatshirt, and sneakers. She stood in front of the door to the suite of rooms on the North side of the house. Reaching up, she felt along the door molding. No key. She fished out the skeleton key from her back pocket and opened the door to Milo's childhood home.

The light switch was modern, and it worked. Pausing to get her bearings, she walked into the living room which had a distinct nineties look: a blond wood coffee table, botanical wallpaper, an overstuffed, dark hunter-green couch, and two cozy side chairs.

A large phone-like device was sitting on a side table. Agnes picked it up. "Game Boy?" she said to herself, reading the name from the front of the device. "Property of Milo Rathkey!" *I wonder if he remembers he left it here. Did he hope he would return one day?*

Walking to the end of a short hallway, Agnes opened the door to a bedroom whose walls were covered with yellow flowered wallpaper. The room was furnished with a double bed complete with a lacy dust ruffle, and a green-striped Queen Anne side chair. From the décor, Agnes thought this was Milo's mother's room.

Agnes checked on Milo's former bedroom. The room was painted blue with sports posters along the walls. Agnes got the feeling she was trespassing and closed the door.

"Now, if I were a stairway to a third floor where would I be?" Agnes asked herself, looking around the room. A closed wooden door lurking in the far corner of the living room seemed to be the likely location. Agnes walked over to it, turned the knob, and pulled. The door was locked. Reaching in her pocket, she produced the skeleton key again. It fit and turned. Agnes opened the door to a stairway. She remembered her trip last year down the dusty, hidden staircase in the library and came prepared with a flashlight and a mask.

The light switch was one of those old push button affairs, but not as old as the toggle switch in the library staircase. She pushed the button. Agnes' eyes grew wide when she reached the third floor. The large, finished room was filled with old furniture, numerous paintings, and two bookcases crammed with books.

"Lakesong, you just go on forever!" Agnes exclaimed in delight.

She moved a finger through the thick dust on one of the bookcases. "You need to be cleaned up and appreciated."

The room itself was the biggest surprise. Agnes expected an attic, but this was a finished room with a beige ceiling and white walls—another living area, at least on this side of the house.

I wonder what this room looks like on Sutherland's side of the house, Agnes thought. *I should have asked him how to get up there.* She took out her phone and called him.

"Hi there," Sutherland answered.

"Did you know Lakesong has a third floor?"

"Yeah, the attic. I've never been up there. I assume you have."

"Yes, I'm here now and let me tell you, it's not an attic. It's a third floor, completely finished, at least on Milo's childhood side."

"What's up there?"

"Old furniture, books, paintings, and dust—lots of dust."

"You're having fun, aren't you? I guess that means Milo will have to keep you on."

"The reason I called is I need to know how to get up to the third floor on your...our side of the house. Your changes upstairs are not recorded on the new blueprints. Is there a third set of blueprints? Did you remove a stairway?"

"I don't remember. I told my dad what I wanted, and he made it happen. I was a teenager."

"Okay, well I'll go look for a staircase that may or may not be there."

"How do you purpose to find it?"

"Knock down all the walls with my sledgehammer and crowbar. Have a nice day." Agnes hung up. Finished with Milo's section, Agnes, on a mission, marched over to what she still referred to as Sutherland's area—the south end of the second floor. She was hoping the stairway upstairs mirrored the location of the one she found in the Milo's area. Opening the double doors, she realized that Sutherland's changes had made any comparison impossible.

She surveyed the living room first, looking for a door, secret or not, that would lead to a staircase. No luck there. She tried the bedroom and bathroom next—nothing. Finally, Agnes went into the exercise room and its closet. She banged on the walls and kicked the baseboards. If Lakesong had another secret staircase, she wasn't revealing it.

§

Arriving back at the cop shop from the forensics warehouse, Milo retrieved the Björklund body snatching file from Gramm, sat down at an empty bullpen desk, and began to thumb through it. There wasn't much. A patrolman did the interviewing, not a detective. In the days after Pearl Harbor many police departments were involved in defense. Leif Björklund's disappearance was not a high priority case.

Milo took a few notes.

The body arrived at the Edelman Funeral Home on December 5th of 1941. It was embalmed in preparation for burial. Sometime on the night of the fifth or the early morning of the sixth the body disappeared. There was no sign of a break-in, leading the patrolman to conclude it was an inside job.

"Inside job? By whom? The morticians? They already had the body, why steal it?" Milo asked himself. Several cops in the bullpen turned to look at him. "Oh, come on, you guys ask yourselves that all the time. Right?" The other cops, being used to Milo, nodded, and went back to their business.

White walked over to him. "Grave diggers?"

"This guy never got to a grave," Milo said. "Someone took him before the funeral. The cop who investigated it thought it was an inside job."

"I don't want to know anything more," White said, returning to her desk.

Milo yelled after her, "The body ended up in Mille Greysolon's closet and stayed there for the past eighty years." That outburst again caused the bullpen crew to gawk.

Gramm walked out of his office and motioned for White and Rathkey to join him. Once seated, he said, "Playtime is over, boys and girls. Deputy Chief Sanders wants to know why we haven't wrapped up this case. He pointed out O'Dell solved his last case in two hours."

"Give me a break," White said. "The perp in his last case, shot the victim in front of two witnesses and a camera!"

Gramm nodded. "I pointed that out."

"And?"

"He said O'Dell has better karma. We need to wrap this up. I've decided to call both Mia Dawson and Gabriel Gibbs in for a serious chat."

"Together?" White asked.

Gramm nodded. "They both have motive. Mia Dawson wanted her husband out of the way and Gibbs was angry Charlie was screwing up this bike thing. I think they killed Charlie Dawson together. It's Gibbs' bike and Mia Dawson's house, giving them means and opportunity. For all we know, Gibbs rigged that bike before giving it to Charlie."

Milo took out his phone. "That's a good theory. Let me check."

"Check with who?" Gramm asked.

"Marsden. He's the guy who delivered the bikes," Milo said, looking at White. "Do you have his cell number?"

She checked her notes, reading off the number.

When Marsden answered, Milo put him on speaker. "Yeah, this is Milo Rathkey. When you delivered the bikes, who decided which rider got which bike?"

"Each bike had a name and address. I boxed them up and had them delivered."

"Who put the names to the bikes?"

"I assume Gibbs. He's the one who knew them all."

"So, the bike Charlie Dawson got was the one Gibbs earmarked for him, right?" Milo asked.

"Yes, I guess so."

"Before you delivered them, did you open up the bike's electronic boxes?"

"No reason to."

Milo thanked him and hung up.

"Even stronger evidence," Gramm asserted. "That bike could have been rigged by Gibbs from the get-go, and he purposely sent it to Charlie Dawson."

"I don't know if Gibbs has the know-how," White said, "but Mia Dawson sure does."

"Any mind lint, Milo?" Gramm asked.

"Everyone lies, but only one person lies because they're the murder."

"Of course. Thank you. Oh, I almost forgot, I set up a meeting for you this afternoon with Dr. Ben Blue, our new clinical psychologist. Hope it helps."

"His name is Ben Blue?" Milo questioned.

"It is, and I have to ask you to not bring any weapons with you into the meeting."

Milo was surprised. "He is the police clinical psychologist, right? Do weapons scare him?"

White laughed. "You'll figure it out."

§

Gabriel Gibbs and Mia Dawson arrived at the police station separately, each with their own lawyer in tow. Milo and Preston sat in their usual ante room behind the one-way glass to watch.

"I'm interested in how they arrange themselves," Milo said.

Preston asked what he meant.

"There are two lawyers and our two suspects. Do Gibbs and Dawson sit next to each other with the lawyers on the outside, is it lawyer, suspect, lawyer, suspect, or..."

"I get it, but why do you care?"

"We know Gibbs and Dawson are having an affair. Are they still together, or is it every suspect for themself?"

"I'm going for the two together in the middle," Preston said.

"I'm going for the split. What's the bet?"

"Nothing."

"You're on."

Mia entered the room first, followed by her lawyer. She took the third chair, her lawyer the fourth. Gibbs entered next but did not sit next to Mia. He took the first chair, his lawyer sat next to Mia. If she was upset, she didn't show it.

Milo looked at Preston. "Pay up."

"Here's nothing," she said, settling in to watch the show.

Gramm and White walked into the room. White sat opposite Gibbs and his lawyer, Gramm opposite Mia and her lawyer. Gramm opened a folder, a bluff on his part because he seldom kept anything in a folder. "Let me tell you what we know so we can get past denials and lying."

Mia smirked.

Gibbs sneered.

"We know that you two have been having an affair. It's not too far a stretch to see that the continuance of your romance was predicated on the removal of Charles Dawson."

White was stifling a laugh. *Where did Gramm get those words, continuance, predicated?*

Mia began to speak, but her lawyer advised her not to. She ignored the advice. "Sure, we are having an affair, a bit of fun. It's not serious. I wasn't planning to marry Gabe, and even if I was, divorce is easier than murder."

White countered, "But a divorce could be costly. Your husband could have ended up with half your assets."

Mia shook her head. "I have better lawyers," she said, glancing at her attorney. "Charlie wouldn't have gotten a dime."

Gramm looked at Gibbs.

"I don't marry. Like Mia said, it was a bit of fun."

Gramm turned a page in his prop folder. "Mr. Gibbs, we understand that you were the one who decided which bike went to which person—an ideal arrangement for rigging one bike to kill."

Gibbs smiled. "You're understanding is crap. I didn't care who got what bike. Do I look like a warehouse worker to you?"

In the observing room, Preston turned to Milo. "He's such an ass, but so pretty."

"My colleague always says everyone lies, Mr. Gibbs," Gramm began, "but only one lies because they are the murderer. I think I'm looking at that one."

Gibbs' lawyer, a tall and imposing man, stood up. "We're leaving. I'm not hearing or seeing any evidence here, Lieutenant. Do you have fingerprints, DNA, anything that links my client to Mr. Dawson's accidental death?"

Gramm closed his folder. "We are gathering that evidence as we speak."

"Good. When you find some call me, otherwise either leave my client alone or explain your continued harassment to a judge. Good day."

Gibbs, Mia, and their attorneys paraded out of the room.

Gramm said, "Well, we know Gibbs is lying. We just have to prove it."

"Continuance? Predicated?" White laughed. "What did you watch last night?"

22

Milo drove to Dr. Ben Blue's office in the east hillside area, next to St. Luke's Hospital. The medical building had its own parking lot which Milo appreciated. Dr. Blue's waiting room, shared with other mental health professionals, was littered with children, their parents, along with two adult patients. Milo told the receptionist he was here to talk with Dr. Blue.

The young, multi pierced woman held out her hand, "Insurance card and ID."

"I'm not a patient, I'm here to talk to him," Milo stated.

The receptionist didn't remove her hand. "That's what he does, talk to people. He's a psychologist. Insurance card and ID, please!"

"I'm here from the police department about a suspect."

Her hand dropped. "Oh, yeah, his other job. I'll tell him you're waiting. Have a seat."

Milo looked around. There were no seats to be had. He leaned against the wall and watched a little boy ram a toy truck into the wall over and over again.

After about five minutes, Dr. Blue, a sandy haired man with a slight 'dad' bod opened his office door to the waiting room and called Milo's name. Milo walked past Dr. Blue and received the stare of death from the truck boy's mother.

Milo entered a beige-on-beige office furnished with blond furniture and bookshelves. He noted that the doctor faded into the background, being a bit beige himself.

Speaking low and soft, Dr. Blue leaned over his desk and offered Milo coffee. Milo declined the coffee. He thought the doctor would have made a good mortician.

"I need to know about psychopaths," Milo began.

"Ahh, psychopathy, how wonderful, it's my clinical specialty, and..." He paused.

Milo waited for the end of the sentence. It never came.

Dr. Blue seemed to return from somewhere. "What is your question?"

"What are the warning signs of a psychopath?" Milo asked.

"To the lay person—such as yourself—there may be no warning signs. The psychopath appears to be friendly, even charming, at first, but push the wrong buttons at your own risk. They will do what they think needs to be done to protect their interests, right a wrong. Psychopaths have little or no conscience. They lie, of course. They're quite good at it. They're rule breakers and have no..."

Again, the sentence stopped. "No what?" Milo asked.

"I'm sorry? What?"

"You said they have no, but you didn't finish the sentence."

"Really? I wasn't aware of that. Anyway, they can be bullies; they have an almost complete disregard for others, and, therefore, most have shallow relationships. Did I mention empathy?"

"No."

"I think I did."

Milo realized why Gramm had warned him not to carry a weapon. "Can they kill over anything?"

"Oh certainly, if the anything is important to them. They can…"

"They can what?"

"What?"

"You said they can, but you didn't finish it."

"People tell me that all the time. I do get caught up in my thoughts. Where were we?"

Shooting you and dumping your body out the window! Milo thought.

"A psychopath often doesn't recognize other people's distress," Dr. Blue continued.

"Do they know what they're doing?" Milo asked.

"Oh, yes. They are often highly intelligent and are excellent scammers and manipulators. They don't care about the consequences of their behavior. These traits can often be traced back to childhood. In fact…"

Dr. Blue stopped in mid-sentence once again. Milo stood up. It was time to leave.

§

Milo was thinking about lunch when Robert, Mille's butler, called. "We have a new wrinkle in our closeted friend, sir."

"He's a skeleton—no wrinkles."

"Very drole sir, but a Mr. Karlsson will be calling on Mrs. Greysolon here at Wardline this afternoon at four. He thinks he knows why his grand uncle Leif spent time in the closet. Mrs. Greysolon would like to have you present for the discussion."

"I'll stop by Wardline on my way home."

"I will leave the gate open for you and a light on in the window, sir."

§

Agnes had abandoned her search for the staircase and was in her office when April Lindstrom called. "April, how are we doing?" Agnes asked.

"Great news! Someone paid the taxes! I can't believe it. That is so great!"

Agnes smiled to herself. "That's wonderful, April."

"Mrs. Pearson wouldn't tell me who it was, but I hope it's someone I contacted. Do you think one of us has a lot of money?"

"Maybe."

"Anyway, Mrs. Pearson said the house could still use some funds, so I am going to stay with the GoFundMe page—just tweak it a little bit. I'll send you the URL. Give what you can."

"I will."

§

Milo's phone rang again. "I'm very popular today," he said to White who was sitting one desk away from him in the bullpen.

"Milo, Bello here," Ron said.

"I need a ringtone for you," Milo complained.

"I'm partial to 'Paperback Writer' by the Beatles," Bello suggested.

"I think I've heard it once or twice."

"Can you come over to my place around six? My publisher would like to have a conference call with us."

Milo sighed. "Why does he want to talk to me? I don't write books."

"It would be a favor to me."

"Wait, check, Ron, are you still alive?"

"I think so."

"*That's* my favor to you."

"Please! He thinks you're quite intriguing and wants to meet you. He's been bugging me about it for weeks."

"Can I convince him to stop you from writing books about me?"

"Give it your best shot."

"What hotel are you in?"

"I have rented that charming bungalow in Lakeside that is owned by a lady who just married a guy who lives in a mansion by the lake."

"Ah, you're living in Agnes' house."

"That would be the one. Six o'clock. I make a great gimlet," Bello lied.

Gramm stepped out of his office just as Milo was hanging up on Bello. "We're stuck," he said to both White and Rathkey. "I would love to arrest the widow and Gibbs, but we have no concrete proof."

"We've been here before," White said.

"Yeah, but Milo comes up with some mind lint and we're off to catch the killer. Milo?"

"I told you, everyone lies."

"Tomorrow, we start this all over again," Gramm said. "Sometimes that works. Reinterview everyone if we have to. Rethink it all."

White sighed. "No fun, but I see no other way."

Gramm waited for approval from Milo who was staring off into space. "Milo? Milo?"

Milo shook his head as if waking up. "What?"

"We start this all over again tomorrow, right?"

"Sure."

"What's going on?" Gramm asked.

"I think I know."

"Mind lint! At last!" Gramm shouted.

"One piece doesn't fit."

§

Agnes waited for Sutherland in the kitchen and pounced on him as he opened the door from the garage. "I want to talk to you about the foundation," Agnes said.

He stared at her and blinked. "I don't think I heard that correctly."

She grinned impishly, took him by the arm and guided him into the gallery to an infrequently used seating area farthest from the family room.

Sutherland blinked again. "Why here?" he asked.

"I don't know," Agnes shrugged. "I just like it; Kinda private in a public space. Cozy."

Sitting next to her, Sutherland didn't mention to her that she was sitting in Laura McKnight's favorite spot.

"So, the foundation?" Sutherland asked.

"Emma Worthington, Jet's former owner, gave money every year to the Woman's League for the purchase of prom dresses and suits for foster kids."

"And I assume that money ended with Emma's death."

"It did. So, I would like the Laura and John McKnight Foundation not only to pick up that slack, but also provide money for school clothes and maybe a couple of scholarships."

Sutherland nodded. "When do they need the prom money?"

"Yesterday."

"Well, the foundation doesn't move that fast. We must meet, look at applications for funds, and decide where the money goes. The next meeting, which will include you, isn't until June."

"Oh, no," said a dejected Agnes.

"But I have a solution. Why don't you and I fund the prom clothes this year, and the foundation can begin funding the rest before school starts in the fall," Sutherland said.

Agnes smiled at him. "I bet you never thought I would be this expensive."

He put his arm around her shoulders and leaned back. "Yes, it's going to be ramen for another month, but we'll manage."

Agnes laid her head on his shoulder. "Those clothes are important."

§

Once again, Milo followed Robert to Wardline's great room where a serious looking man, with reddish-blond hair and a well-trimmed beard, was in Milo's usual chair. The man jumped up and introduced himself as Nils Karlsson. Recognizing the name as the relative of Leif, Milo thanked him for helping Doc Smith with the DNA test.

The man's serious exterior dropped away as Nils beamed. "I have more than just my DNA, I've brought glogg," Nils said, raising his glass of red liquid.

Glogg was new to Milo. *I hope it tasted better than lutefisk*, he thought, sitting down in one of the chairs Robert brought it over to form the friendly foursome.

"We've been discussing how my great uncle might have ended up here in Mrs. Greysolon closet."

Milo was all ears.

"Oh, me first, Nils. Me first." Mille interrupted.

Milo wondered how much of the Glogg had already been consumed.

"As I mentioned, my mother always told me Uncle Sidney did something horrible to Leif Björklund. Being an imaginative child, I assumed that meant he murdered him. But in chatting with Nils, she may have meant something completely different. Mother was always extremely religious. In her world, denying Leif a proper burial could have been the horrible act."

Nils could contain himself no longer. "I didn't have any family legend about Leif Björklund that was passed down to me. No one ever mentioned him. I loosened Mom's tongue yesterday with some of this wonderful warm glogg."

Mille tossed a few raisins in her cup and poured herself another glass full of the warm red liquid. Robert raised an eyebrow. Mille saw the questioning look but ignored it.

Nils continued his story. "On her second cup Mom began chatting about Leif and Mille's Uncle Sidney. I got a story that you will not believe. You must realize my mother is Leif's niece but was a baby when this happened. She has no memory of it herself, but growing up, she remembers her mom and dad talking about it with their friends. You know how kids listen when adults reminisce. According to her, Leif was ill and knew he was dying. He told the family that, when his final day came, he wanted to go out in a blaze of glory. Mom loved telling me this part." Nils grinned and shook his head.

"According to her Uncle Leif demanded—are you ready—a Viking funeral. His mother was appalled, calling it pagan. Every time it was mentioned, she would take to her bed. Apparently, Great Uncle Leif was not moved by her hysterics. He insisted his friends grant him his last wish. That included his best friend, Mrs. Greysolon's Uncle Sidney."

"That explains the disappearing body," Milo said, watching Mille drop raisins in her now empty cup, and dispense more glogg.

Karlsson finishing his second glass of glogg was eager to continue. "Mom thought the friends had stolen Leif's body and burned it in a funeral pyre. Obviously, that never happened, as Leif has been waiting patiently in the closet."

"We now know who took him and why," Robert said, "but why not follow through? Why was he abandoned?"

"I know! I know!" Mille was getting excited. "According to Dr. Smith, Leif died on December 5th of 1941. His body disappeared on the sixth, and on December 7th Pearl Harbor happened."

"Nice historic timeline, but what does that have to do with Leif and the closet?" Milo asked.

"Timing, Milo," Mille said. "I know my Uncle Sidney immediately joined the Marines. They all joined up. Uncle Sidney probably thought he would come back and then they could give Leif his send off. Unfortunately, he didn't. Sidney died on Guadalcanal. If any of his buddies made it back, I don't think they knew where Uncle Sidney had stashed Leif. I can only guess that my mother knew that Leif's body was taken. He never received a proper funeral. That was what was so horrible. Not that Leif was murdered."

"She never guessed that Leif was so close by," Robert said.

Milo started to laugh. "That is one of the greatest stories I've ever heard!"

Mille's eyes sparkled. "It is, isn't it. Now, I think it is our duty to carry out the late Leif Björklund's final wish. He has, after all, lived with us so long, he's like one of the family."

Milo looked at Nils.

"I called my mother before you arrived. She's not only on board, but she's already researching Viking funerals."

"Really, sir?" Robert asked.

"I left her a bottle of glogg and a box of raisins," Nils confided. "We're set."

Milo felt his work was done. He left Nils, Mille, and Robert to plan Leif Björklund's send off, and traveled up to Ron Bello. After that story, a good gimlet would be welcomed. Walking into Agnes' former home, he looked around at the total lack of change. "I love what you've done with the place, Ron."

"Always a smartass," Ron charged. They walked to the kitchen where Ron mixed Milo's gimlet.

Milo took a sip. "Acceptable, but not great. A little less lime juice."

The two men sat at the kitchen table where Bello had set up his computer in anticipation of a Zoom call with James Random, Bello's publisher. Milo envisioned a serious New York executive with a no wrinkle, expensive suit, and well coifed hair. What he got was a man with big ears, a full head of fly-away, wavy, black hair, and a salt and pepper beard. Milo thought a sculptor could have fun with the crags in his face.

Random was adjusting his screen so his black-coat sweater with a black-plaid scarf could clearly be visible. "Milo! Great to meet you at last!" the man grinned. "I'm James Random and before you ask, I am not the Random guy of Random House."

The publishers' opening gambit usually broke the ice. Milo didn't laugh.

"Never mind," Random said, "Ron warned me you were often on a different track."

Milo didn't like his drink, didn't like Random's humor, and especially didn't like being told he was on a different track. Why was he here?

§

Chatting with Agnes, Sutherland lost track of time. Ten minutes before six, he ran upstairs, threw on his biking gear, grabbed a water, and switched on Gibbs' bike. Gibbs was already on the monitor waiting for everyone to log on.

"Glad to see you could all make it. Let's go!" Gibbs shouted. The group began pedaling.

§

"So, Milo, have you ever thought about writing? Maybe mysteries?" Random asked.

Milo shook his head. "I read them—enjoy the puzzles. If I write them, I'll already know the solution. No fun."

"With Ron's book, you're becoming a household name. There could be good money in it."

"I have money," Milo said.

Random shrugged. "You can't blame me for trying. Ron is currently writing another, I'm sure, best seller involving your latest case in which you stopped the perpetrator on a runway or so I understand."

"If he makes the book about me, I'll shoot him in both knees," Milo threatened.

Bello leaned into the computer screen. "He's mellowing, James. Last time he threatened to choke me like a chicken or was it feed me to the carp?"

§

"Come on people! Keep up!" Gibbs shouted, when he noticed the others were falling behind.

"What's with you Gibbs?" Leah Davis demanded. "Your pace is ridiculously fast!"

"I agree. This is supposed to be fun," Nora Swenson added.

Sutherland, a more experienced rider, wasn't having a problem keeping up with Gibbs. The others were.

"I'm trying to finish this! It's the last twenty miles, people," Gibbs shouted. "The faster we do this, the faster we're done."

"They're volunteers, Gibbs!" Marsden said, slowing a bit. "They don't work for you."

Gibbs ignored him.

§

Milo's phone vibrated. He answered. A female voice asked him to hold for a police forensics conference call. "I gotta take this," he said, putting the gimlet down, thinking what a waste of good vodka. He answered the call, knowing it was rude, but not caring. *Maybe I'm a psychopath.*

"Michelle Holden here, do we have Lieutenant Gramm, Sergeant White, and Consultant Milo Rathkey on here?"

All three said they were on.

"Milo is working on another fascinating case," Bello whispered to his publisher as Milo listened to the call. "A guy who was electrocuted on a bike."

James Random cocked his head. "I see the cover. Green background, white lettering, *Murder on the Bike Path.*"

"No path," Bello explained. "It's an experimental, new-concept, exercise bike."

On Milo's call, Holden was getting right to the point. "We are ninety percent sure that the wires on the switch device in Charlie Dawson's bike were connected…"

"So just one dead guy?" James Random asked Bello.

"Yeah," Bello whispered, "he was part of a group testing a new bike."

"But only one guy died?"

Milo put his finger in his ear to shut out Random and leaned closer to his phone, "Sorry? Connected to what?"

"To the mileage counter," Holden repeated.

"No, no, no, Ron!" Random shouted from the computer screen. "In the book it will be much better if the murderer kills 'em all! Bikes snapping, zapping…"

Milo's eyes opened wide. Holden was still talking, but the back of Milo's brain lit up and screamed to the front. He looked at Random's face in the computer screen and demanded, "What did you say?"

"Ron and I were talking about your current case."

"What did you say! Dammit!"

Random was taken aback. "I suggested it would be better to kill 'em all. Sorry if that offended…"

"Crap!" Milo shouted, standing up and yelling into his phone. "Ernie get to Gibbs Industries now! Get everybody off those bikes!"

Milo disappeared out the front door, Bello's publisher, looking surprised and perplexed by the turn of events, laughed, and asked, "Was it something I said?"

"It was, and I get the feeling you will get a mention when I write the book," Bello mused.

§

Sutherland looked down at his mileage, nineteen miles, one to go. *I'm not going to miss these rides. They're no longer fun,* he thought.

306

The program was showing the riders on a bike path through the Pyrenees. The scenery was gorgeous, but the bikes were not doing well. The other riders in Sutherland's monitors were flickering, and Gibbs was frozen in the front monitor.

"This bike is damn mess!" Gibbs was shouting. "It's embarrassing!"

Milo slammed his recently acquired flashing blue light on top of the Honda and flicked on the siren. Racing down the hill to Lakesong, he called Agnes.

"Yeah, Mi..."

"Get Sutherland off that bike now!" he screamed into the phone. "It's going to kill him! Stop his ride! Now!"

Agnes ran from the gallery to the stairs, taking them two at a time, hitting the top of the stairs, bursting through the double doors, knocking them against the walls. Building momentum, she ran through the exercise room door shouting for Sutherland to stop. Headphone wearing Sutherland was oblivious to her presence. With full on force, she charged at him, both hands connecting with his upper torso, sending him flying off the bike and crumpling into the left side monitor.

Sutherland screamed as he landed in a heap.

"Everybody stop! Stop now!" she shouted.

Gibbs stopped as did the others. He turned his body to look behind him and saw Agnes' head in the rear monitor. "Who the hell are you?"

Driving at breakneck speed, Milo called Martha, shouting for her to open the gate and the front door now. Martha didn't ask questions. She pushed the buttons on the intercom. Milo drove through the gates, around the drive, and launched the car up the first step before jumping out and running into the house. An out of breath Milo joined Agnes in the exercise room.

Sutherland was lying by the bike, not moving. Agnes was bent over him trying to stem the blood gushing from his forehead.

"What the hell is going on?" Gibbs demanded.

"All the bikes are rigged to kill!" Milo shouted. "Everybody! Get off now!"

Looking at the side monitors, Milo saw two empty bikes. The rear monitor showed an angry Marsden still pedaling.

Leah Davis yelled, "Marsden stop!"

Gramm, who had just arrived in the pinball conference room with White, looked around but did not see any bike except Gibbs'. "Where the hell is Marsden?"

"In his office," Milo yelled.

"Where is that?" Gramm asked.

Leah once again implored Marsden to stop.

Marsden smiled. "I'm still going to win, Gibbs!" Marsden stiffened. There was a crack milliseconds before his image on the monitors went black.

Gramm looked at Gibbs. "Let me repeat the question. Where is Marsden's office?"

Back at Lakesong, Milo was on his phone. "I need an ambulance…"

23

Gibbs led Gramm and White to Marsden's office down the long hall to the back of the building. When they were a few feet from the door, Gibbs recoiled, turned on his heels, and complained about the awful smell. White told him to wait down the hall. She and Gramm used her tube of odor blocker and entered Marsden's office.

They found him on the floor, tangled in the rear monitors. From the smell and the burn marks on his hands, it was clear Marsden met the same fate as Charlie Dawson.

Passing Gibbs, White ran to direct the ever-growing police presence in the building. Seeing officers Preston, Butler, and Hughes, she ordered them to make sure the building was secure. "No one in or out."

She told Officer Young to position herself outside the conference room where Gibbs had been riding his bike. "No one comes in the room."

Gramm called Doc Smith who grumbled about people dying at an inconvenient time but said he would be at Gibbs Industries within the hour. Gramm then called forensics head, Michelle Holden and filled her in on the evening's events.

"Should I consider all the bikes to be dangerous?" Holden asked.

"We're working with that hypothesis."

"I will get a team moving to you. Meanwhile, contact everyone and get them away from those bikes. I mean at least a room or two away. No one touches them for any reason. We will began picking them up tonight."

"Tonight?" Gramm asked.

"They should be considered deadly weapons—like loaded shotguns. See you in a bit."

White was making her way back to Gramm when she was accosted by an angry Gibbs "What's going on here? What are you people doing?"

White keyed her radio. "Preston?"

"Yes, boss?"

"Would you come down the hallway outside the conference room to escort Mr. Gibbs to the lobby? Bring another officer."

"It's my damn building!" Gibbs shouted. "I don't need an escort."

White showed no emotion as she said, "Your building has a dead body in it. It's a crime scene. You *will* be escorted by Officer Preston. The only question is with or without handcuffs. Your choice."

Preston and another patrolman arrived and took Gibbs in tow. "Stay with him," White ordered. "If he attempts to flee or gives you a problem in any way, cuff him and place him under arrest."

"Charge?" Preston asked.

"Disturbing the peace," White answered.

"What? Are you crazy?" Gibbs shouted.

White walked up to him. "You love to throw that word 'crazy' around Mr. Gibbs. I wonder why."

"I want my lawyer!"

"Call him." White returned to Gramm in Marsden's office.

"Make sure Swenson and Davis are okay," Gramm said. "Forensics said to get them away from their bikes—at least a room away."

White took out her phone and called Nora Swenson. A shaky voice answered. "Yes?"

"This is Sergeant White, are you okay?"

"Yes."

"Where are you?"

"On my bed."

"In the same room as that bike?"

"Yes! I only have one room!"

"Get out of there now!"

"I only have one room!" Swenson shouted.

"Are you upstairs or downstairs?"

"Upstairs."

"Get out of your room and sit on the steps. Don't touch the bike," White instructed.

Gramm leaned into the phone. "Police technicians will be there shortly to take the bike."

"Now? Tonight? My landlady will have a fit."

"Can't be helped," Gramm said.

White added, "Go to the stairs now!"

"I'm going."

White hung up and called a less shaken Leah Davis.

"What is going on?" Davis answered. "Is that Marsden guy okay?"

"Listen to me. I want you to get out of the room where you have that bike."

"I'm out. I'm in my kitchen."

"Good. Police technicians will be coming to your house shortly to pick up the bike. Do not touch it. Do not move it. Do not be in the same room with it."

"Should I leave the house? Am I in danger?"

"No, as long as you stay away from that bike. Stay there, you need to let in the forensics people."

§

Sutherland, still in the exercise room, was regaining consciousness as the EMTs were moving him to the stretcher. They assured a hyper focused Agnes that the profuse forehead bleeding looked bad but was minor. They put strips across the wound to temporarily close it.

"Where are you taking him?" Agnes demanded.

"To St. Luke's."

"I'm going with him," she demanded. "I'm his wife."

The EMT nodded.

"What's going on?" Sutherland asked, looking around. He winced in pain.

"Lie still," the EMT ordered.

"You can bounce him down the stairs," Milo advised "but as fun as that would be, we have an elevator. Follow me."

A slow elevator ride later, Sutherland was placed in the ambulance with Agnes sitting beside him.

Milo returned to the house and called Gramm.

"Where are you now?" Gramm questioned.

"I thought I'd go for a walk." Milo snapped. "Where do you think I am?"

"Sitting by the fire?"

"I'm headed to the hospital."

"Are you hurt?"

"Not me. Sutherland."

"You didn't get to him in time? What's going on?"

"Agnes knocked him off the bike, really took him out. He hit the monitors and the floor. He'll be okay, but he'll hurt for a while."

"Oh good. Look, who is left there?"

"Me and two cats."

"Stay there. Holden is sending people to pick up that bike. Don't go back into that room."

"I need a drink."

"Good idea. Get a drink. Wait for the forensics people." Gramm hung up. Milo made a good gimlet and waited.

After his last sip, two technicians and a driver came through the gates of Lakesong with a large truck. Sporting rubber boots and thick rubber gloves, they unplugged the bike, labeled all the parts 'McKnight,' and loaded it, the monitors, and all the connecting cables into the elevator and then into the truck.

Doc Smith arrived at Gibbs Industries at the same time as Holden and her team. Together they began to process Marsden's office.

"I have a question," White said, looking at the body of Marsden.

"Just one?" Gramm asked.

"How did this happen?"

Milo screamed all the bikes were rigged to kill," Gramm said.

"Did Marsden not hear him?" White wondered.?

Gramm called Milo who complained that he was leaving for the hospital. Gramm ignored his complaint. "This is a mess. Tell me your mind lint. Who's the killer? To my weary eyes, Gibbs is the only one left standing."

"It's Marsden." Milo hung up.

Gramm looked at White. "Milo says Marsden."

"My money is still on Gibbs. Has his bike been checked?"

"Now there's the question," Gramm said. He asked Holden to have someone check Gibbs' bike immediately to see if it was rigged before he returned to the lobby to interview Gibbs.

White radioed Young to let forensic people into the conference room, but not to go in herself. She then joined Gramm.

Gibbs was sitting in one of the visitor's chairs. "Let's chat," Gramm said.

Gibbs' lawyer burst into the lobby hurling all sorts of legal jargon and demanding the police vacate the building.

"So, you want to dispose of the charred body in the back office?" Gramm asked sarcastically.

"Body? What body?" the lawyer asked, looking quizzically at his client.

"One of my lesser employees was electrocuted." Gibbs sneered.

"Your step-brother." White said.

The lawyer said he needed a minute to talk to his client.

Gramm and White stepped away. Gramm called Milo again. "I need to know why you think it was Marsden. All my evidence points to Gibbs. Hang on a minute, I have Holden calling me."

Milo considered another gimlet but thought better of it. He still had to drive this evening.

Gramm came back on the line. "The evidence implicating Gibbs is piling up. Holden's people just checked his bike. His bike is not rigged. Not rigged! Did you get that Milo?"

"Of course not!" Milo said, munching on a cheese sandwich. "It all fits. How about the other bikes?"

Gramm sighed and called Holden again, asking if the technicians were checking the other bikes as they picked them up.

"Of course," Holden said.

"And?"

"McKnight's and Swenson's are rigged. We're just getting to Davis' house. I'll let you know."

Gramm clicked back to Milo. He repeated Holden's report. "We're still waiting on Davis."

Milo shook off a moment of distress hearing Gramm say Sutherland's bike was indeed rigged to kill. He knew it had to be the case but didn't like hearing it.

"If it's Marsden, what was his motive?" Gramm asked.

"His goal from the beginning. The destruction of Gibbs. It stems from his mother."

"What?"

"Psychopathy"

"You want to speak English Milo. I don't have a gimlet. I do have another charred body," Gramm shouted.

"If we check, I suspect we'll find Marden has been treated for psychopathic tendencies. He hated Gibbs, plotted to destroy him."

"By killing people he didn't even know?"

"Dr. Blue says people like Marsden don't experience guilt."

White broke in. "But Gibbs is volatile, impulsive. He equates humans with lawnmowers. Talk about non-caring."

"He's all those things, but the bottom line is that it was Marsden who checked those bikes and lied, saying they were safe."

Gramm agreed. "Yeah, I get it. Everyone lies but only one lies because they are the murderer."

§

Milo drove to the hospital to check on Sutherland. He found Agnes waiting in one of the curtained off areas of the emergency room. "How's our boy?" he asked.

Agnes looked up. "Hi Milo. They're checking him for a possible concussion. If he's okay, we can take him home."

"Good. I drove the SUV. We can throw him in the back."

"I think his separated shoulder might complain about being thrown."

"Not a problem. He has the strippers, Ginger and Turmeric."

Agnes shook her head. "I think he's going to need something stronger. I know I am."

"I should alert Martha to the situation. I think breakfast should be delayed," Milo said.

"I already texted her."

"What did you say?"

"I knocked Sutherland off his bike. We had to go to the hospital."

Milo laughed. "And she accepted that."

"She texted back, '*Understood*.'"

§

Gramm and White returned to Gibbs and his lawyer. "All the bikes are rigged to kill except yours, Mr. Gibbs. Care to explain?" Gramm asked.

Gibbs, who was sitting in a lobby chair staring at the floor, looked up. "How can I explain something I didn't do? I didn't rig anything."

"Are you going to charge my client?" Gibbs' lawyer asked.

"Not at this time."

24

Milo awoke to find Jet lying on his chest, squeaking, and Annie at the foot of the bed making loud, discontented meows. *How do they get in here?* Milo asked himself, vowing to solve that mystery one of these days. The undue attention by the fuzzy felines continued throughout his morning rituals until he and his cavalcade of cats walked through the gallery into the family room.

Sutherland was lying on the couch with his arm sling and his forehead bandaged, "You look worse than I did last summer when I fell off that trail bike into the rocks," Milo said.

"You only had gravity. I understand I had Agnes, this lovely lady sitting right beside me. And I'm so grateful I did," Sutherland paused. "Did I say that correctly?"

"Nicely done," Agnes nodded.

Jet jumped up on the coffee table to get a closer look.

Sutherland stared at the young cat. "What's on your mind?"

Jet squeaked as Jet does. He turned to Agnes, put his head down, and rubbed it against Agnes' hand, licking her gently with his sandpaper tongue.

"Hey!" Sutherland complained, "I'm the injured one here. Why are you getting loved up?"

"He thinks you break too easily," Milo said, sitting down at the family room table and thanking Martha for his breakfast. "Clearly you got in a cat fight and came out the loser."

Agnes petted Jet under his chin, on the top of his head, and smoothed back his whiskers. Eventually, he jumped down, presumably to inform Annie of the damage.

"Again, I'm so sorry I hurt you," Agnes apologized to Sutherland.

"Sorry?" Milo said, almost shouting. "You saved his life."

"I'm right here in the room," Sutherland complained.

"That's my line," Milo said. "So, what's the damage?"

Sutherland sighed. "Five stiches in my forehead, I'll have a scar." Sutherland tried to hide the pride in his voice.

Agnes rolled her eyes.

"I also have a separated shoulder," Sutherland added, gently tapping on his left arm. "Along with an ugly thigh bruise, plus other minor scrapes."

"And you're planning to milk it, right?" Milo asked.

Sutherland grinned. "I am. I must, a little. I got knocked on my butt…"

"By a girl," Milo added.

"A girl that would look good in Viking purple," Sutherland suggested.

"Packer green and gold," Milo corrected as his phone did the Ernie Gramm ring. Before picking up, Milo shouted to Martha, "I think Gramm and White are going to bust through the gate for a late breakfast."

"Got it!" Martha yelled back.

"Rathkey," Milo answered the phone.

"I know it's Rathkey. That's who I dialed." It was eleven in the morning and a sleep deprived Ernie Gramm was irritable.

"You're coming over, right?" Milo asked.

"Yes. Robin and I didn't wrap it up until about three. We need some questions answered, and it will help my mental state if I could have one of Martha's comforting breakfasts."

"Tough life. I'll order you both extra comfort. Meanwhile, what does Robin want for breakfast?" Milo asked. He could hear White's response in the background. "Eggs, sunny side up, and hash browns."

Milo relayed the order, getting Gramm a half lumberjack identical to his own and adding extra-comfort toast to White's order. Wincing, Sutherland turned to take a sip of his protein shake that Agnes insisted he drink because she believed extra protein helped the healing process.

Fifteen minutes later, Gramm and White arrived at the front door. Milo led the human parade into the family room.

"Wow! You're a mess!" Gramm said to Sutherland.

"I was assaulted."

"In my defense, I was ordered to get Sutherland off that bike immediately, and I did." Agnes said.

"She saved his life," Milo explained. "Took him out."

"Into the monitors and onto the floor," Sutherland added, clutching his arm for sympathy. He didn't get any.

Gramm and White thanked Martha as she delivered their extra-comfort breakfasts to the family room dining table. "I wondered why Mr. Rathkey was in such a panic to have me open the gate and the front door last night," Martha said.

"There wasn't time to explain," Milo said.

"You didn't ask?" White wondered.

Martha laughed. "In this house? It's business as usual. Glad I have a fast finger."

"Double that woman's salary," White said.

A smiling Martha left to set up dinner, wondering how many people would be dining.

"Okay, Milo," Gramm said, pushing his eggs through the ketchup, "we're all on a Zoom call with Holden, and the next thing I know you're screaming 'stop the bikes!' How did that happen?"

"Unlike you, I was on two Zoom calls—yours and one with Bello's publisher," Milo said.

Gramm took a bite of his toast and chewed. "So what?"

Milo broke off a piece of bacon and gave it to Annie who was threatening to scratch a groove in his leg. "Holden said the trigger was the mileage counter. At the same time, Bello's publisher shouted, 'Why not kill 'em all?'"

White dipped her toast into an egg yolk. "How does a stranger's 'kill 'em all' become our 'kill 'em all?'"

"Remember I said I thought I knew who did it, but I was missing a piece? That piece was motive. I couldn't figure out why Marsden wanted to kill Charlie Dawson. He barely knew him. When the publisher screamed 'kill 'em all,' it clicked. Charlie Dawson wasn't the target. Marsden wanted to kill all of them and blame Gibbs."

"Why?" Gramm asked.

"His hatred for Gibbs was psychotic. Ironically, when I went to talk with him to get the low down on Gibbs, Marsden accused Gibbs of being a psychopath. He used the term 'psychopathy.' Any of you know what that means?" Milo asked.

"I suspect it has to do with the treatment of psychopaths," White said.

"Sounds good. I don't know. All I know is Dr. Blue also used it when he was telling me the traits of a psychopath. Why would Marsden know and use that term? Maybe he read his own file? Maybe he's been treated and learned the lingo? He told me he had a past filled with problems."

"Okay, let me ask this question. If Marsden's plan worked and everyone died together, how was he going to talk his way out of claiming the bikes were safe?" Gramm asked.

"He wouldn't have to. Dawson's dying early screwed up the plan. If it had worked like it was supposed to Marsden wouldn't have had to claim anything."

"But Dawson did die early, and Marsden had to declare the bikes safe. What was his plan after that?" Gramm insisted.

"He could play dumb. Maybe say the wiring was done so well, he simply missed it."

"But we have a picture of Charlie's bike before his electrocution. It clearly shows that trigger device!" White insisted.

"Exactly, but Marsden didn't know we had the picture," Milo countered.

"Was Marsden always planning to kill himself?" White asked.

Milo shrugged. "I don't know."

Sutherland raised his good arm.

Milo acknowledged him. "Your turn Sutherland, and someone give him a point for class participation."

"Marsden had a leg cramp on the first ride and stopped pedaling. His meter was behind the rest of ours."

"Clever, It gave him a mile or two cushion," Gramm said. "That would set up his end game with him alive."

Milo nodded. "His plan was for everyone to die but not Gibbs and not him. His bike was rigged, Gibbs' bike wasn't. Gibbs goes to jail, and Marsden wins,"

"But he lost," White said. "He kept pedaling. He had to know what he was doing."

"The way I see it now," Milo said. "When people started shouting to get off the bikes, Marsden figured it was over."

The room fell silent.

"He didn't even know me…" Sutherland mumbled as his eyes closed.

Agnes put a blanket over her dozing husband and suggested they take their breakfasts back into the morning room.

Jet and Annie stood up with the humans not understanding why everyone kept changing rooms. They followed the group into the kitchen, where Martha collected the empty plates and then into the morning room where the humans lined up for more coffee. Annie realized that morning bacon was over and left for her Guiana Tree. Jet hung around a few minutes more, but the humans were boring. He too disappeared.

"How close did they come…I mean how many miles were left before…you know?" Agnes asked.

"Gibbs said they had less than one tenth of a mile," White said.

Agnes closed her eyes and sat down at the table.

White continued. "Gibbs thought twenty revolutions—maybe a little more."

"Hence your push," Milo said to Agnes.

"What a twisted plan," White said.

"And it would have worked," Milo added, "if Charlie Dawson had not broken the rules, rode his bike when he wasn't supposed to, and died too early."

Agnes rose and went back to sit close to the now sleeping Sutherland.

§

"Thanks to Agnes McKnight we will be able to provide clothes for all the foster children this year," Sunny Upton told the assembled Women's League group at their monthly Nokomis Club. "She also assures us that we will be in the running for a permanent grant from the McKnight Foundation next year."

"She's a go-getter, a doer, a perfect person to join our group," Lydia Olson said.

Sunny shook her head. "I asked her, but she begged off. She's quite busy with a full-time job."

"Really?" another woman asked. "Where does she work?"

"I understand she's a personal assistant."

"To whom?" Lydia asked.

"Milo Rathkey."

"That detective who solved the Harper Gain thing? I just finished reading that book!"

"I guess so," Sunny said. "How many Milo Rathkeys can there be?"

"Agnes McKnight sure lives an interesting life," Lydia mused.

Mrs. Pearson always hoped that one of her girls would get a seat at the table. "You know," she said to the group, "you don't know what a child is going to be until they become it."

§

Gramm and White departed.

Milo stood in the doorway watching Agnes and Sutherland. "How are you doing?" Milo asked.

Agnes looked up. "I've…I'm fighting hysteria. I'm as happy as I've ever been, but to have that happiness almost taken away by someone who didn't even know us—I'm just… can't catch my breath."

"But it wasn't taken away," Milo said. "You stopped it. You ran up those steps. You stopped Sutherland from turning those pedals."

"Honestly, I hardly remember any of that. I took your phone call and the next thing I knew Sutherland was in a crumpled heap at the bottom of his bike. Then there was the ambulance and the emergency room. I felt like I was on autopilot."

"But you saved his life. If you weren't the most important thing in his life before, you sure are now. Remember, Lakesong likes you."

Agnes smiled. "Thank you, Milo. After both of us sleep for about a month, Mr. Broken Body here, may have your next case."

Milo smiled. "What's that?"

"Sutherland has an aunt."

"Aunt? I didn't know John had a sister."

"Not his dad, his mother."

"Laura had a sister?"

"Named Lana."

"Where has she been?"

Agnes explained the story. "Might finding her be interesting enough for you."

Milo nodded. "I'm curious. So, yes. But when are you and sleeping beauty going to start making that upstairs a home?" Milo asked.

"I think I'd rather hide in the basement for a few months."

Milo shook his head. "In the wine cellar or the vault?"

"The vault, it seems secure enough to keep the world out."

"May I make a suggestion?"

Agnes sighed. "Sure, why not?"

"Forget a month in the vault. Get started on the remodeling."

"Maybe, but you need to sort through your things first."

"What things?"

Agnes looked up and yawned. "I found one of your old gizmos while walking through."

"Old gizmos?"

She laid back down. "I think it's called Gameboy."

"Oh, that. No big deal. I forgot I had it."

"Why did you leave it?" she asked snuggling under the blanket and drifting off.

"Not a good look at basic training."

Agnes didn't respond.

Milo left them and went up to the second floor, finding his Gameboy on the end table where he left it thirty years ago. Picking it up, he said, "Hello old friend. I'm back. Now where were we?" He went to his old bedroom and found the charger still plugged into the wall. "So, what was playing all those years ago? Tetris? Works for me."

25

A somewhat smoky Milo arrived back at Lakesong Friday evening to find Sutherland stretched out on his new place to be, the sofa in the family room. Sutherland slurped the last of his protein smoothy while Agnes sipped a dirty martini.

"Not drinking alcohol?" Milo quizzed.

Sutherland shook his head. "On pain killers."

"Protein," Agnes said. "When you love someone, you give them protein to help them heal."

Milo sat down in a chair opposite the sofa. Agnes sniffed the air. "Did you attend an Artic barbeque or a house fire?"

"I was at the Leif Björklund Viking funeral. It was a fitting end to my first interesting case."

"Please don't tell me you burned a body in a massive bonfire on Lake Superior." Agnes was aghast.

Milo shook his head. "Sadly, no. There are laws against that. His relatives had his bones cremated, and we placed the ashes on top of the bonfire."

"Did you roast marshmallows?" Sutherland asked.

"Sutherland!" Agnes admonished.

Milo's eyes darted from side to side.

"Oh no, you didn't?"

"It wasn't my idea," Milo said. "It was Mille's and Leif's family and it was fun. How's the tackling dummy?"

"I still hurt, but Agnes is keeping my mind off of it by going over our remodeling plans."

"We're working on plans for that third floor!" Agnes said.

"There you go, a two-story apartment, and you have the elevator," Milo added.

"Are you sure you don't mind? I sometimes agree to things and then regret it."

"Well, I expected you to regret marrying Sutherland but not this quickly."

"Very funny," Sutherland mumbled, readjusting the bag of frozen peas on his shoulder.

Nodding toward the peas, Milo said, "When you get paid next, buy one of those proper ice thingies."

"Yeah, but this is so much more fun."

"What's your mother's maiden name?" Milo asked.

"Freskin. Why?"

"Agnes said you have an aunt."

"Oh yes. I haven't thought about her in years."

§

Milo retired to his office to begin the search for Lana Freskin. The search didn't take long. *Sutherland could have done this himself,* Milo thought. He found her in Scotland still using her maiden name. Lana Freskin was still alive. She had founded an environmental group dedicated to stopping the shipping industry from polluting the oceans.

Milo clicked past several articles before he found a picture of her. He sat in stunned silence. "Oh, Sutherland, I'm not so sure you're ready for this. I'm not so sure I am."

SNAP, ZAP, MURDER!

*If you wish to contact the authors, email us at
authors@dbelrogg.com or leave a message at
www.dbelrogg.com.*

If you enjoyed this book, please leave a review on Amazon.

BOOKS BY D.B. ELROGG

GREAT PARTY! SORRY ABOUT THE MURDER

FUN REUNION! MEET, GREET, MURDER

MISSED THE MURDER. WENT TO YOGA

MURDER AGAIN! HAPPY NEW YEAR!

SNAP, ZAP, MURDER